White House Pet Detectives

White House Pet Detectives

Tales of Crime and Mystery
at the White House
from a Pet's-Eye View

edited by
CAROLE NELSON DOUGLAS

Cumberland House Publishing
Nashville, Tennessee

Published by
    Cumberland House Publishing, Inc.
    431 Harding Industrial Drive
    Nashville, TN 37211
    www.cumberlandhouse.com

Cover design: Gore Studio, Inc.
Text design: Lisa Taylor

Library of Congress Cataloging-in-Publication Data

White House pet detectives : tales of crime and mystery at the White House from a
pet's-eye view / edited by Carole Nelson Douglas.
        p. cm.
    ISBN 1-58182-243-X (pbk.)
    1. Detective and mystery stories, American. 2. White House (Washington, D.C.)—
Fiction. 3. Washington (D.C.)—Fiction. 4. Historical fiction, American. 5. Pet
owners—Fiction. 6. Pets—Fiction. I. Douglas, Carole Nelson.
    PS648.D4 W44 2002
    813'.087208362—dc21

                                                                      2002007585

Printed in Canada
1 2 3 4 5 6 7 8 — 07 06 05 04 03 02

Contents

Introduction

O ver the years, it's estimated, the families of sitting presidents have
included almost four hundred pets and something under two hundred dependent children.

It's not surprising that presidential pets outnumber presidential offspring by two to one. Most presidents attained the nation's highest office
later in life when their children were grown. And most of these, presidents
and pets, resided in the White House, beginning with John Adams in
1800.

In 1790 George Washington signed an Act of Congress declaring that
the federal government would reside in a district "not exceeding ten miles
square on the river Potomac." Washington and city planner Pierre L'Enfant
chose the site for the new residence now known as 1600 Pennsylvania
Avenue, and Washington oversaw construction of the house, whose cor-
nerstone was laid in 1792.

Once the White House was established as the official residence, along
with the parade of constantly changing First Families came alligators,
goats, parrots, ponies, bears, and plenty of the usual suspects, cats and
dogs. The Theodore Roosevelt menage, amply supplied with both animals
and children, was a veritable Noah's ark of presidential pet-owning, including representatives from almost every species that ever called the White
House home.

This anthology features twelve new stories and one reprint about thirteen of these chief executives and the apolitical animals in their lives. It

even visits the most unusual American president, Jefferson Davis of the Confederate States of America, who never lived in the White House, but who owned the most stalwart of the presidential pets, a dog named Traveler.

Also visited in this collection are Ulysses S. Grant's horse, four-footed representatives of two Roosevelt administrations, Founding Fathers' feathered friends, and assorted alligators. The stories, written by an equally diverse group of award-winning writers, range from late eighteenth- to late twentieth-century settings. It is fitting that the first story, featuring George and Martha Washington, was written by the dean of American mystery short fiction, Edward D. Hoch, named in 2001 a Mystery Writers of America Grand Master and given a Lifetime Achievement Award from the Bouchercon World Mystery Conference.

White House Pet Detectives

Martha's Parrot

Edward D. Hoch

A s soon as she arrived at the three-story President's House in New York
on May 27, 1789, Martha Washington knew that the Cherry Street
mansion was a very good one. George had been there nearly a month without her, since his inauguration on April 30th as the new nation's first president. Now, satisfied that the rented mansion was handsomely furnished
and suitable for his wife, he had summoned her from Mount Vernon, and
arranged to meet her in New Jersey to escort her on the presidential barge
for the final leg of the journey across New York harbor. Two grandchildren
from her previous marriage, orphaned and living at Mount Vernon, had
accompanied her.

"'Tis a pity you were not here for my inauguration," Washington told
her. "That was quite an occasion. Afterward I walked up Broadway with
some members of Congress for a worship service at St. Paul's. In the
evening there were huge backlit transparent paintings of patriotic themes
erected around the city."

"Were there fireworks?" the boy Tub asked.

"Yes, two hours of fireworks. The streets were so crowded I had to walk
back here. My carriage could not get through."

In front of the house, Martha's servants were unloading her belongings.
She went to meet them and returned carrying the parrot cage. "I don't
think Polly enjoyed her journey very much."

Washington gave a sigh. "Patsy, couldn't you have left that bird at
Mount Vernon?"

He liked to call her Patsy, and hearing the name softened somewhat this latest attack on her parrot. "She is good company for me when you are out and about on the nation's business."

"You didn't need her with you at Valley Forge," he reminded his wife.

"I was younger then, and so were you." She was fifty-eight now, one year older than her husband, and they had been married for thirty years. The harsh winter they'd spent together at Valley Forge seemed a lifetime ago.

Though she missed her home at Mount Vernon, Martha made the best of their new home during the months that followed. Her ten-year-old granddaughter Nellie began taking piano lessons, and Martha organized Friday evening receptions for men and women that became the talk of New York society. For his part, President Washington followed a British tradition of holding Tuesday afternoon "leeves" from two to four, for men only. They were largely dull affairs at which the president wore his sword and carried his hat, items of dress he dispensed with during Martha's livelier receptions. On Thursday evenings the head steward served up elegant dinners for specially invited guests. He also supervised a household staff of twenty other servants, including the four coachmen and two grooms who had charge of the president's cream-colored coach, pulled by six horses. Washington justified the seeming extravagance of it because the coach had been a gift to Martha from the governor of Pennsylvania, and had been used regularly at Mount Vernon. He took great pride in his horses, instructing his grooms to brush their teeth each morning.

By the end of that year, when it became obvious the president needed a larger house, arrangements were made to rent the Macomb mansion at 39 Broadway, where they moved on February 23rd, the day after his 58th birthday. Washington seemed to relax some of his customary stiffness as his wife continued to shine in New York's social circles. He'd always been aware that he towered over her physically, six feet two inches tall while Martha was barely five feet, but she had the knack of soothing the men while charming the ladies. Abigail Adams, the vice-president's wife, sat at her right during parties and receptions, and was quick to praise her, even while she occasionally criticized the splendor of the president's domestic arrangements.

Martha's dark hair had turned white with age but her teeth and large hazel eyes were still beautiful. One morning, examining her hair in the mirror, she asked, "George, have you ever realized that you and Hamilton and Jefferson all have red hair?"

Washington chuckled. "This hair of mine is rapidly turning white, my dear. Why do you ask? Do you think we should start some sort of red-headed league?"

"No, it just seemed something of a curiosity."

"One that history will ignore, I assure you."

At that moment Polly chose to utter one of her unpredictable repetitions. "History! History!" she cackled.

*   *   *

In January of 1790, with Congress back in session, an unforeseen problem had arisen to threaten the new nation's solidarity. Alexander Hamilton, Secretary of the Treasury, submitted a plan to the House of Representatives for federal assumption of state debts from the Revolutionary War. Washington hardly expected anyone to balk at this official generosity, but one Tuesday afternoon following the usual "leeve" James Madison remained to talk about it. Madison was a friend of Washington's and had played an important part in both the drafting and ratification of the Constitution. Now a Virginia congressman, he was a man whom Washington respected.

"You see, Mr. President," he began, choosing his words with care, "in our state and some others much of the war debt has already been paid. Secretary Hamilton's proposal would unfairly discriminate against us."

"I understand that," Washington replied with a slight smile, "and I also understand that you and others put little trust in New York bankers. You have been unhappy ever since our capital was established here."

"I make no secret of that," Madison admitted. "A nation's capital should be centrally located. It is almost nine hundred miles from Atlanta to New York, and that very distance works a hardship on our southernmost states."

"I imagine Virginia would be the perfect place," the president agreed.

"We are from the same state, sir. Would you not prefer a President's House closer to your Mount Vernon home?"

"Someday soon I will return there. In the meantime I serve where my country needs me."

"I must tell you I will speak out in the Congress against Hamilton's proposal for assumption of state debts."

"So be it."

Two months later, on April 12th, the measure was defeated on a preliminary vote in the House by 31 to 29. Washington had long admired Hamilton's work but the young Treasury Secretary seemed especially haggard and dejected when he spoke with the president as the date for the final vote approached. "New York firms have been buying southern securities since last summer," he admitted. "They hold nearly three million dollars in South Carolina, North Carolina, and Virginia obligations. They would have made huge profits had the federal government assumed the debt at six percent interest. Following my proposal in January there was a mania of speculation in public securities. One of my own assistant secretaries Cyrus Wilmer resigned recently, having used advance knowledge of my January proposal to promise profits to small investors. Surely Madison will use this information as a weapon against us when the final vote comes."

"Can we do nothing about this man Wilmer?"

"Invite him to one of your dinner parties so I can wring his neck," Hamilton replied.

It was upon leaving the President's House that Hamilton came upon Thomas Jefferson on his way in. Jefferson, the country's first Secretary of State, was startled when Hamilton begged him to reassure southern congressmen on the necessity for assuming the states' war debts. He went so far as to offer his help in moving the national capital out of New York.

When Washington heard of this, he suggested to Jefferson that both of them be invited to dinner along with Madison, to work out an agreement if one was possible. Jefferson considered this. "First let me have Madison and Hamilton to dinner at my house in Maiden Lane. Then we will come here a few nights later with some preliminary thoughts."

The plan was agreed upon, and later in the day Washington conveyed the information to Martha. "We will be eight for dinner on Thursday. Madison, Jefferson, and Hamilton will be joining us."

"Oh dear! What will we do for women? Jefferson is a widower and Madison is not yet married. What about Hamilton?"

"His wife was with him when he took the oath as Treasury Secretary. I believe her name is Elizabeth."

"Good, but we need two other women." She considered the possibilities. "I will invited my friend Daisy Ward. I know you enjoy her company."

"Indeed I do," Washington agreed with a smile. Daisy was an attractive young woman in her twenties who owned a millinery shop a few blocks down Broadway. "Perhaps you might invite Abigail, too. John is in Rhode Island for the statehood celebration." The state had finally ratified the Constitution on May 29th, the last of the thirteen colonies to do so. Washington would have been there himself, but he was still recovering from a bout of pneumonia suffered two weeks earlier.

"I will do that," Martha agreed.

A sudden thought came to him. "Let us also invite Cyrus Wilmer, one of Hamilton's former assistants at the Treasury Department. It might be a perfect opportunity to speak with the man. I will inform him that Hamilton will also be present."

Martha was exasperated. "Now we have five men and four women."

"We will include your granddaughter Nellie. She is almost eleven, and can be quite charming. When he is a bit older we can have Tub, too." He was thinking that the child's presence would keep the conversation light, avoiding any conflict between Hamilton and Wilmer, at least until the men adjourned for brandy and cigars.

"Very good."

"And Patsy, move that parrot of yours into my study for the night of the dinner. Our guests will find it more pleasant without Polly's cackling."

* * *

Dinner at the President's House always began early. Washington was just slipping into his striped waistcoat when Jefferson and Madison arrived. While they awaited the others he took them out to the stables to show off his stallions. "Nelson here is my favorite," he said, feeding the horse a taste of sugar.

"How many do you have?" Jefferson inquired.

"Fourteen when I'm home at Mount Vernon, plus ten hound dogs." He turned away from the stallion, handing the reins to one of the grooms. "Here, Chester, put him in the stable. I won't be needing him tonight."

It was Madison who first broached the subject of the dinner with Hamilton. "All went well the other night," he confided. "I think we can reach an agreement this evening."

"Perhaps," Washington replied. "However, I invited another gentleman who may shed some light on this matter. He is Cyrus Wilmer, who made a small fortune by using knowledge he gained as Secretary Hamilton's assistant. I want to hear in his own words what went on prior to Hamilton's proposal to assume the war debts of the states."

Jefferson was troubled by the news. "Does Hamilton know this man will be here?"

"Yes, I told them both."

"It may be unwise."

But Washington was adamant. "Thomas, we are talking about moving the capital of this new nation. It is not a decision to be reached in haste. I must consider all the facts."

Martha called to them and announced the arrival of Cyrus Wilmer. Washington went back inside and greeted Wilmer, a short balding man who wore a brown suit and striped waistcoat similar to Washington's own garment. "It is a pleasure to meet you, Mr. President," Wilmer said, shaking his hand.

"We have never met before?"

"Only briefly at the Treasury Department, on the day Secretary Hamilton took the oath of office."

Washington tried to make casual conversation, delaying any serious talk until after dinner. "I see we have the same taste in waistcoats."

"What? Oh, you mean my vest." Wilmer peered at the president's garment. "Yes, they are virtually identical."

"What was your history before working under Hamilton at the Treasury?"

"I was with the Commissioners of Forfeiture in Westchester County. As you may know, more than fifty Loyalist landowners had their property forfeited and acquired by tenant farmers that had been renting it. You can imagine that I was not a popular person."

"And now?"

"I was lucky enough to make some wise investments in our new nation, but I am open to any new offers of a government position."

Washington realized the man expected to be rehired for something. He was already regretting having invited him. But the rest of the guests were arriving then, led by his new friend Daisy Ward, and he put the matter of Cyrus Wilmer out of his mind for a moment.

"Daisy! How good to see you again," he said, taking her hand.

"And so good of you to invite me, Mr. President." Martha had been the first to make her acquaintance at the millenary shop, and had invited her for tea one afternoon. Washington was immediately taken with her fresh appearance and lively personality.

"You are always welcome here, Daisy. This evening you will be meeting some important members of my government."

"I am deeply honored."

Jefferson and Madison came in from the stables and he introduced them, along with Wilmer. At that moment Hamilton and his wife arrived. As the maid was showing them in, Washington's groom hurried in from the stable to hand Jefferson a snuffbox he'd dropped. It was a confusing moment and Washington saw the color drain from Wilmer's face as he caught sight of Hamilton.

Before anything could be said, Abigail Adams arrived. "Thank you for inviting me," she told Martha. "I feel lost with John away."

"Will there be nine of us?" Elizabeth Hamilton asked, taking a quick count of the guests.

"My granddaughter Nellie is making a tenth. She's a charming young lady."

The steward, Samuel Fraunces, an impressive black man with a powdered wig, served his usual bountiful and elegant dinner, and Martha was pleased to see that even young Nellie seemed to enjoy it. She was seated to Washington's right, with Daisy Ward on his left. Across the table, Martha sat between Jefferson and Madison, with Abigail Adams to Jefferson's right. The table talk was light and filled with the diners' impressions of New York. The theaters were open again and a new racetrack, the Maidenhead, was operating in lower Manhattan. Hamilton, who'd been quiet through much of the meal, commented that perhaps the Treasury would be better off with the bookmakers at Maidenhead.

After dessert the men adjourned to Washington's study for private conversation. "Why can't we come, too?" Daisy wanted to know.

"Because male conversation is very boring to the fair sex," Washington assured her. He followed the others into the study and took down a bottle of his finest brandy from the shelf.

Martha hurriedly appeared in the doorway. "Excuse me, gentlemen. I neglected to cover Polly's cage." She pulled the pink silk hood over the cage and retreated quickly from the male domain.

"That bird!" Washington grumbled. "Would it surprise you if I served roast parrot at out next dinner?"

Madison chuckled. "I believe you are too humane for that."

"I have a parrot myself," Cyrus Wilmer told them. "But yours, sir, seemed especially colorful."

"If the bird was mine I would make you a gracious gift of it, but 'tis Martha's pet."

"Why did you bring us together, Mr. President?" Hamilton asked, coming right to the point.

Washington lit his cigar from a candle before responding. "Secretary Jefferson and Congressman Madison have discussed the matter of moving the nation's capital to the south. As you knew, this has been a delicate matter for some time, and it has become entangled with the issue of the federal government's assumption of the individual states' war debt. Virginia and other southern states oppose this because part of their debt has already been paid off through the issuance of their own bonds. It is unfortunate that speculation in these bonds has created something of a scandal in financial circles."

Hamilton cast a glance at Cyrus Wilmer. "There was a lapse in my department shortly before I made my proposal to the Congress. Word got out and set off needless speculation. A great many innocent people lost money."

"What do you know of this, Cyrus?" Washington asked him, not unkindly.

"I may have let something slip," the balding man admitted. "If I did, I have paid dearly for it. The loss of my position with the new government has been a decided blow to my family."

"Are you thinking of appointing this man to another government position?" Hamilton asked, suddenly concerned with Washington's motives.

Washington sensed that the conversation was getting out of hand. "I am merely trying to clear the air before we get down to our real business of locating the future capital of our nation."

It was Jefferson who took over the conversation at this point. "I suggest the president and I confer with Congressman Madison for a few moments in private. Then we will return here."

Washington and Madison, heeding his suggestion, followed him from the room. Hamilton started out too, before he realized he had not been included. Instead he turned toward the parlor where the ladies had gathered. Wilmer remained in the study and called out to Washington. "May I look at your parrot?"

"Certainly, sir," the president responded, and saw the balding man lift the silk cover from the bird's cage.

He joined Jefferson and Madison in Martha's sewing room, not the best place for such a conversation, but at least it was private. "Was your plan to confront Hamilton with his past mistakes, Mr. President?" Jefferson asked.

"No, only to remind him of them. We need Hamilton's support if we are to reach a compromise on this issue of the states' debts. He is, after all, our Secretary of the Treasury."

"He is not a Virginian like ourselves," Jefferson remarked.

"A bastard child of the West Indies—," Madison began, but Washington immediately cut him off.

"We will have no such language in the President's House. No man is more loyal to these United States than Alexander Hamilton."

"Will he support a compromise to move the capital out of New York?" Jefferson asked.

"I believe so," Washington said.

The discussion continued and the framework of the compromise began to take shape. Washington himself would choose the site for a new capital city, possibly along the banks of the Potomac River. It would take perhaps a decade to build, and in the meantime the capital would be moved to

Philadelphia, giving some appeasement to the southerners who mistrusted New York.

They were about to return to the meeting with Hamilton and Wilmer when the sound of a woman's scream reached them. Fearing something had happened to Martha, the president hurriedly led the way to the parlor. The scene that greeted him was beyond imagining. Daisy Ward was slumped on the floor by the study door while Elizabeth Hamilton attempted to revive her. Beyond her, on the floor of the study itself, Washington could see the bloodied body of Cyrus Wilmer.

* * *

When she revived and was helped to her feet, Daisy Ward told of having left the other ladies to look over the president's bookshelves. Upon hearing a sort of thump from the study, she called out to the person inside. There was no answer and she opened the door to find Cyrus Wilmer's body, the bloody knife by his side. He had been stabbed more than once, and she realized that he was dead.

The room had another door leading down some steps to the servants' quarters and the stables. Everyone was quickly accounted for with the exception of Hamilton, who'd gone outdoors to explore the stable area.

It was Martha who joined the men in the presidential study, though Washington tried to block her view of the body. "This is no place for you," he said.

"Nonsense! I have seen dead men at Valley Forge. But we must notify the authorities."

She was bending down to retrieve the silk cover from the parrot's cage when Polly gave a screech and said, "Westchester!"

Martha and the men froze in place, as if expecting the bird to reveal the name of the killer, but it only repeated its geographic message. "Westchester!"

"What does it mean?" Madison asked.

"Polly usually repeats a word or phrase that is spoken loudly or with emphasis. It is something she heard spoken here when Wilmer was killed." She glanced at Washington for confirmation.

"That is so," he agreed. He was remembering Wilmer's previous position with the Commissioner of Forfeitures in Westchester County and he wondered if that might have played a part in his death.

Washington's groom had been sent in search of Alexander Hamilton and returned with him. "I found Secretary Hamilton in the stable, Mr. President," he reported.

The president told Hamilton what had happened while Jefferson knelt by the body, examining the bloody kitchen knife. He extracted something from the dead man's waistcoat pocket, being careful to avoid the bloodied areas. "It is a wad of currency," he said, holding it up. "British pound notes. There must be several hundred pounds here."

"Strange that he would be carrying so much money on his person," Madison said.

"Not so strange," Hamilton observed. "He was a gambling man."

"You knew him better than the rest of us," Washington said. "Can you think of any reason why someone would want him dead?"

"No one other than myself," Hamilton admitted. "He betrayed a confidence by revealing the proposal I was about to make to the Congress."

Washington asked grimly, "Did you kill him, Alexander?"

"I did not, sir. I was inspecting your stables at the time it happened."

Jefferson paced the floor, carefully avoiding the body. "We must get to the bottom of this matter, and quickly. How many servants do you employ, Mr. President?"

Washington turned to Martha for the exact figure. "There are twenty-one," she said, counting them off on her fingers. "The coachman, two footmen, the head groom and five other stablemen. Then there is the steward, Black Sam, whom you saw at the dinner table, also a French confectioner and a French valet for my husband, along with his young body-servant. I have my long-time attendants, Mollie and Oney, along with our cook and five housemaids for various chores."

"Is Black Sam a slave?" Jefferson asked Martha.

"No, he is Samuel Fraunces, a well-known New York tavern owner from the Indies. We did bring seven slaves from Mount Vernon, including my two attendants who are very close to me, but they do not come in contact with the public. We have arranged that all be freed upon our deaths."

"But any of them might have slipped in the back door and stabbed Cyrus Wilmer."

"Any of us might have, too," Martha countered.

"But weren't you women all together?" Hamilton asked. "As were the men."

"We were indeed together, except for Daisy who went to examine the library before she found Wilmer's body."

"As were we, except for Hamilton," James Madison offered.

Washington closed the door to the outer rooms and sat down at his desk. "Tell me about the Westchester business," he said.

Behind him, the parrot squawked, "Westchester!"

*　*　*

The Westchester land forfeiture by property owners loyal to the King had been pretty much as Wilmer described it. All of the original landholders had fled to Canada and it was doubtful that any had returned to New York. Even if they had, no one could imagine them entering the President's House to kill Wilmer when the crime could have been accomplished so much easier elsewhere.

"He had that money in his waistcoat pocket," Madison reminded them. "The killer may have wanted it. Hearing Miss Ward at the door might have scared him off."

"We must speak with the servants," Martha decided, "but first let me cover this." She spread a quilt over the body and then went off to summon them. Hamilton followed along.

"Might it have been Alexander?" Jefferson wondered. "Perhaps the two men struggled and—"

"No," Washington said firmly. "I will not hear of it!"

"Then one of the servants—"

"Most have been with us for years," Martha said, returning from her errand. "And what motive could they have?"

It was Jefferson who raised another possibility. "This woman Daisy Ward, who found the body—could she be involved?"

"How do you mean?" Washington asked.

"She was looking at the books. Might she have slipped in here, stabbed him with a knife she'd obtained earlier, and pretended to have heard his falling body?"

"No, no," Washington insisted. "Daisy is not a woman who could hurt a fly."

"You wish everyone innocent, Mr. President, but surely it was not the hand of God that struck down this poor man."

"Westchester!" Polly said.

Washington showed his frustration to Martha. "Cover that bird, Madam, or surely we will have roast parrot for tomorrow's sup."

"George, my Polly is trying to tell us who the killer is."

"Do you converse with the creature, then?"

"Enough to know the villain's identity. And you should, too."

*   *   *

Washington summoned his groom and asked that a rider be sent to inform the authorities of the killing. There was some confusion as to whether the local police department or the military police would have jurisdiction, but that was a matter for others to decide. Although Edmund Randolph of Virginia served as Washington's Attorney General, the post did not have cabinet rank. Still, Randolph would have to be consulted on the matter and Washington began drafting a letter to him, seated at the dining room table.

Suddenly there was the sound of scuffling from the study. The president rose to his feet. "Jefferson?" he called.

"We have him, sir. It's just as Mrs. Washington said."

"Just as Polly said," Martha corrected, coming in with a lamp from the next room. Jefferson and Madison had pinned someone to the floor next to Wilmer's body. As she held up the lamp they saw that it was Washington's groom, Chester.

"Polly said *Westchester*," Madison objected.

"Not *Westchester* but *Vest, Chester*," Martha told them. "After the first knife wound Mr. Wilmer was trying to inform his killer that the money was there, in his vest pocket. You'll remember he used the term *vest* rather than the British *waistcoat*. But Chester delivered a second fatal wound, and only realized a short time ago what Wilmer's dying words meant. That's why he came back here now, as we thought he might, to search his victim's waistcoat pockets before the authorities arrived."

Chester, his face pale and frightened, tried to speak. "I knew him from the Fraunces Tavern. He told me in December about speculating on bonds to cover the state war debts, and promised to double my money. I gave him everything I had, and then he lost his position at the Treasury Department. He didn't know I was working as the president's groom until he saw me tonight. Later when I confronted him with a kitchen knife I thought he was reaching for a weapon and I stabbed him."

Washington nodded and told the men, "I saw the color drain from Wilmer's face and thought it happened when he saw Hamilton. But he knew Hamilton was coming so that was hardly the cause. It was the sight of my groom Chester entering at the same time that panicked him. Also, of course, Hamilton was in the stable at the time of the murder yet Chester had not seen him. That was because Chester himself was otherwise engaged, sneaking into my study through the back stairs while Wilmer was looking at our parrot."

The murder at the President's House was never publicly revealed, and Chester pleaded guilty to a lesser charge, going quickly off to prison. It was not until sometime later, after Congress had approved the compromise that moved the nation's capital to Philadelphia while the new city on the Potomac was being built, that Martha reminded the president of what he'd said that night.

"You called Polly our parrot, George. Do you remember that?"

"She is a good old bird," he admitted. "And probably too tough to eat in any event."

A Mimicry of Mockingbirds

Lillian Stewart Carl

The evening was fine and warm in a last lingering imitation of summer. Through Tom's open window came a distant strain of harpsichord music, accompanied from time to time by a woman's voice. He would have preferred hearing the salutations of the muse of law, as he was at this moment preparing a difficult case. He pulled his candle closer to *Littleton's English Law with Coke's Commentaries.*

A song, an echo of the original, trilled from the tree outside. Tom looked up with a smile. He liked the voice of the mockingbird, *mimus polyglottos*, the American nightingale. Mockingbirds were clever little fellows, modest as widows in their silver and gray suits. . . . Voices shouted, the harpsichord and the woman's voice ceased abruptly, and with a flutter of wings the bird flew away.

Tom dipped his pen and turned to a fresh page in his commonplace book. "As our laws so have our vocabularies been shaped by the customs of our sovereign Britain. Such collective nouns as 'an ostentation of peacocks' or 'a parliament of owls' amuse our fancies and remind our intellects of the deep roots of our mother tongue. And of its insularity, that such a charming creature as a mockingbird has no such appellation. . . ."

A knock drew his attention. "Come!"

His landlady opened the door. "Mr. Jefferson, are you working still?"

"Indeed I am, Mrs. Vobe. My colleague Patrick Henry will soon argue a case of inheritance, for which I have promised him a complete brief."

"He does go on, Mr. Henry does. Why, you'd think he was preaching revolution!"

"So one might think," Tom returned, without venturing to express those grievances of which he as well as Mr. Henry were sensible.

Mrs. Vobe was wiping down a long-necked wine bottle with her apron, causing its blue glass to wink gaily in the light. "Here you are, Mr. Jefferson. Shocking, the dust from the streets, but I reckon it repels the flies."

"Thank you." Tom placed the bottle at the far end of his desk, away from his books and papers, noting as he did so that despite Mrs. Vobe's best efforts with the apron, her own fingers, tacky with the baking and basting due her position, had left smudges upon the glass. "Did I hear voices exclaiming in the street just now?"

"Aye, that you did. Mr. Bracewell's been taken sick, very sudden, and his wife's sent for the doctor."

"Which Mr. Bracewell, Nicholas the merchant or his brother Peter?"

"Nicholas, the elder."

"I hope he recovers speedily."

"And if he don't, well then, there's work for you in proving his will."

"Which is a duty I should gladly forgo, for I have quite enough work without wishing ill of one of my fellow citizens. There are greater matters at hand than such domestic ones as wills and properties. And yet," Tom turned back to his books, "such domestic matters are as vital to those whom they closely affect as are the present debates on taxation to the citizens of all His Majesty's colonies."

He heard the door shut as Mrs. Vobe went on about her business and left him to his.

*   *   *

Raindrops sifted down the back of Tom's collar as he stood with his hat in his hand. But he took no more notice of them than he did of the odors of mortality, smoke and cooking food and ordure, which hung in the misty air. Beyond the churchyard the various buildings of the town seemed little more than suppositions, allowing him to imagine them as fine palladian structures, not the serviceable but disagreeably ramshackle houses of Williamsburg.

"Earth to earth," intoned the rector, "ashes to ashes, dust to dust. . . ."

Eliza Bracewell attended the dark gash in the earth that was her husband's last resting place, her child clasped against her skirts. At her side stood Peter Bracewell and his wife. Nicholas had owned property and served his time as juror. If not representing the upper stratum of society, still he'd been of the solid middling sort. Now a goodly number of Williamsburg's citizens stood around his grave, eyes downcast in seemly sobriety.

To Tom's mind came the words of Cicero: "What satisfaction can there be in living, when day and night we have to reflect that at this or that moment we must die?"

A child was more likely to come to its funeral than to its marriage. Those souls who lived long enough to marry seldom made only one such contract. Tom's old school companion Bathurst Skelton, for example, had recently died, leaving his charming wife, Martha, a widow. Anne Bracewell, Peter's wife, had been the relict of James Allen, a planter from Surry County.

And now dire misfortune had deprived the other Mrs. Bracewell, Eliza, of her husband. Surely Peter, despite his reputation of caprice and instability, would remember his obligations to his nephew and provide for his education just as Tom's uncle had provided for his after the untimely death of his father. Although Eliza could be expected to marry again. She was a comely young woman, her complexion pale beneath the brim of her fashionable bonnet but of a pleasing plumpness.

"Amen," said the rector. In a soft wave of sound the gathered people echoed the word.

Eliza directed her steps toward the gate, awkward as a marionette, supported less by her brother-in-law on the one side than supporting her child on the other. Peter's wife walked just behind. By the draping of her skirts Tom perceived Anne was with child, and politely averted his eyes.

Every few steps Peter paused, inviting the socially select amongst the mourners to share the funeral feast at Nicholas's house. "Mr. Jefferson, we should be honored by your presence."

"Thank you, Mr. Bracewell. I should be honored to attend."

The rain thickened, dripping in resonant thuds down upon the coffin.

Three mockingbirds perched along the wall of the churchyard, the notes of their song passing from the one to the next and then to the next in an avian symphonic composition. An exaltation of larks. A watch of nightingales. A mimicry of mockingbirds. . . .

Tom found his creation pleasing, and promised himself he would write it down as soon as may be, after the funeral courtesies had been observed.

*   *   *

A cold wind blew dried leaves into the house. Hastily the servant closed the door and accepted Tom's hat, cloak, and gloves. Tom strode briskly through the hall, past the staircase, elegant in its austerity, to George Wythe's familiar office with its intoxicating scent of books.

"Mr. Jefferson, how very amiable of you to attend me." Wythe greeted his former pupil with a hearty handshake. His high forehead and eagle's-beak nose caused the lawyer and jurist to seem a veritable new world Aristotle, intellect personified.

"I always come to this house with great pleasure and fond memories, Mr. Wythe. How may I assist you? Is it a case of law?"

Wythe gestured Tom toward an empty chair and returned to his desk, stacked high with papers. "That is for you to tell me."

"I beg your pardon?"

"Allow me to set forth the facts of the matter, beginning with a question. How well were you acquainted with the affairs of Nicholas Bracewell, who was taken by death only two days since?"

"More by reputation and rumor than by actual discourse," Tom answered. "I confess it is his younger brother's reputation of which most rumor has reached my ears."

"There is no surprise in that," said Wythe, "when Peter has spent a rather longer time than most young men in sowing his wild oats."

"And so has found himself without the means to reap them?" Tom returned. "Mrs. Skelton, with whom I was conversing most amiably at the Governor's palace last week, said she should not be surprised if Peter had married the former Mrs. Allen so that the property left to her by Mr. Allen might assist in the payment of his debts."

"Be that as it may, debts Peter has yet, many contracted upon the expectations of an inheritance from his brother."

"Have you read out Nicholas's will and made an inventory of his personal property, then? Has something gone amiss with one or the other?"

Wythe leaned forward. "Something has gone amiss, yes. Not with the will or the inventory but with the heirs themselves. And with, I fear, the circumstances of Nicholas's death."

"Indeed?" Tom frowned, not caring for the direction of Mr. Wythe's conversation but intrigued nonetheless.

"Three days since, Nicholas sat at his desk tending to his accounts, as was his habit of an evening, when he was afflicted suddenly by a severe gastric fever. Mrs. Bracewell assisted him to his bed and summoned Dr. de Sequera, but the usual remedies availed nothing, and Nicholas died soon after dawn. May God rest his soul."

"Fevers are not infrequent this time of year."

"Neither are disputes between heirs, at any time of the year. This one, though, goes well beyond most such quarrels. Both Mrs. Nicholas Bracewell and Mr. Peter Bracewell have waited upon me, separately, each to accuse the other of murder by poison."

"Murder!" exclaimed Tom.

"Disagreeable as we may find it to be, that is the word exactly. At root, as you may expect, are the contents of Nicholas's will."

"And, I would presume, the contents of his last meal as well?" Tom smiled, thinly, as befit the circumstances. "Has Nicholas left Eliza less than her widow's third, so that she intends to renounce the will for her dower rights?"

"Not at all, no. He has left her the majority of the estate, property and business both, and Peter but a small settlement. Peter asserts, however, that Nicholas intended writing a codicil to his will that would ensure him a full two-thirds of the estate. He suggests that Eliza killed her husband before he could do so. Eliza, in turn, asserts that Peter killed Nicholas believing that the codicil had already been written, reluctant to wait till nature had in the course of time worked its will upon his brother."

"Many a man has teased his family with implications of the contents of his will," offered Tom.

"True enough."

"But are these infamous charges true? Have you any evidence that such a terrible crime as murder was actually committed?"

"Not one jot or tittle of evidence, no. This is why I sent for you. I know how you enjoy digging into a case and discovering evidence."

"And yet no case is to be seen, Mr. Wythe, only the suspicions and accusations of dissatisfied heirs."

"As yet, yes. But if the citizens of Virginia are to live under the rule of law, as is their right, then such suspicions must be answered. I'm asking you to research the matter, Mr. Jefferson. Then if you believe that no case exists to be brought before judge and jury, there the matter will rest."

"Very well," Tom returned. "As reason is the only sure guide which God has given to man, I shall apply my reason to the problem."

"Good," said Wythe. "I trust you to find its solution."

*   *   *

Tom made his way up Duke of Gloucester Street, envisioning himself a small boat tacking against the wind. His cloak fluttered like a sail. He secured his hat with one gloved hand. What he at first took to be a swirling red leaf settled upon a fence and revealed itself as a redbird.

So were man's senses deceived. Had the Bracewells allowed such distasteful motives as jealousy and greed to deceive them as well? Indeed, Tom himself had wondered at the stiffness between Eliza and Peter after Nicholas's funeral, each offering the other courtesies so exaggerated as to be mocking.

Death struck too easily and too swiftly to hasten anyone into his arms. Murder must out. Tom must not only prove a case of murder but bring its perpetrator to justice, lest doubt besmirch the community as surely as mist had smeared the streets the day of the funeral.

He turned into Dr. de Sequera's gate. There was the man himself, plucking globes of red, yellow, and green from several windblown bushes. "Doctor!"

De Sequera looked around. "Mr. Jefferson! What brings you out in such a gale?"

"A serious task. Eliza Bracewell and her husband's brother, Peter, are each accusing the other of the murder by poison of Nicholas."

"Well, well, well." De Sequera's thick black brows arched upward. He picked up a basket that was half-filled by smooth round fruits. "Come inside."

The two men walked up the steps and into the still silence of de Sequera's house. Tom looked about as eagerly as he always did when waiting upon his friend, finding great interest in the array of scientific instruments and medicines in their glass bottles. One of de Sequera's refracting lenses had so intrigued Tom he'd ordered a copy from England for himself, to magnify the vexatiously small print in his books. "What have you there?" he asked, indicating the basket. "Tomatoes?"

De Sequera held up a rosy red globe. "Yes. I eat them often."

"But are they not of the nightshade family?"

"They are, yes. And yet despite their mimicry of less salubrious fruits, they are tasty and nutritious. The food we eat determines our state of health. And nowhere more so than with Nicholas Bracewell, it appears. Tell me what you have heard."

"Very little, in truth." Tom repeated what Wythe had told him and concluded, "You treated Nicholas. What symptoms did you observe?"

"During the autumn I see many fevers of the remitting and intermittent kind. Nicholas was taken by a very sudden fit of gastric fever, with vomiting so severe I had no need for the usual vomits and purges. I administered snake root and Peruvian bark, but to no avail. This particular fever did run its course uncommonly swiftly, but each body is heir to its own."

"Vomits and purges. Those would also be the symptoms of some poisons."

"So they would."

"I should hate to ascribe to malice what could have occurred by accident. Could Nicholas have eaten food unsuitable for consumption? Not tomatoes, I warrant," Tom added with a smile.

"According to his relations, he took his dinner with friends at Weatherburn's Tavern, then supped lightly on the same bread and cheese eaten by his wife. If poison had been introduced into either meal, Nicholas should not have been its only victim. 'Tis more likely the poison found its way, by whatever means, into a cup or glass from which he and he alone drank, not long before he was struck down."

"I see." Tom nodded. "Arsenicum produces such symptoms, does it not? And antimony, the favorite of Lucrezia Borgia?"

"Both are elemental metals. Antimony, though, does not dissolve in food or water and tastes bitter. If Nicholas were indeed poisoned, I should think arsenicum a more likely means, as it readily dissolves and leaves no taste."

Tom knew he must not be afraid to follow the truth wherever it may lead. "Is it possible that Nicholas dosed himself, thereby taking his own life?"

"'Tis possible. But if I were to make my own end, I should choose a method much quicker and tidier. 'Tis certainly against our deepest instincts to cause ourselves suffering."

"Yes," Tom agreed. "How unfortunate that it is not always against our deepest instincts to cause suffering to another. Thank you for your help, doctor."

"If I can be of further assistance, please let me know." De Sequera hoisted his basket onto his arm. "Till then, I have a recipe to perfect, a sauce of tomatoes and herbs, served over fowl, perhaps. Will you join me in such a culinary experiment?"

"If you can eat tomatoes with a smile upon your face, then I shall gladly join you, and prove scientifically that they are a wholesome and delectable fruit." Shaking his head—the good doctor might be somewhat eccentric, but his methods were sound—Tom walked back out into the cold.

So Nicholas had indeed been hurried to his grave by poison. Now to discover whence the poison and how it was dispensed. Those considerations must, Tom hoped, bring him in due course to the hand that had dispensed it.

* * *

Nicholas Bracewell's parlor was small but in every particular fashionable. The porcelain figurines lining the mantelpiece were as superior a quality as any found in the best houses in Williamsburg. Tom doubted Nicholas, a pleasant but less than polished individual, had selected such tasteful furnishings. As the daughter of a planter possessing no more than an acre or two, it was Eliza who had by marrying a merchant risen above her origins.

Mrs. Bracewell's countenance was colored prettily now, but her fine dark eyes displayed a rigidity approaching haughtiness. In her black silk dress, its bodice softened by a white fichu, she reminded Tom of a magpie. "Allow me to offer you refreshment. Tea?"

Tom held that the present tax on tea was not so much an absurd expense as an affront to colonial rights. Bowing, he refused the tea but accepted a chair. After a few moments of polite conversation he came to the point of his visit. "Mr. Wythe has told me of your allegations against Mr. Peter Bracewell. And of his corresponding allegations against you."

Eliza flicked open her black-trimmed mourning fan and with it concealed her lips as she spoke. "He cannot even present you with a reasonable falsehood. Why should I kill my husband and render myself a *femme sole*, alone in the world?"

"Was the poison introduced into Nicholas's food, do you think?"

"No. No one else fell ill. I expect it was mixed with his wine."

"Wine?"

" 'Twas his custom to take a glass or two of wine in the evenings as he looked over his accounts. He fell ill with the bottle and the glass still before him, or so I found him when I answered his cries of distress."

"You were not with him when he was taken ill?"

"No. I was here, endeavoring to learn the words of a new song. My husband took pleasure in my singing, whether or not I had the advantage of tutors in music and deportment in my youth." Her voice took on a mocking edge.

Tom nodded. "May I see Nicholas's office, please, Mrs. Bracewell?"

"Surely." Furling the fan, Eliza led the way down a narrow hall to a closet at the back of the house.

A bookcase, a desk, and a chair filled the tiny room. Two ledger books lay upon the desk next to an inkwell and pen. A blue wine bottle and a glass occupied the far corner, beyond several bills of lading. A child's toy horse lay next to the door. "This is how the room appeared when Mr. Bracewell was taken ill?" Tom asked.

" 'Twas necessary to wash the floor," said Eliza.

"Ah." Tom had no wish to press Nicholas's wife as to the unfortunate details of his illness. He picked up the bottle, recognizing the same vintage he kept for his own use. 'Twas merchant Josiah Greenhow's best, evinced by Greenhow's seal, a glass medallion affixed to the bottle just beneath its shoulder. The cork that plugged the bottle's mouth was still damp and firm. A small amount of wine splashed back and forth inside. "This bottle is new, is it not?"

"I purchased it at Mr. Greenhow's store little more than an hour before my husband drank from it."

"Did you first draw the cork? Did you note whether it were sound?"

"I drew the cork, which was quite sound, with my own hands, to ease my husband's way for him."

And so was his way eased across the Styx, Tom said to himself. "Who, then, could have entered the room between the time you brought the bottle home and the time he drank from it?"

Eliza's plump face took on the appearance of a dried apple. "Our cook and housekeeper, Sylvia, was away that night. But Peter lives just there, on my husband's sufferance, and comes and goes in this house as though we lived here on his." She gestured toward the window.

It overlooked the house's dependencies, kitchen, dairy, smokehouse, and privy. Beyond the small structures lay a garden, set out with a trellis and a row of fruit trees in design very like the Wythe's garden. Over the few remaining leaves of the trees rose the roof of Peter Bracewell's cottage. A narrow path ran between the two properties, for the convenience of the servants, no doubt. "Nicholas owns the house where Peter and his wife make their home?"

"He did, yes. Now Peter owns it, for it and it alone was left to him in the will."

Tom set the bottle back down. "What then, could be the motive for murder, Mrs. Bracewell?"

"My husband's other properties, not to mention his business, all of which have now come to me. Peter desires to live in leisured dignity but has not the means to do so. I must confess he is no stranger to the gambling tables, and in other ways lives well beyond his income. All is status and show to him."

Tom offered no response to that statement.

"The evening before the one my husband was taken from me, he and his brother fought most bitterly over Nicholas's refusal to pay Peter's debts. They spoke so loudly I could not help but overhear, walking as I was outside the door."

"Did Nicholas advise Peter that he intended to make his will more favorable to him?"

Eliza's chin went up. "Nicholas told him he had already made the change, hoping to encourage Peter to mend his ways and turn his hand to business."

"But Nicholas did not in fact write the codicil?"

"No. He did not. 'Twas Peter's pride and avarice that led him to believe Nicholas's ruse, as though Nicholas would compromise his own son's inheritance in favor of a blaggard such as Peter!"

"And so you believe Peter hastened Nicholas to his grave."

"I do not believe it, Mr. Jefferson. I know it."

"The facts of the matter have yet to be proved," Tom told her. "May I have the use of this bottle and its contents?"

"To pour away, I should hope, lest some other unfortunate soul should drink from it."

Tom's intentions were otherwise, but Mrs. Bracewell had no need to know his true purposes. "I should greatly appreciate the loan of a basket in which to carry the bottle. And may I interview your cook?"

Eliza, her color high, stared him up and down for a long moment, then quit the room.

Tom turned to the desk. Despite the sunlight outside, the room was dusky, and he had no means by which to light the lamp now sitting cold upon the desk. Still he inspected the desktop, books, and empty glass as best he could. Yes, by Jove, a few grains of a chalky white powder were caught in the hinges where the desktop could be folded away. Tom wet his forefinger at his lips and pressed it to the spot, so that a particle or two adhered to his flesh. Making a face indicative of doubt and caution mingled, he put his fingertip first close to his nostril, then passed it across his tongue. The substance had neither smell nor taste. It was neither sugar nor flour.

The light from the door was blocked by a woman's entrance into the room. By her simple calico garb, white headcloth, and ebon complexion,

Tom deduced that she was the cook and housekeeper. She proffered a wicker basket filled with straw, her hands trembling so severely the straw rustled. "Mrs. Bracewell sends you this, Mr. Jefferson."

"Thank you," he said, and accepted the basket. "Sylvia is your name?"

"Yes, sir."

"Were you in the house the night Mr. Bracewell was taken ill?"

"No, sir. 'Twas my night out, so I went visiting with my daughter at Mr. Randolph's house. I was nowhere near this room, no sir."

As this statement could be readily investigated, and as Tom was eager to ascertain the cause of the woman's agitation, he moved on to another question. "Do you have any knowledge of poisons, Sylvia?"

Her eyes widened, surpassing agitation and achieving outright fear. "No, sir. I never poisoned Mr. Nicholas. Why would I do that?"

"Indeed, Sylvia. An excellent question." As an enslaved person, Sylvia's testimony would not be allowed before a court of law, giving her no reason to lie about the circumstances in which she found herself. Indeed, to murder her master would have gone against her best interests, for even with her inheritance Eliza might have found herself obliged to make economies, and an experienced cook like Sylvia would bring a good price in that market for human flesh Tom found so troubling.

"Sylvia, you need fear no retribution if only you tell the truth. What do you know of Mr. Bracewell's death?"

"Nothing, sir," the poor woman stammered. "Only that he was taken terrible sick just after I brought arsenicum and soft soap into the house."

"Arsenicum and soft soap?"

"Mrs. Bracewell bid me buy them at the market, so as to clean the bedsteads and rid them of bedbugs. But within a day they was gone and Mr. Bracewell was dead."

"Did you by any chance overhear Mr. Bracewell and his brother in disputation over the younger gentleman's financial situation?"

"Oh, no sir, I never heard anything of the sort. Not that I'd be listening, mind."

Nodding, Tom placed the wine bottle in the basket and slipped the handle over his arm. He found a small coin in his pocket and pressed it into Sylvia's hand. "Thank you. Please give my respects to Mrs. Bracewell, and tell her that I am continuing my investigations into the matter."

Her manner mollified, Sylvia showed Tom to the door.

*   *   *

Tom walked round the corner of the street toward Peter Bracewell's front door. Two households, as Master Shakespeare had said, both alike in dignity, and no less given to feuding, or so it seemed by Eliza Bracewell's testimony.

Black birds swirled like cinders in the wind, stooping over a field at the edge of town. Ravens or crows, most likely, although at this distance Tom could not ascertain which. An unkindness of ravens, he said to himself. A murder of crows.

The bottle and basket hung from his arm. He should not allow his next witness any knowledge of what the previous one had said. He concealed the basket behind a patch of tobacco which, despite the time of year, still flourished between the cottage and the street. Then Tom stepped up to Peter Bracewell's front door and in a matter of moments was seated in another parlor furnished a la mode, complete with an elegant French mirror above the mantel.

Peter himself, in truth only a half-brother of Nicholas, had always had more of a taste for culture than had the bluff merchant now deceased. Tom himself had recently spent a most agreeable musical evening in this house, playing his violin whilst Peter played the harpsichord and his wife sang like a lark. The cold supper had been the equal of one served at the palace itself, a calf's head displayed as the centerpiece of a veritable cornucopia of dishes.

Today Peter stood before the fireplace warming the tails of his coat, his handsome face soured by recent events. "Mr. Jefferson, I have given the matter much thought, and have concluded that my brother's death was an unnatural one. Fevers abound in these climes, yes, but for him to suffer one so conveniently defies belief."

"His fever and subsequent death were convenient?" Tom asked.

"On the day before his death, Nicholas stated his intention of paying my debts. He also informed me he'd added a codicil to his will leaving much of his property and his business to me, as a reward for my hard work in its pursuance. So Holy Scripture instructs us to welcome home the prodigal, he said, and congratulated me on mastering my baser appetites. But his wife has always been jealous of Nicholas's affection toward me, thinking it better directed to her own son."

"And who can blame a woman who wishes to protect her child?"

Peter's mouth twisted in a satirical smile. "No one at all. But not when she imposes upon Mr. Wythe, and through him upon you, the vilest of falsehoods—a charge of murder laid against an innocent man."

"Why, then, should Mrs. Bracewell accuse you?"

"If she were to eliminate me, then would not Nicholas's entire estate fall to their son, and through him, upon her? Who's to say she does not have her eye and her cap set already toward a new husband, one of greater property and therefore greater prospects than my poor brother?"

"What are you suggesting, Mr. Bracewell?"

"That Nicholas was indeed murdered. But by his own wife."

"How then, do you think Mrs. Bracewell could have accomplished such an outrage?"

"With poison from her own kitchen. My own wife saw Nicholas's Sylvia purchasing arsenicum and soft soap, and remarked upon it, whereupon Sylvia admitted to the infestation she hoped to combat." Peter paced across the room, drew an arpeggio from the keyboard of the harpsichord, then looked out the window at Nicholas's roof. "Less than an hour before my brother's death I passed Eliza upon the street outside Mr. Greenhow's establishment, her basket upon her arm and the neck of a wine bottle protruding from it. Nicholas was accustomed to taking a glass or two before retiring. How easier to introduce a poison to him but to no one else?"

"You saw her carrying a bottle such as that one?" Tom indicated two blue glass bottles sitting in the corner cupboard, close beside several stemmed glasses.

"Very similar. Those, though, are my own private stock. Nicholas, with less of a palate than God saw fit to give me, drank from the common store." Peter presented one of the bottles for Tom's inspection.

The common store was quite acceptable for everyday consumption, in Tom's considered opinion. But he kept his own counsel and noted only that yes, the glass medallions on the bottles were indeed imprinted with Peter's name, not with that of merchant Greenhow.

"Surely you will not object to telling me, Mr. Bracewell, how you were employed between the time Mrs. Bracewell brought home the new bottle and the time her husband first felt the pangs of—his illness."

"I found employment just here, Mr. Jefferson, practicing the new minuet by Corelli, neglecting even to take my supper, for my wife and I intend to hold yet another musical evening very soon. We should be honored if you would join us. I shall," he added with a sly smile, "extend an invitation to Mrs. Martha Skelton as well."

Tom concealed his expression by inspecting his shoe buckles. Delightful as she was, blessed with a voice as lovely as her form, Mrs. Skelton was not party to this problem. "Thank you, Mr. Bracewell. I heard your playing myself that night, accompanied by your wife's most agreeable singing."

As though summoned by his words, Mrs. Anne Bracewell entered the room. She too, had no doubt happened to be walking outside. Her silk wrapper was more highly colored than her complexion, which was very pale, as befit her delicate condition. "May I offer you dinner at our table, Mr. Jefferson? Our cook is not the equal of my sister-in-law's Sylvia, but she does tolerably well."

"Thank you, Mrs. Bracewell, but I expect Mrs. Vobe has already prepared my usual dish of vegetables." Tom rose to his feet. "I was complimenting your husband on your singing, which was cut so lamentably short the night of Mr. Nicholas Bracewell's death."

"I was fortunate to have had the advantage of tutors in music and deportment in my youth." Anne inclined her head with grave propriety, but Tom did not imagine the edge of mockery in her voice.

He heard the echo of Eliza's words in Anne's. Yes, Anne's family was of a higher status in Virginia than Eliza's, a fact of which both women seemed only too aware.

Making his excuses, Tom found his way to the street. There he retrieved the basket and stood for a moment listening to a mockingbird singing in a nearby tree. Just now it seemed to be repeating no particular melody. He wondered whether he could teach one of the little creatures a song, an Irish or Scottish air, perhaps, even though its duplication could be but a counterfeit of the original.

Just as the support Peter Bracewell had given Eliza at her husband's funeral was counterfeit, or perhaps as Peter's indignation or Eliza's excuses were counterfeit. The bird, though, did not purpose to deceive with its mimicry.

*   *   *

After stopping to speak with several other citizens, Tom returned to his lodgings and amazed his landlady by asking to purchase one of the chickens that occupied a pen behind her kitchen. "An old one will do, one destined soon for the pot," he explained.

"Well, then," replied Mrs. Vobe, "have that old cockerel in the far corner, the one's grown weary of his life and is pondering dumplings and gravy."

This chicken would not follow its relatives into dumplings and gravy or even into de Sequera's exotic sauce. The good doctor might be content to experiment upon himself, but Tom intended to take a safer course. He isolated the chicken in a small pen and set before it a dish of corn laced liberally with a draught from Nicholas's wine bottle. Leaving the animal pecking away at the food, he sat down to his own dinner, a splendid *potage a pois*.

He had had little need to inquire of the Bracewells' neighbors whether they heard the music of harpsichord and voice the night of Nicholas's death. With the windows standing open, he had heard both himself. He did, though, ascertain that Peter had recently, if reluctantly, turned his hand to Nicholas's business, and that the relations between the brothers had not always been so cordial as Peter would have Tom think, as the issue of his own debts caused a constant friction.

Mrs. Randolph had assured Tom as to the whereabouts of Eliza's Sylvia at the fatal hour. And Josiah Greenhow, who'd readily testified to Eliza's acquisition of the infamous bottle of wine soon before her husband's death, asserted that its cork had been fixed and whole when it left his hands.

Nothing, then, that Tom learned from the citizens of the town led him to believe either Bracewell a liar and therefore a murderer.

He returned to Mrs. Vobe's yard to discover the chicken in its death throes. Before he could do it a mercy by wringing its neck, it expired in a shuddering heap of feathers. Tom poked and prodded its lifeless body, but unlike a Roman haruspex of old declined to inspect its internal organs. He'd proved that the poison, probably arsenicum, had been introduced into the bottle of wine in the brief interval between its arrival at the house and Nicholas's pouring it out.

There should be some way of formulating a more exact test, to indicate not only the presence of poison but its specific sort. Then no uncertainties would remain on the mind, all would be demonstration and satisfaction. . . . No. Science could not illuminate the shadows of the human heart. It could identify the poison but not who placed it in the bottle. The question, as always, was *cui bono*, who benefited from the crime?

Peter might well have killed his brother to gain enough income to pay his debts and to live in the style to which he had accustomed himself. He, though, could not have been playing his harpsichord and poisoning the wine at the same instant.

Eliza might have killed her husband to prevent her own income from being diminished, as oftentimes widows found themselves obliged to take in lodgers or depend upon the kindness of relations, which, considering the demeanor of Eliza's relations, was not an alternative. But then, if Eliza had made good with her first marriage, why not make better with her second, especially with her first husband's estate as bait?

A squawk made Tom glance around. Mrs. Vobe's cat was crouching in the door of the kitchen, its fur forming a bristling ridge down its back. A mockingbird stood only a few feet away, wings half extended, cawing its contempt at its nemesis. No wonder it was named a "mocking" bird, when it not only copied but teased.

If the season had been spring, Tom would have thought the bird intended to draw the cat away from its nest. Such was always the maternal imperative, to protect the child even at the forfeit of one's own life. But the season was autumn. Perhaps the bird fancied the cat encroached upon its territory, which passion was also a human trait.

Tom considered that Nicholas's child was as much a motive in his death as his territory, his possessions. Eliza and Peter would each benefit from the other's demise, as Nicholas's property would go to his son, and the surviving adult, whether mother or uncle, would have control over its use.

But both Peter's and Eliza's accounts rang true. Neither countenance displayed any guilt or sly regard. Indeed, both seemed quite sincere. And yet one of them must be false. Tom needed more evidence, evidence that could be demonstrated to everyone's satisfaction.

The cat leaped forward. The bird launched itself into the air and flew away, evading the extended claws by inches. A thin dust swirled lazily into the air and then drifted back to earth. The cat slinked back into the kitchen, admitting to no defeat. Its paws left a spoor in the dust.

Frowning, Tom strolled closer to the site of the momentary battle. Had he not seen it for himself, still he could have reconstructed the affray from the marks in the dusk, the spiky prints of the bird's feet, the pugmarks of the cat, and the twin furrows where the bird's wings had brushed the earth upon its abrupt departure.

Tom's eye then turned to the wine bottle, still sitting where he'd laid it, on a shelf inside the chicken coop. A fine layer of dust and chaff shrouded its gleam. He remembered Mrs. Vobe, at the very moment poor Nicholas was hastening toward his mortality, entering Tom's room wiping another bottle with her apron. No doubt Greenhow had done the same, cleaning the bottle Eliza purchased of dust and dirt. . . .

If his mind could stretch itself to invent a new collective noun, it could also invent a new scientific test. One that could identify the hand that had poured the poison. Taking great care to lift the bottle by its lip, Tom held it up to the light and squinted at its smooth glass sides.

*   *   *

Tom waited politely as George Wythe seated his guests around the green baize-covered table in his office. Mrs. Nicholas Bracewell twitched her skirts away from Peter Bracewell's buckled shoes, whilst Mrs. Peter Bracewell folded her hands in her lap and looked about with little expression. Her husband and sister-in-law bent upon each other expressions of distrust and disdain, each complexion colored as pinkly as though Mr. Wythe's fire burned with much greater heat.

"Mr. Jefferson," said Wythe, seating himself in the remaining chair.

Stepping forward, Tom placed a clear pane of glass on the table between Eliza and Peter. "Would you each be so kind as to press your thumbs and fingertips firmly against this glass?"

"I beg your pardon?" demanded Peter.

Eliza said haughtily, "An exceedingly strange request, Mr. Jefferson."

"If you please," Wythe said, "indulge my young friend's scientific endeavors. He has explained his reasoning to me, and it rings true in every respect."

With indignant murmurings, first Eliza and then Peter did as he requested, even suffering Tom to apologetically roll their thumbs back and forth against the glass. He carried the pane closer to Wythe's lamp, scattered it with the fine dust he'd collected in Mrs. Vobe's yard, and blew the excess into the fireplace. He then inspected the resulting smudges through his refractive lens. "It seems as though the oils inherent in human flesh leave marks upon all they touch, in a process not dissimilar to the way marks are made upon paper by the metal type and ink of a printing press. These marks can be readily distinguished on such a hard, smooth surface as glass, be it this pane of glass I borrowed from Mr. Geddy's workshop, or the glass of a wine bottle, which must be grasped firmly lest it fall and break."

Not the least murmur or rustle of fabric came from any of the gathered souls.

Tom turned to the sheet of paper resting upon the corner of Wythe's desk. He'd employed the afternoon sunlight in scrutinizing each print upon the bottle and painstakingly sketching its patterns, so that now he had before him a gallery of whorling designs like miniature labyrinths. "I theorize," he continued, "that each human fingerprint is as distinct, albeit subtly, as each leaf upon a tree, or each snowflake falling from the sky in winter."

There, yes, one pattern matched those made by Eliza's fingers. Another matched the set he'd taken from himself, and a third matched that of Josiah Greenhow, who'd agreed with good humor to the test. Wythe himself had provided a wax seal pressed by Nicholas Bracewell's thumb, from which Tom had been obliged to extrapolate the rest of the dead man's grasp. But nowhere upon his paper was a copy of the pattern Peter had just this moment impressed upon the glass.

So then. The presence of Eliza's prints proved nothing, as she'd already admitted touching the bottle. The absence of Peter's prints, though, proved that he'd never touched it at all, and was therefore innocent of pouring the arsenicum into its narrow mouth.

Tom might perhaps have settled then and there upon Eliza as the perpetrator, except he had yet one set of designs upon his paper for which he could make no attribution. Was it possible that Eliza and Peter were both telling the truth, and the murderer was someone else?

He could hardly test the fingertips of every citizen of Williamsburg who'd passed by the Bracewell's house during the fatal hour. But no. *Cui bono*, he reminded himself, and turned toward the group of people seated around the table. The disgruntlement of heirs.

From the chill twilight beyond the windows came the chirrup of a mockingbird, so gentle he would have found it hard to believe the same bird capable of the harsh squawks he'd heard this afternoon had he not heard them for himself. . . .

The answer winged into his mind like a mimicry of mockingbirds winging amongst the trees. He himself, not to mention the neighbors, had heard a woman's voice singing whilst Peter played the harpsichord. All had leaped to the assumption, as the cat had leaped toward the bird, that the voice belonged to Anne. But, as the cat had missed the bird, so assumption had missed fact.

Eliza had been practicing a song at that same hour. Without study, who could tell the song of one mockingbird from another? Who could tell Eliza's song from Anne's, particularly as Eliza had been endeavoring to copy Anne? That Anne had been privileged to possess tutors in music and deportment was a fact with which each woman mocked the other.

Tom considered Anne Bracewell's lacy cap, which was presented to his gaze as her own gaze was directed to her lap. From modesty or from guilt?

Any mother, avian or human, would put her child's welfare above her own. She would be compelled to defend any encroachment into her territory, even though such defense meant the risk of her own life. Eliza might have killed her husband to provide for her son, but Anne, too, had a child who wanted provision. As a *femme coverte*, her property might belong to her husband but his belonged to her. And to their child.

Anne had remarked upon Sylvia's purchase of arsenicum. Anne would have known Nicholas's and Eliza's habits as well as Peter. Anne, going about her lethal errand, might have deliberately started singing every time Eliza paused, so that music accompanied her trip through the dusk from house to house and back again as though in a tragic opera. It would have been the work of only seconds for her to steal the arsenicum from the kitchen on her way into the house and to dispose of its packaging in the privy on her way back.

Tom set his pane of glass on the table in front of her. "If you please, Mrs. Bracewell, might I have the impressions of your fingers as well?"

"What is the meaning of this?" Peter demanded, and again Wythe remonstrated.

Slowly Anne raised her hand and set it against the glass, so limp and feeble that Tom had to push her fingertips down with his own. A moment later he had ascertained that the remaining marks upon the poisoned bottle were indeed those of her hands. Glancing up, he met Wythe's solemn eyes, and received a nod of encouragement.

"Facts are stubborn things," Tom said. "The fact of who poured arsenicum in Nicholas's wine is now revealed. Mrs. Peter Bracewell left the marks of her fingers upon the bottle. Her husband, intent upon his music, was never sensible of his wife's brief absence from the room. Mrs. Nicholas Bracewell, intent upon hers, was never sensible of her sister-in-law's brief presence in her house."

Eliza's eyes darted to Anne's bowed head, and her countenance suffused with understanding. Peter's countenance went red. "You accuse my wife of murder?"

"I do, yes," said Tom. "Mrs. Bracewell no doubt intended Nicholas's death to be thought a natural one. And so would it have been, had you and Mrs. Nicholas Bracewell not chosen to contest the estate. In time Mrs. Anne would have discovered an opportunity to destroy the dregs of the poisoned wine, and no one would ever have been the wiser."

"But, but," stammered Peter. "Why?"

"For the child." Anne rose unsteadily to her feet, her complexion as pale as ash. Her hands rested upon the swelling of her belly. "I could not bear our child being born to less than the income he deserved, an income which his uncle permitted his own child but denied to ours. Now it is the child that I shall plead before the court. . . ." She fell as a curtain falls when the hooks are torn away, folding to the floor.

Eliza knelt over Anne and cradled her lolling head even as disgust wrote its lines across her features. Peter stared from Wythe to Tom and back again, as though they were capable of changing the situation in which he found himself.

"I shall send for the sheriff and his constable," said Wythe, his sober mien becoming grim. "I see no need, however, to conduct Mrs. Bracewell to the jail. She may stay in her own home until after the trial. Until after the delivery of the child."

Tom turned toward the window. Yes, all had been demonstrated. But he found little satisfaction in his demonstration. And yet his failure to solve the problem would have caused a different set of uncertainties to remain upon his mind.

Against the darkness he could see only his own shape reflected imperfectly in the glass. He could still hear, though, the song of the mockingbird outside. So men, he said to himself, often imitate the finer sentiments, but defectively and with less pleasure to those nearby than the mockingbird mimics music.

* * *

Tom threw open his window upon the bright, soft spring day. There were his little friends, perched amongst the new leaves of the tree just outside. Tom sang a few lines of "Barbara Allen" and first one, then the other mockingbird repeated them, heads tilted to the side, throats swelling, eyes shining like obsidian beads. When he completed his property at Monticello, Tom intended to populate it with mockingbirds in the most comfortable cages he could devise.

He considered also that his new house was in need of a mistress. Indeed, he had only this morning copied into his commonplace book Milton's lines celebrating the felicities of marriage, which, along with the joys of books, friends, and music, gave the lie to old Cicero and his dissatisfaction with living. Death came soon enough. Life was meant to be embraced.

As was Mrs. Martha Skelton. . . . But it was a truth universally acknowledged that a widow in possession of a good fortune might not necessarily be in want of a new husband.

He meant to convince Martha that he wanted her not for her fortune or her social position but for herself, just as he enjoyed the mockingbirds for themselves, and not because he intended to submit them to gravy or de Sequera's delectable tomato sauce. He scattered a few dried berries on the windowsill, and laid out several long red hairs from his own head.

In such a context he could not help but remember the Bracewells. Anne had come to trial and been found guilty of murder, but the sentence of the court had not been carried out by human hands. Just past the new year she'd died as so many women died, bringing new life into the world.

Now Peter was courting another widow, this one with both children and fortune, who had expressed herself glad of Anne's daughter. Eliza, on the other hand, had settled down with her middling income and declared her intentions never to remarry.

One bird lit softly upon the sill and picked up a berry. The other seized upon the hair and flew away to build its nest, the task set before it by natural law. That same natural law that gave men the free will to covet and to murder. Or to do neither.

Was it not simply reason that no one ought to harm another in his life, health, liberty, or possessions? Was it not simply reason that all men were created equal, and that a government existed for men, not men for government? It went against the law of nature that the laws for the citizens of Britain should be the just laws, and those for the citizens of the American colonies only imitations, more imperfect in equity and justice than any song repeated by a mockingbird.

Tom leaned against the frame of the window and watched the mockingbirds weaving the long red strand amongst the twigs of its nest, building for the future.

Alligator Tears
Bill Crider

It was clear that Louisa didn't like the creature in the bathtub. She said, "I don't see why you would want to have a thing like that, John."

John Quincy Adams, sixth president of the United States, looked down at the beast that reposed just under the surface of the water in the bathtub. He had to admit that it was ugly, with its leathery blackish-green skin covered in tough pimples, its unprepossessing snout filled with spiked teeth, its unseemly lethargic manner.

"It is not a thing," he said. "It is an alligator. The name comes to us from the Spaniards, who called it *El Lagarto*, the lizard."

Louisa sniffed, an action for which she had a certain flair. She said, "It is, no matter what its name or the origin of its name, most unattractive, and certainly not suitable to be a resident in the home of the president of his country."

A lesser man than John Quincy Adams might at that point have had an uncharitable thought about his wife and her own suitability for the presidential mansion, but if such a thought occurred to Adams, he repressed it at once. He had made his marriage knowing that he would stay with Louisa until one of them died, no matter what their private relations were. That was simply the way things were.

"It is," he said, "as suitable a resident as some people would be." While not willing to engage in harsh thoughts about Louisa, Adams was quite content to engage in them about certain others, particularly one of his opponents in the presidential election. "I believe that I shall name this alligator Andrew Jackson."

Louisa rewarded her husband's comment with a small smile, the only kind of which she seemed capable.

"There is a certain resemblance," she said.

"Yes. Both are wild and rough; both would bite the hand that fed them; both are savage and unrelenting killers."

"Now, John, perhaps you go too far."

"Perhaps I do, but I go no further in my accusations than Jackson has gone in his. The very idea of saying that I have filled this house with gambling paraphernalia!"

"He did not say that himself," Louisa pointed out.

"No, of course not. But his followers did, and that is not the worst lie they have told."

Adams's bitterness was well-earned. No candidate in the presidential election having received a majority of the electoral votes, Adams had been chosen president in the House of Representatives, and the followers of Jackson, who had received the most electoral votes, had immediately mounted a campaign to drag Adams's name and reputation through the mire.

They said that Adams was undeserving of his office and had become president only because his father had been president before him, implying that the Adams family was trying to establish an American monarchy.

They said that to satisfy the lust of the Russian Tsar, Adams had turned Pander and had procured for him a lovely American girl.

And they told the story of the gambling paraphernalia, which happened to be nothing more than a billiard table.

"False rumors may blacken your name temporarily," Louisa said, "but they can have no lasting effect on the reputation of a true gentleman."

Adams, though he would once have agreed with his wife, was now not so certain that she was correct. Rumors were like the teeth of the alligator, sharp and dangerous and capable of tearing the flesh from the bones.

"I suppose you should keep your pet," Louisa continued. "And its name. It will serve to remind you of your great enemy and how dangerous he is. And of how as long as you stay safely away from him, he will do you no harm."

"It would certainly be quite a mistake to bathe in the same water with him," Adams said.

"Indeed," Louisa said. "But tell me, John, are such creatures as this found in the Potomac?"

It was well known in Washington that, during the bathing season, Adams strolled to the river each morning, sometimes before dawn, and swam in the nude for as long as two hours. It was his favorite form of exercise.

"Have no fear," he said. "The alligator is native to the southern extremes of the country. And, after all, I was a champion swimmer in my youth. There is no possibility of danger in the Potomac."

"I am most glad to hear it," Louisa said.

But as it turned out, her husband was wrong.

*   *   *

Adams arose the next morning as usual, around four-thirty. After reading his Bible he went outside. It was going to be a warm and humid day, and he looked forward to his matutinal swim. The early morning was the one time of the day he could call his own, for much of the rest of his time was taken up by a wearying succession of people who importuned him to grant their various wishes: men complaining about the laws, women seeking pardons for imprisoned husbands, members of Congress who hoped for this favor or that, Indians complaining about injustices to their tribes, ministers from Britain or Mexico or France, also hoping for favors though offering little in return. From the middle of the morning until around five in the afternoon, all his time was taken. Adams knew that he had a responsibility to be available to the people, but there were times that he regretted it. His only real time for reflection and thought was in the early dawn hours, and he treasured the time alone. He was not in the least socially inclined.

When he reached his usual swimming spot, he found it deserted, as always. That was the reason he had chosen it. He removed his clothing, laid it neatly on a large, flat rock along with the clean napkins he had brought to dry himself. He was, at age fifty-eight, a trim, compact little man, not much given to smiling. But he allowed himself a small smile now as he entered the water and thought of the two hours of solitude he had ahead of him.

The water was cold at first, but he soon became used to its lapping around his ankles, and launched himself into a dive beneath the surface. The water closed over his head, and he glided along beneath it, letting it flow over him in a comforting stream. This was by far the best part of his day.

He was swimming strongly along parallel to the shore, mentally composing a sonnet to the dawn, when something clutched at his ankle.

A sharp thrill coursed through him, and Adams thought about the teeth of the alligator. He imagined them taking their fatal grip on his foot while the alligator shook him and rolled him beneath the water until he was drowned. His stomach knotted, and for just a second his arms and legs refused to follow their usual discipline. They flailed and splashed, sending water-drops flying, but he soon gained control of his limbs and dismissed thoughts of an alligator as the merest fancy. There were, as he had assured his wife, no alligators in the Potomac.

What had made a feeble grasp at his anatomy had not been sharp teeth, he realized, but something else altogether, something that felt more like the cold fingers of a dead hand than teeth.

Adams turned in his course and dived under the clear water, his eyes searching for whatever had touched him, and in seconds he saw her, a young woman devoid of clothing. She seemed to be standing there, arms outstretched, her body white as marble, and her wild black hair writhing about her head like the serpents of Medusa.

Adams knew at once that she must be drowned. He could do nothing for her, but he could at least remove her from the river. He surfaced to get his breath, shook water from his face, and looked along the shore. There was still no one there. He inhaled deeply and dived again.

He swam to the woman and grasped her cold, upraised hand, trying to pull her to the surface, but she did not move. Diving deeper, Adams saw that her right foot was wedged between two rough stones. He was able to move them with only a little effort, and when that was done he drew the woman to the surface and pulled her to the shore.

First he dried himself and then covered her nude body with the napkins as best he could. There was nothing offensive in the sight of her, for to

Adams death was merely the appropriate end to life and not something to be feared or to arouse disgust. As he covered her face, which was flushed as if she burned with fever instead of being inert and cold, something tugged at his memory.

He raised the napkin. The woman looked up at him with dull black eyes that might have been carved from stone, and he realized that he knew her. Or had met her. She was Mrs. Morrison, and she had been to see him only two days earlier to plead for the life of her husband, who had been convicted of mail robbery.

* * *

Mrs. Morrison was a formidable woman, and her eyes had not been dull at her first meeting with Adams. They had snapped with dark lightning as she spoke:

"Hubert Morrison is my husband, sir, and an honest tradesman," she said. "He has done nothing wrong, nor would he ever. He was falsely accused by others of a crime he never committed. You must find a way to pardon him so that his innocent blood will not be on the conscience of the state."

Adams knew a little of Morrison's case, and he was aware that convincing evidence had been found secreted in the man's house. He said, "Mail robbery, madam, is a serious crime, and I believe that it deserves the fullest punishment that the law provides."

"And we heartily agree," said Mr. Harlin Morrison. He was Mrs. Morrison's brother-in-law, a sharp-eyed, sharp-toothed little man who seemed quite sincere in his assertion. "However, my brother Hubert could never have committed this crime. He is as honest as the day is long. His probity is renowned among all, as this paper will prove."

With those words he had produced from the pocket of his coat a petition for the release of his brother. It was signed by no fewer than thirty respectable persons of their town, all of whom appeared convinced that Mr. Hubert Morrison was indeed a paragon of honesty, a man of utmost integrity.

"Could a man so well thought of by his neighbors be guilty of mail robbery?" Mrs. Morrison asked as Adams perused the paper. "I think not!"

Although he was known as a hard man, Adams had always experienced difficulty in resisting the solicitations of women, but he said, "There must be those who dislike him, or they would never have accused him."

"Yes," Mrs. Morrison said, "but they were his enemies. You of all men must know what a man's enemies will say about him."

Adams thought of Andrew Jackson's supporters and the lies they had spread. He said, "I know that very well."

Mrs. Morrison gestured to the paper that Adams held. "The good people of our town signed their names to show what they believe about my husband. See if his accusers would do the same!"

"And who are these accusers?" Adams wanted to know.

"Ah," Harlin Morrison said, with a rueful smile. "There you have found the crux of the matter. No one knows. The blackguards have neither faces nor names. That alone shouts out my brother's innocence."

"A man has the right to face his accusers," Adams said.

"But these were anonymous, never showing their faces or revealing their names."

"And the evidence found in your home?" Adams asked Mrs. Morrison. "How did that come there?"

She shook her head. "That I cannot answer. I know only that my husband did not put it there. Perhaps his accusers would know."

"But you do not."

"No. I did not see it done."

"It could have been anyone," Harlin Morrison said, spreading his large hands. "There are no servants in the house, and we are frequently absent. Hubert's enemies could have—"

"And who are these enemies?" Adams asked. "Are they as faceless as the accusers?"

Harlin Morrison reddened. "Are you saying that I am a liar, sir? For I assure you that—"

"I am saying nothing of the kind," Adams told him. "I am merely asking a question."

"My husband is a printer," Mrs. Morrison interjected. "There are those who do not like what he prints. They believe that it goes too far." She paused. "He is not fond of Mr. Jackson."

She nodded to her brother-in-law, who reached into his coat and brought out a handbill which he then passed to Adams. On it was a crude drawing of Jackson firing a rifle at a blindfolded man in uniform, a reference to Jackson's having executed several deserters during his time in the army. The inscription under the picture contained only one word: *Murderer*.

Adams could understand all too well why someone might not be fond of Jackson, even though the charge depicted on the handbill was as ridiculous as the charges Jackson's followers leveled at Adams.

"Your husband does indeed seem like a forthright man," Adams said, returning the handbill. "And you, Mr. Morrison, do you share your brother's views?"

"I work for my brother and share his roof as well as his views. His enemies are my enemies."

"But you cannot name them."

"No, sir, I cannot."

"And you, Mrs. Morrison?"

"No," she said.

Adams was about to drop the subject when Harlin Morrison raised a finger.

"There is one, I suppose," he said. "A certain George Greene. He is a Jacksonian of the worst sort. He has even threatened to burn the print shop. I believe that he is mad, but that may not be so. I do know that he is capable of any evil, though I cannot say for certain that he was my brother's accuser."

Adams had heard of Greene, an unsavory character indeed, quite possibly guilty of any number of crimes, including vote fraud, though convicted of none. It would not be a surprise to learn that he was involved in mail robbery or in a plot to ruin another man and destroy his property.

Still, Morrison, by all accounts, had been fairly tried and convicted. Adams said, "Did not the people who signed this paper speak for your Mr. Morrison at his trial?"

"They did," Mrs. Morrison said. "Almost the entire lot of them."

"And did he not speak in his own defense?"

"He refused to speak," Mrs. Morrison said.

Adams was surprised. "What? He said nothing?"

"That is correct," Mrs. Morrison said. "Nor would he allow me to speak in his behalf."

Adams looked at her brother-in-law, who shook his head.

"Nor I," he said.

"A stubborn man, then," Adams said.

"Yes," Mrs. Morrison said, "but a good and a loyal one."

"That may be," Adams said.

Being a stubborn man himself, he could appreciate the trait in others, but he knew there was a difference between stubbornness and being bull-headed. And while he valued loyalty quite highly, there were times when a man had to speak in his own behalf no matter the consequences.

He voiced none of these thoughts, however. Instead, he said to Mrs. Morrison, "I will consider your petition. Return in two days hence in the afternoon for my answer."

"But my husband is in prison, in fear for his life."

"I believe that I may give you some hope of hearing the answer you desire," Adams said. "But I must have time for consideration."

"And so you shall," Harlin Morrison said, taking his sister-in-law's hand to draw her from the room. "And so you shall. We will leave you to it."

As soon as he passed out of the door, however, he turned back and returned alone.

"I am sure you will do the right thing," he said to Adams in a confidential whisper. "I know you for a man of principle, and principles matter in an affair such as this."

Before Adams had a chance to respond, the man turned and was gone.

*　　*　　*

And now Mrs. Morrison was dead, on the very day she was to have met with Adams for word of her husband's fate. Worse, it appeared that she might have taken her own life in despair. Adams was doubly sad because her death was entirely unnecessary. He had reached the conclusion that he would grant her petition and pardon her husband.

He sighed as he placed the napkin over her face once more, reflecting on the melancholy lives that some people led and the ends that they found for themselves. As the napkin was about to drop into place, Adams noticed livid bruises on Mrs. Morrison's neck. He supposed she might have injured herself while struggling to remove her clothing, though that seemed highly doubtful. He sighed, let the napkin fall, and stood up.

He knew that it was his duty to notify Harlin Morrison of his sister-in-law's unhappy demise, but that would have to wait. First he would find her clothing, which he knew must be nearby. And indeed it turned out to be so. Not far from the rock where Adams had laid his own clothing, he saw something sticking out from beneath a large flat stone. The stone was quite heavy, and he struggled to move it. When at last he succeeded, he found the dead woman's clothing stacked neatly beneath it. He had heard that those who took their own lives often removed their garments, as if wanting to pass from this world in the same state in which they had arrived. But was that the case with Mrs. Morrison, or did someone merely wish people to think so?

Leaving the clothing where it was, Adams turned his steps in the direction of the town, wondering if Mrs. Morrison had really taken her life because she had given up hope of gaining her husband's liberty or if she been killed by someone, someone like George Greene.

* * *

Greene had presented himself to Adams on the afternoon of the same day that Mrs. Morrison had brought her petition. He was short, shorter even than Adams, and thin as a fence rail, with a beard so black and tangled that his wild and staring eyes appeared to be peering at Adams from a thicket of dark brambles. He looked as if he would be more at home lurking in the swamps with the ancestors of Adams's alligator than in the parlor of the president. The words rushed out of his mouth, and his delicate hands waved as he spoke.

"I know she has been here," he said, looking all around him. "I can sense her presence in this room. It reeks of her."

"And who might you mean?" Adams asked.

"Mrs. Morrison, the wife of the mail robber," Greene said, his hands moving, the delicate, long-nailed fingers twitching as if they itched to find themselves around someone's neck. "The wife of Hubert Morrison, the justly imprisoned man whose life she came here to beg you to spare. I hope you have not been persuaded by her perverse arguments, sir. Surely you must realize that the man is as guilty as Satan! The evidence was found in his own home, placed there by his own hands! I believe that his wife might have taken part in the robbery, which is why he refused to speak in his own behalf at his trial. I know that he—"

"I believe he may well be innocent," Adams said, interrupting the torrent of words. "Many of his townsmen have vouched for him and signed their names to a petition in his behalf. And he has been neither convicted nor accused of any other crimes."

Greene glared at him with his hot, half-hidden eyes as if wondering whether he had been insulted. Adams offered him nothing more than a bland look.

"You have been bewitched by the woman," Greene said. "She is comely and well-spoken, and she has clouded your judgment with lies."

Adams held on to his temper and said, "You are vastly mistaken in your assumptions."

"Bah. And of course her husband is one of your political supporters."

"That is as it may be," Adams said, his face flushing. "I have never spoken to the man, so I cannot say for certain. Even if he were, I would never free him on that account."

"You will free him to spew his venom again," Greene said. His face, or that small part of it that Adams could see, was suffused with red. A vein pulsed in his forehead. He pointed a quivering finger at Adams. "I will not have it. I will not see it done."

"It is my decision," Adams reminded him, his voice rising only a little. "And mine alone. You have nothing to do with it."

"You will see," Greene said. "Justice will be done, will ye, nill ye!"

He fairly screamed the final words, then turned abruptly and rushed from the room, leaving Adams only a few moments to compose himself before spending an hour listening to his Secretary of State, Henry Clay, complain about the state of his health.

* * *

Remembering Greene's final words, Adams looked down once more at

Mrs. Morrison's body. Did she, after all, take her own life, or was it not likely that there be more to the story than that?

That was, perhaps, not his concern. What he must do first was find a member of the constabulary and inform him of the death. He walked until he found a small boy fishing on the river bank. He sent the boy for a representative of the law and returned to watch over Mrs. Morrison's remains.

The constable, when he arrived, huffed and puffed and blustered. His was a mostly peaceful existence, and he was not a man accustomed to dealing with dead bodies.

"I say, sir," he said to Adams. "What have we here?"

Adams told him that it was the body of a woman.

"And did you find her here like this?"

Before answering that question, Adams explained who he was.

The constable was not overly impressed.

"I say, it's a pleasure to meet you, sir. Indeed it is. Very much so, I'm sure. Are you really the president?"

Adams said that he was.

"Well," said the constable, wiping his brow, "that's all very fine, but who is this young woman, then? And, please, how did she come here, and how did you come to find her?"

Adams described the circumstances as best he could.

"You come here to bathe every day?" the constable said.

"In the bathing season."

"Very odd, sir, if I may say so."

"You may, but I do not find it odd."

The constable looked skeptical for a moment and then turned his eyes to the still covered body.

"Killed herself, suppose. Drowned herself in grief about her husband, poor woman."

Adams was not so sure that was true. He said, "You might want to question a man called George Greene. He was her husband's enemy, and he might bear some responsibility for this."

The constable shrugged off Adams's remarks. He seemed to have made up his mind about what had happened.

"I will see to things from here," he said. "You may go about your business, sir."

Adams started to say more, but he felt it would be useless. He left the constable there with the body and walked back to town in the direction of the presidential mansion, mulling over the problem of Mrs. Morrison as he prepared to deal with the day's round of meetings.

Before he reached home, he reached one decision. He would not seek out Harlin Morrison. He would wait until their scheduled appointment and then tell him as kindly as possible of his sister-in-law's end. Somehow he would have to deal with his suspicions of Mr. Greene, but first he had another day of meetings to deal with.

* * *

When Adams arrived home, he broke his fast with sausages and bread, read two chapters of Scott's Bible commentary, and paid a visit to his alligator. The beast seemed unaware of his presence. It was absolutely still just under the surface of the water, as uncommunicative as if it had been carved from stone. And yet Adams, who was not a man given to fancies, had the odd feeling that it was trying to tell him something. He looked at the creature's eyes, but they were closed, whether in sleep or meditation Adams had no idea.

The alligator's claws rested on the bottom of the bathtub, and Adams was reminded of the long nails on Greene's fingers, and he imagined those fingers wrapped around the neck of Mrs. Morrison.

Adams shook himself. He did not like to indulge in morbid imaginings. He left the alligator to its deliberations or its nap and went to meet with Mr. Rush, his Secretary of the Treasury. But the meeting was interrupted before it had hardly begun by the entrance of George Greene, who burst into the office unannounced. He appeared completely distracted, waving his hands and raving about justice and death and destruction in a most incoherent fashion.

Adams and Rush tried to calm him, but the man bounded around the room like a wild animal.

"We must put a stop to this," Adams said, and Rush agreed.

They subdued Greene easily, as he was small and frail, but not before Rush's face had been scratched by the overlong nails of Greene's fingers.

While Rush held the struggling Greene in a bearish hug, Adams went for help. He sent one servant for the law and brought another back to the office, but the man was not needed. Greene had calmed himself and was speaking almost rationally, though Rush still held him in a tight embrace.

"You must not pardon Morrison," he said when he saw Adams had returned. "The man is a criminal, under a just sentence, and he must be punished as the law declares is fit."

"You are the one who must face the law now," Adams said. "Mrs. Morrison is dead."

"Dead?" Greene said. He stared wild-eyed around the room as if looking for some means of escape, but there was none.

"And you, sir, are to blame," Adams said. "You killed her in the hope that I would not pardon her husband if she were dead. You thought no one would find her, or if she were found that she would be thought to have taken her own life. But you were wrong, wrong in everything. You chose a deserted spot to kill her, but she was found. You thought to indicate self-murder, but I saw the marks of your fingers upon her throat."

At Adams's words, Greene struggled mightily to break free of Rush's grip, but the secretary held on. Then a constable came in. He was not the same one that Adams had encountered earlier.

"What's the trouble here?" he asked.

"This man is a murderer," Adams said. "Take him to the jail."

"With pleasure," the constable said, smiling as he advanced on the hapless Greene.

* * *

Having disposed of Greene and Rush almost at the same time, Adams devoted the rest of the day to his other appointments, feeling rather good about himself for having caught Mrs. Morrison's killer, though at the same time feeling sorry for her husband. Adams would certainly pardon the man now. He had, with his wife's death, lost as much as any man could, short of losing his own life.

Somehow, however, Adams's good feeling did not last until his appointment with Morrison. For reasons he could not define, his thoughts kept drifting to his alligator, and to Greene. It was almost as if they were trying to tell him something, something he could not quite make out.

The afternoon drifted from one meeting to another. The only one that Adams enjoyed was with Bulfinch, the architect who was overseeing the building of the Capitol, and Persico, the sculptor who was working on the pediment of the east portico. Adams had not been pleased with Persico's first design, and it had been discarded. The president now felt that for the first time they were making real progress toward the figure's completion.

After the sculptor and architect had left, Harlin Morrison appeared. He seemed in low spirits, and Adams thought that the man must know already about the death of his sister-in-law. But that turned out not to be the case. Morrison knew only that she had disappeared.

"I have sought her for most of the day," he said. "I cannot fathom what must have happened."

Adams said only, "When did you see her last?"

"Near nightfall yestereve," Morrison said. "She wanted to walk around the city and see the buildings. I was feeling unwell and did not join her. For all I know, she never returned."

"Indeed she did not," Adams said, "nor will she ever."

"What can you mean?" Morrison asked, and Adams went on to relate his grisly discovery.

"My God, sir!" Morrison said when the story was concluded. He wept unashamedly and wrung his large, rough hands. "Did she drown herself from sorrow?"

"I do not believe so," Adams said. "I believe that she was killed."

"Who would dare to do such a thing?"

"George Greene, I believe," Adams said, and when he spoke Greene's name, he thought of his alligator again. Several other things leapt into his mind as well, and it became suddenly clear to him that he had made a dreadful mistake.

He stepped away from Morrison and said, "Stop your tears. For it was not Greene, after all. It was you. You killed Mrs. Morrison as surely as you stand before me."

"You jest, sir," Morrison said. "I could never have done such a thing."

"That is the point," Adams said. "Or the reverse of it. *Greene* could not have done such a thing. But you could have."

"I do not take your meaning," Morrison said, his voice cold, his tears already dry.

"I believe you do know. Mrs. Morrison was a stately woman, whereas Greene was small. She quite disliked him, and for her to wander off with him would be unlikely. For him to overpower and strangle her would be less likely still. Had he done so, surely the marks of his sharp nails would have been on her throat, but there were none. Besides that, his hands were too thin and delicate to have done the job. Even if he had killed her, he could hardly have moved her body into the water and wedged her foot between the rocks. Mrs. Morrison would, however, have gone for an evening walk with you, a man she mistakenly trusted. I believe you accompanied her on her walk, and during the course of it, you killed her, hiding her body beneath the waters of the river where you hoped it would not be found."

"You are quite incorrect in your assumptions."

"I do not think so. Greene could never have moved the rock under which I found Mrs. Morrison's clothing, but you could have. And I see that your hands are roughened with recent labor, of a kind unlikely to have been done in a print shop." Adams looked at his own hands. "Having recently moved the same rock, I can vouch for the coarsening of the skin that such work causes."

"But why would I kill her? There is no reason for me to have done so."

"You did it because you are like an alligator, though lacking its claws," Adams said. "You are cruel and would bite the hand that fed you. You betrayed your own brother, who let you live under his roof and held his peace to save you. You, sir, were the mail robber. Who could have placed the evidence in his house more easily than you? I suspect that you are the faceless informer, as well. And though your brother had protected you, you feared that he might have second thoughts were he to gain his release.

"You then killed his wife in the hope that her death would seal his fate, biding your time in watchful silence until you struck."

"You are raving," Morrison said.

"Oh, no. Greene was raving, and that is why I thought he was the killer. I should have known better. It is the quiet ones, the ones who lie in wait and then cry false tears who are the more deadly."

Unlike Greene, who had grown more agitated as the question of his guilt was pursued, Morrison grew calmer with each passing second.

"I dare say you can prove none of your assertions," he remarked. "And no one will believe your unsupported word, for all that you are the president. Why, after all, would I come to plead for my brother's life if I wanted him to remain in prison?"

"When I think back over our conversation of yesterday, I see that you did not plead so much as try to lead me to certain conclusions, one of them about Greene. Were you planning even then to kill Mrs. Morrison?"

Morrison stiffened. "I will listen to this no longer," he said. "You have no proof of any of your wild accusations."

He turned and walked from the room. Adams watched him go.

* * *

That night, after Adams and his wife had dined, they went to look once more at the alligator. While they stood beside the bathtub looking at the warty brute, Adams told Louisa about Greene and the Morrisons.

When he had finished, she said, "And yet you let the one man go free and sent the other to jail?"

"I have had Mr. Greene released," Adams said. "I believe that he might be mad, or near it, crazed by his hatred, but he had no hand in Mrs. Morrison's death."

"How can you be sure?"

Adams went through the evidence step by step, and Louisa stated that she was convinced.

"But," she said, "Mr. Morrison has not been punished, and will not be. As he said, you have nothing that amounts to convincing proof of his guilt in the matter."

"And he is correct, to a certain extent. It all depends upon whom one is trying to convince."

"I was speaking of a magistrate."

"And I was speaking of Morrison's brother, to whom I shall give two things: a pardon and a letter telling all that I know and suspect. It will be up to him to decide what to do. He remained silent once to protect his brother. I do not believe he will remain silent now."

"And what if he does more than speak?" Louisa asked.

Adams did not answer. He looked down at the alligator and imagined it sliding out of the water and mangling its prey before dragging it to some secret spot underneath the water to rot and become all the better to eat.

Louisa broke the silence at last. "I still do not feel that an alligator is an appropriate animal to have under one's roof."

"Better than some," Adams said. "One can learn a lot from an alligator." He gave one of his rare smiles. "Even one named Andrew Jackson."

The Greatest Sacrifice

Brendan DuBois

On an October day in 1900, Charles H. Ransom, a correspondent for the Boston *Post* newspaper, stood in an overgrown field on the Gulf Coast of Mississippi, smoking a cigar, wondering how in God's name it could be so brutally hot at this time of year. At home in Boston, a day in October like this one meant leaves falling on the cool Boston Common, hot drinks and companionship at the Parker House, and late nights with boon companions, gossiping about politics and the future of the country, on the cusp of a new century. But here, even close to the ocean, the heat was oppressive, making him sweat through his cotton shirt and suit coat, his feet swell in his leather shoes, and wishing for his own pleasant home back north.

He walked through the field, looked back at the small house called Beauvoir, rising up on brick pillars above the ground. He had earlier toured the eight rooms of the home, after having taken a train from New Orleans for the express purpose of visiting this home, the last residence of one of the great traitors to the Union, one Jefferson Davis, dead these past eleven years. Charles wasn't sure why he had gone out here on the Louisville & Nashville Railroad, coming out from New Orleans, but that swamp of a city had depressed him, with its strange population, the even stranger patois of French Creole and Southern English, and the hint of spirits and voodoo all about in the air. Having spent two days in that wretched place, he had an urge to go someplace out in the country, away from the swamps and the strange buildings. He had earlier come to New Orleans on a mail steamer from Havana, where he had written a series of articles about the new government of Cuba, wiring them north to his newspaper. He had even toured some of the battle sites and had seen the rusting hulk of the *Maine* in Havana Harbor. Now, on his way back to Boston, he strolled through the overgrown fields, looking about the last home of a man who had died not even a citizen, for his citizenship had been taken away from him following the great Civil War.

And such a war it had been, and he had grown up, playing in the fields of Marshfield, listening to the tales of his fathers and uncles, of how they had marched south for Mister Lincoln, to preserve the Union. They didn't talk much all the time, but during the family celebrations, when the whiskey and wine came out, and the tongues were loosened, he would sit by their feet and listen to the tales of courage and heartbreak and dedication to the Union.

He paused in his walk and saw an old man, stooped over, seemingly resting his arms and head on a shovel. The old man had worn pants, a rope belt and patched shirt, and frayed straw hat. Charles nodded at the man but he said nothing in return, and feeling put out, he decided to go back to the house and wait for the time to pass, to take the train back to New Orleans. At least in the home, raised up and with large windows, he might catch an ocean breeze, might cool down in this terrible heat. Perhaps, if he was fortunate, he could secure a cold drink of some kind from the residents now in the house.

Charles turned and started to walk, and just as quickly, his foot caught on a stone and he fell awkwardly on his face. He cursed to himself as he rolled over, cigar still in his hand, and then he stared up in shock and perhaps a bit of fright, as the old man stared down at him. The old man had gray and white stubble on his face, and tobacco juice stained his chin. "You hurt there, fella?" he asked.

"No, not really," Charles said.

The old man nodded, spat out a stream of tobacco juice, and said, "Give you a hand, mebbe?"

"Yes, thank you, that would be kind." Charles held up his hand, surprised at the grip of the old man, and he was raised up. The old man looked him over and said, "Yankee, eh?"

"Yes," he said. "Boston."

The old man slowly nodded and rubbed at his chin, saying, "Yep . . . them Massachusetts boys, they was good fighters, most of 'em. Can't rightly say anything bad about 'em, even if they was abolitionists. They had a job to do and so did we . . . most of 'em did all right agin' us."

"Oh," Charles said, feeling warm and embarrassed. "You fought in the war, then."

" 'Course I did," he said, holding out a hand. "Caldwell Boone, at yer service."

He shook his hand. "Charles Ransom. Honored."

"What you be doin' here at Beauvoir?" Boone asked, eyeing him strongly, and Charles bit off what he was going to say, that he had this odd compulsion to see the last home of the last great traitor, the man who had led the Confederacy through four bloody years that had torn the country asunder, that had come so close to snuffing out that bright light of freedom and liberty that had been lit in Lexington and Concord, all those years ago. He felt sorry for the old soldier, looking worn and tired, out here in a field that had seen better days.

Instead of saying anything about the rebellion and the great traitor, he said, "I'm a student of history, Mister Boone. I had some time in New Orleans before my ship left for Boston, and not wanting to have my fortune told or to lose my money at cards, I decided to come here, to see Mister Davis's last home."

Boone spat another stream of tobacco juice. "Don't get many Yankees here, you know. You must be the first in quite some time."

"I imagine," Charles said. "Are you the groundskeeper?"

" 'Scuse?"

"The groundskeeper," he said. "A man to keep the greenery trimmed and neat."

The old man cackled, revealing just a few teeth, and said, "No, not hardly. I come here and do what I can, try to keep the wild things at bay. Nobody pays me. Just my way of showin' some respect to Mister Davis. You see, my family grew up in this part of the land, got to know Mister Davis and his family quite well. And how about you? What is your line of work?"

"A newspaper man. For the *Post*, from Boston."

"Well, that be a curious profession."

"True," Charles said, and added, "And speaking of curious, I'm curious to see what caused me to fall."

He moved some of the grass away with his boot and noted a small, elaborately carved tombstone. Chiseled out in the center, face up, were the letters T-R-A-V-E-L-E-R. He looked up at the old man. "Am I reading that right? Is this the tomb of Traveler?"

"That it is," Boone said.

Charles turned around, taking in the Gulf Coast estate. "But why on earth would Robert E. Lee's horse be buried here, at Jefferson Davis's home?"

"Ah, that be a common mistake," Boone said. "This ain't the buryin' place of Traveler the horse. This is the buryin' place of Traveler, Mister Davis's dog. And a more finer dog I've never met."

"A dog? I didn't know he had a dog. Did he have it when he was president of the Confederacy?"

"Nope. Much later."

"But you knew Mister Davis?"

Boone nodded. "Knew the whole family, 'specially his pets," he said. "Like I said, me and my family lived a ways away, my momma did some cleanin' about the place, and I'd do some chores, some yardwork. But I always saw Mister Davis and how much he loved his pets. You see, Mister Davis, he did have a soft spot for his creatures. Especially his peafowls, and Missus Davis, she was always upset that in his coats and dressing gowns, he also had scraps or grain for his peafowls. He'd walk out by the back steps in the mornin', walkin' back and forth, back and forth, and he said that it was the same length as his exercise path, back in prison. It was a hell of a sight, seein' all those big birds followin' him around, like soldiers followin' their general."

Boone spat out another stream of amber juice. "But it was that damn big dog that he really loved. He got that dog, years after he was let out of prison. . . . The dog came from a family called the Dorseys, Samuel and Sarah. 'N fact, Mister Jefferson Davis, he ended up buyin' this place from Mrs. Dorsey. But the Dorseys had Traveler first, and bought 'em on a trip to Switzerland, that place with the Alps. Ol' Traveler was a cross 'tween a Bernise and a Russian bulldog, and he was one tough son-of-a-bitch. You see, the Dorseys were world travelers, and Mister Dorsey could always depend on Traveler to protect his wife. Once in Arabia, in the desert one night, ol' Traveler chewed on an Arab who was goin' to do Missus Dorsey some harm. And in Paris, so the story goes, a jewel thief breakin' into her room had his throat torn out by the dog, and he died 'fore even being arrested."

Charles saw that his cigar had gone out, and relit the stub with a match. "My word, he sounds like a vicious brute. How did the Davis family end up with such a creature?"

Boone shook his head. "Oh, Traveler could be a devil on paws if he felt you was threatenin' him or Mister Davis, but he was real gentle about Mister Davis's kin. One of his nieces, I forget her name, she could tussle with that dog all day long and he wouldn't even growl. A couple of times, she even rode him around the yard like a tiny little pony, if you can believe that. Even strangers here, visitors, would be treated jus' fine by Traveler, but only if Mister Davis said so."

"How's that?" Charles asked, fascinated by the story of this dark traitor, this former president of the defeated Confederacy, and how such a man could enjoy the pleasures of a family, of a devoted pet. He had heard curses and complaints about Davis as a child from the menfolk of his family, and Davis was considered the spawn of the Devil himself. But to think that the man had a dog, a companion . . .

Boone said, "Well . . . it was real easy, and if I didn't see it myself, I wouldn't believe it. Mister Davis, he'd have the dog come up and he'd put one hand on the dog, and one hand on the stranger's shoulder, and he'd say, 'Traveler, this is my friend.' And ol' Traveler would sniff the stranger, like he was sizin' 'em up, and that was that. That stranger was now part of the family."

Charles took a deep pull off his cigar, wondering if this strange little tale could possibly be something to write up for the *Post*. Something light to go with all the Cuban stories he had written, about the hard work to rebuild that country after years of Spanish oppression.

"It sounds like Mister Davis had found a true friend," he said.

Boone nodded. "Ain't that the truth. Traveler would walk along with 'em, whenever Mister Davis wanted to walk by the waves, and Mister Davis, sometimes he'd be lost in thought. You know, it was tough times for him and his family, even in a pretty place like this. And when Mister Davis got thinkin', he wouldn't know where he was or nothin', and he could easily get in the waves and drown. But Traveler wouldn't allow that . . . he'd tug at Mister Davis's pants, pull 'em back from the water's edge. It was somethin' to see."

"It sounds like the dog saved his life," Charles said, and he was amazed at what happened next, when the old man nodded and tears appeared in his red-rimmed eyes. Boone sniffled and said, "By gum, he certainly did, especially towards the end. Traveler really did save Mister Davis's life."

"What do you mean?"

Boone took his shovel and gently tapped the stone on the ground between them. "What I mean is look at this, at this stone . . . how much it cost . . . and let me tell you, Traveler, when he died, he was placed in a real wooden coffin, like he was a child or somethin'. And that's 'cause besides being a part of the family, he really and truly did save Mister Davis from death."

Charles puffed on the cigar and then reached into his coat pocket, for a notepad and pencil, knowing he finally had to put some words down, for this would make a magnificent tale for his newspaper. But Boone shook his head at what he saw Charles doing.

"Nope. Not gonna happen. I'll tell you the story, mister, if you want, but it ain't gonna appear in your Boston paper, or anyplace else."

Charles smiled and made a show of putting the notebook away, thinking to himself that he would no doubt be able to rebuild this conversation on the train journey back to New Orleans, but it was like the old Confederate soldier was reading his mind, like some damn voodoo thing, for what he said next.

"And I'll tell you this," Boone said, "I tell you what happened and I find out that the story appeared in Boston, and I can do that, no matter how far away that might be, well, then I'll come up to Boston and thrash you."

Charles tried to make his smile wider, to disarm the old man. "Please, there's no need for threats."

Boone's face darkened, like a cloud had suddenly appeared in the warm sky. "It ain't no threat, youngster. In my stronger days I thrashed a lot of Yankees, in lots of places, from Virginia to Georgia, with my rifle and my bayonet and my bare hands, and it wouldn't take much to take care of the likes of you. So. You want to hear the tale, or not?"

Charles didn't like being threatened by the old man, but he had a weakness for stories, especially wild tales like this one. He took a final puff off his cheroot, dropped it to the grass and ground it in with his heel.

"Fine," he said. "I do want to hear the tale."

"All right," Boone said. "Here it is."

* * *

His name was Traveler and his world was the House, the Fields, the Bad-taste Water, the Sand, and the Man and his mate and the Man's pack. He loved the Man and would do anything for him and his pack, and he felt at peace when he made them laugh, when he made them take notice, and when he protected them at night from the strange sounds and beasts out there in the world beyond the house. He could remember many things and many smells and many shapes over his years of life—the hot sands, the cold mountains, and the big ships that went over the Bad-taste Water that made him sick—but never in his life had he felt such joy at being here with the Man, and protecting the pack. The days were filled with walks along the sand and by the Bad-taste Water, chasing after strange hard-back creatures with no fur or feathers, and playing with the young pups that were part of the Man's pack.

He would be at the Man's side at all times of the day, and when the Man traveled without him, Traveler would sit by the main entrance, waiting for the Man to come back. Sometimes the Man came back with friends, members of his pack as well, and they would talk late into the night. Traveler could detect scents from these males as well, scents of old battles, old conflicts, of blood spilt and wounds made into flesh. From the way the talks went and the scents he smelled, he knew that the Man had once been a great leader of a great pack, and he could sense that as well, from the polite talk and greetings he would receive from his visitors. Oh, how they could talk, and sometimes the talk and the scents of old battles would upset him, would make him growl and pace the floor, but the Man was never angry at him for what he did. The Man was gentle and fed him and rubbed his head and belly, and he gave not only love back to the Man, but protection as well. He defended the grounds and the house and the pack, and at night, he would go to each door and each window, to ensure they were closed, that they were sealed to protect the house and the pack. That was his responsibility, one he was proud of, as he walked the wide porch of the house.

But now he could sense there was a wrongness with the Man, something he couldn't protect against. The Man was more quiet than usual, sitting by himself and staring out into the darkness, where the creatures roamed. Traveler learned a lot about the Man and his kind over the years, especially that they were Scent-dead, that they had no idea of the Scents that went through and about the air and on the grass and on the trees, Scents that told incredible stories, if only you knew how to find them. Stories of battles and great chases and survival, and of fierce lives, lived out there in the dark and in the woods and the brambles. But there were other stories as well, and the Scent he was detecting from the Man was one of despair, of darkness, of bad things coming and coming soon.

He tried to cheer up the Man, by playing about his feet, by fetching sticks and dropping before him, and by rolling on his back, exposing his belly to the Man, hoping for deep rubs and scratches.

But none of it worked. The Man would walk out to the Bad-taste Water and look out there, and sometimes in his walks, he got too close to the waves and Traveler would tug him away with a firm jaw to his leg. Sometimes Traveler would lay before the Man, sighing and moaning, for he did not know what he could do to help the Man.

And one morning, the bad scents, the very bad thing, came into the Man's home, just as the first meal of the day was being finished.

Traveler recognized the other male who came to see the Man, knew him as someone who lived a ways down the road. The male had a package in his arm, a package that he unrolled before the Man. The male and the Man then got into a spat of words, barking at each other, raising voices and pointing fingers, and Traveler got between them, growling, trying to make the fighting stop. But the Man tugged him away by his collar, forced him to lay down, and Traveler looked up again at the Man and the male, and growled, feeling the fur bristle up around his neck. The package was in rolled paper, and even through the paper, Traveler could sense the Badness there. There was Badness in there and the male had presented the Badness to the Man. The Man picked up the package and Traveler growled, and the Man turned and said, "Traveler, sit."

Which he did. But he still wasn't happy. He looked at what the Man had in his old hands, saw that it was a piece of food, some kind of meat, but there was a Badness in the meat. The Man was talking again to the other male, who was now weeping, and the Man said something sharp to him and the male stalked out of the room. Traveler stood up, trembling, looking at what was in the Man's hands, smelling the Badness coming out of the meat, and when the Man raised the meat to his mouth, Traveler lept and knocked the Man down. The meat fell to the floor and the Man shouted at Traveler, and made to go to the meat, and Traveler wasn't sure what was happening, but he knew the Man had to be protected, had to be protected at all costs, and he raced forward across the floor, and in three large bites, ate the meat, ate the Badness.

He turned, now afraid, as the Man came towards him. He trembled in his fear, wondering if the Man would strike him for the first time, would cast him out into the darkness, would actually kill him.

But the Man knelt down, held Traveler's head against his chest, and then he started weeping. Traveler still trembled, scared at what had happened, and then the Badness caused pains in his belly, pains that made him toss back his head and begin to howl.

* * *

Charles looked down at the carved stone, surprised to feel tears rolling down his cheeks. He had written about train wrecks that had made orphans of entire families, raging fires that had destroyed entire neighborhoods, and had been in the slums of Havana and seen the destitute there, living among the misery and ruin of the old Spanish rule, but none of the stories he had ever written about made him do this. A story about an old dog, and an old traitor.

"Poison," Charles said. "Someone tried to poison Jefferson Davis and

Traveler protected him. Am I right?"

The old man said nothing, just nodded, looking down at the stone. Charles recalled the tale he had just heard and said, "Wait. Wait just a moment."

"Eh?"

He moved around, so he could get a better look at Boone. "Why hasn't this story been told before? Why?"

"Mister Davis was a private one, that's why," Boone said. "He'd never say anything about what had happened that night. Nossir. That's why you and nobody else, 'specially the Yanks, know anything about it."

Charles said, "But hold on, sir. You knew about it. You knew enough about it to tell me the entire tale, from start to finish, about the attempt on Jefferson Davis's life."

Boone shifted the shovel from one hand to the other, and Charles stepped back, wondering just how many Union soldiers the old man had killed in his younger days, with those same gnarled hands, but still he pressed on. "It was you. You said there were two men in the room. Just Mister Davis and the other man, and Traveler, the dog. Am I right? Were you trying to poison Jefferson Davis?"

The old man raised his head, and Charles flinched at the hatred and anger in his look. "Stupid, thick-headed, bluebelly . . . If it weren't for your cannon and navy blockade and damn factories, we'd've won, would've won our freedom."

"Freedom?" Charles shot back, surprised at facing down the old rebel. "What freedom was there for your negro? Eh?"

Boone spat out another stream of tobacco juice. "I don't wanna talk 'bout slavery. I'm talkin' about Jefferson Davis, the greatest man of the Confederacy."

"But a man you wanted to poison? Correct? A plot only stopped by his dog?"

"Great Moses, you are stupid," Boone said. "I don't know why I should continue. Yes, I was there . . . damn you . . . but there was no plan on my part to poison him. Nossir. And you print that, I'll murder you dead, Yankee. Understand?"

Charles rubbed at his chin. "But . . . but you said yourself, that the other man was in the room, he brought in some poisoned meat. That had to be you. What happened, then? Was it an accident?"

Boone seemed to think about that for a moment, and then sighed and turned his head, to look at the buildings of Beauvoir. "No, 'twern't no accident. . . . It was poisoned meat, just as I said. . . . I brought it to the house 'cause Mister Davis demanded it, that's why. . . .Would not take no for an answer, and trust me, you couldn't say no long to Mister Davis. . . ."

Charles felt like the heat and the still air was making his head spin. "What in the world did Jefferson Davis want with poisoned meat?"

Again, Boone looked at him, with hate and contempt. "So he could end his life, that's why."

He found he could not say a word. The old man sighed again and went on. "You're too young to remember, you damn pup. . . . When Lee surrendered and the Confederacy collapsed, President Davis—not Mister Davis!—President Davis was forced to flee, for hundreds of miles, until he was captured by Union cavalry. For a while you Federals kept 'em in manacles and chains, like some common tramp. . . ."

Charles interrupted. "After all, he was a traitor. Wasn't he? He was lucky he wasn't hanged after the war."

A fierce shake of Boone's head. "For all his faults, and he had 'em, lots of 'em, he was a patriot. A patriot who thought the Union was made up of a group of independent states . . . states that could leave whenever they wanted to and form their own country, if need be . . . but . . ." Boone looked down at the ground. "I'm too old to start fightin' that war agin' . . . saw too many friends get killed . . . but President Davis, he was a patriot, and he spent more than two years in prison after the war . . . and then . . . what?"

"Excuse me?" Charles asked.

Boone said, "What do you do, after you was president of a country? You still have bills to pay, a family to support . . . what do you do? Poor Mister Davis . . . he invested in copper mining, trading in cotton and tobacco . . . hell, he even worked for a while for the Carolina Life Insurance Company . . . but all for naught. He lost money, he was poor, thought 'bout even selling furniture to make some money, and he was lookin' at his wife and children, with no future . . . no hope . . . and his friends . . . days like that, a man broods some, broods when he feels his only friend is a dog. . . ."

Now he understood. Charles cleared his throat. "Suicide. For the insurance money."

Boone coughed and cleared his throat. "Yep. Suicide . . . but Mister Davis wanted to do it right. . . . Somethin' that would look like he got dead 'cause of natural causes, so that his enemies wouldn't gloat that the great Jefferson Davis took the coward's way out. My mamma . . . well, she was wise with things to do with roots and herbs, and asked me to devise a way of poisoning a meat sausage . . . the way he figured it . . . he would have it with his breakfast and expire later that day . . . his family would do well with the insurance. . . ."

Charles gently toed the grass around the gravestone of the faithful dog. "But Traveler sensed something was wrong, from what you told me. He grabbed it and ate it instead."

"True. And right after that, Mister Davis, oh, how upset he was. Traveler hung on for a few days, gettin' weaker and weaker . . . Even the best physician in the area was brought in, but nothin' worked. . . . It was so damn sad, and you could see how guilty Mister Davis felt, day after day, as that poor dog just wasted clean away. . . . Oh, it was so sad, right up to the morning when poor Traveler died, his head on Mister Davis's lap. . . . I was there when it happened, and Mister Davis, he laid Traveler out on the rug and said, 'I have indeed lost a friend.'"

"So he was buried here," Charles said.

"Yep. Put in a box like a regular coffin and everything . . . and Mister Davis, well, I don't know. I thought what happened would just make him try agin', try to kill himself and do it right this time. But instead . . . he seemed to have this energy later . . . like he realized that Traveler had made the greatest sacrifice for him . . . not only to protect his life, y'know, but his reputation . . . and that's when Mister Davis started writing his history of the Confederacy. All two volumes, Yank, and they sold well and made history and made him and his family comfortable. And when he did that, his reputation was saved. Forever, and all because of this dog."

Charles knew he should say something, but he couldn't think of the words to put together. A wordsmith by trade, his mouth and tongue suddenly felt young and clumsy.

Boone wiped at his eyes and said softly, "Forget what I said earlier, about thrashin' you. If you want to write your damn story, go ahead. I don't care. It's been long enough already."

And with that, Boone turned and walked away. Charles watched him disappear silently into the trees, like the old Confederate soldier he once was. When he could no longer see him, he took his notebook out and a pencil, and was going to write, write a mysterious tale about a traitor and his near death, and how everything had changed because of a simple animal.

But nothing happened. For the first time in his life, the words would not come to him. He slowly put the notepad and the pencil away, back into his coat pocket, and he bent down and gently traced the carved name in the headstone. TRAVELER.

He stood up, brushed some dirt from his knees, and strode back to the house of the old president of a failed country, a traitor, and a man who owed everything, even in death, to the faithfulness of his dog.

Tabby Won't Tell
Jan Grape

P a, Pa! Soldiers come back." Tad Lincoln rushed into the Oval Office, ignoring the cabinet members sitting around the room, and ran straight to his father's lap, climbing up the long legs. "The soldiers came back. They are setting up all their tents."

Abraham Lincoln fondly tousled his son's dark hair. "I told you they would be back today, son." He could scarcely hide his smile at his youngest son's excitement. Thomas Lincoln, better known as Tad, was dressed in the Union army uniform given to him by Edwin Stanton, the Secretary of War. Tad wanted to wear it every day.

"I was 'ascared they would march on by and not stop, Pa."

President Abraham Lincoln, in the midst of a meeting with Secretary Stanton and Secretary of State William Seward, never seemed upset when one of his young sons came rushing into the Oval Office. Especially when it was Tad who interrupted. Tad, at age eight, was the youngest and in many ways the most like his father. Stanton and Seward were used to meetings which could be invaded by Tad or by William Lincoln, age eleven. The men realized how high-spirited the boys were and, although their father was the president of the United States, they knew the White House and its grounds constituted the boys' play areas.

"Have you spoken to Cook about what surprise we might add to our fine 'Bucktail' regiment's dinner tonight?" asked Mr. Lincoln.

"No sir, but I will, I will." Tad had a slight lisp but no one took major notice of it except a stranger. Undoubtedly the Lincolns thought it in the child's best interest to ignore it and that probably was best. "I'll go tell Cook right now." Tad gave his father a fierce hug and dashed from the room, heading for the White House kitchen to order Cook to make a special dessert for the troops. Tad thought nothing of ordering the White House staff around. He often drilled and marched them outside when they weren't too busy.

When Tad reached the kitchen he snuck up behind Rosa, the evening cook. "Miss Rose," his voice squeaked.

"Good heavens, Master Tad." Rosa had heard the boy running down the hall but pretended as usual to be surprised. "You scared me half to death, child. I should box your ears."

"Must catch me first," Tad said and giggled when she patted his shoulder. He watched for a moment as the woman chopped potatoes and dropped them into a pot. "My father, the president, says you must make peach cobbler tonight. And give some to the soldiers out back."

"And when am I supposed to find time to do that, young master Tad?"

Tad shrugged and squirmed up on a stool to watch as Rosa finished with the potatoes.

When she finished she began making pastry for the cobblers. Tad watched but didn't say much. He could be unusually quiet when Willie wasn't around. The two of them together often sounded like banshees. Before Rosa could ask where Willie might be, the young man in question appeared.

"Willie," said Tad. "You been helping Ma?"

"Yes. She had one of her headaches while shopping for those new drapes for Papa's bedroom, and she felt most unpleasant on the ride home. She's gone up to lie down now."

"Then we can play?" Tad asked.

"Yes, in a few minutes. I promised Ma I'd bring up some tea." Willie turned to Rosa, who had already reached for the kettle. The boy got out a cup and the tea can. When the tea was ready Willie took it up to his mother.

"Let's get Nanny and Nanko," said Tad when Willie returned. "Put ropes around their necks and tie them to a chair. They can pull us like we're in a sled."

"Are you sure? Goats are not ponies, you know."

"I know but Mama would never let the ponies in." He seemed to have forgotten the soldiers out on the south lawn.

"Okay," agreed Willie. "It is a splendid idea."

A short time later, their laughter rang out in the long hallway leading to the kitchen as Tad and Willie let the goats pull them all the way from the front of the house, down the hall and through the kitchen, where they then turned and went back to the front again, shrieking with laughter.

Suddenly Tad spied Tabby, his favorite cat. He stopped his chair, grabbed the cat, pulled him aboard and continued down the hallway. Tabby looked as if he'd jump and run at any moment, but the boy scratched him under the chin and the cat settled down to his harrowing ride.

Rosa shook her head at the boys as she pulled the cobblers out of the oven and called her husband, Ned, to load up a cart to take the cobblers outside to the soldiers' mess tent.

When Tad saw what Ned and Rosa planned to do, he hopped off his chair-sled, spilling Tabby, who ran and hid in the pantry.

"Me help, me help," the boy said.

Willie said he'd help too. He untied the ropes and put the goats outside, leaving the chairs in the middle of the hallway.

When Ned had the cart loaded, he and Tad and Willie walked out on the south lawn to the soldier's tents.

The evening was clear and cold and an icy wind blew from the north. Some of the older staff people said it would snow before morning. Rosa had dressed the boys warmly, in coats and hats and boots, knowing Mrs. Lincoln would never forgive her if the boys took cold.

Colonel Smith thanked Ned and the boys and said he was most grateful for the special treat. "If the opportunity presents, will you please tell the president I will be over in the morning to thank him in person?" The colonel turned to a young soldier nearby. "Private Bell?"

The young private saluted the colonel. "Sir?"

"You are hereby appointed sergeant of the peach cobblers. You must help this fine presidential envoy see that some pie gets served to each and every man."

Tad and Willie laughed at the colonel. Times were hard and war was tough, but this man's knack for keeping morale high among his men was well documented.

Tad and Willie helped Ned and the private pass the desserts to each man. Ned would hold a cobbler and Private Bell would spoon a fair helping on each soldier's plate. Tad and Willie were supposed to be helping push the cart along but after only a few minutes Tad stayed at one table, talking to the soldiers.

"Where you been? How many Rebs did you see? Did you shoot your gun?" Tad fired questions as quickly as he could and they answered back quickly, sensing that the boy's curiosity was boundless. "Aren't you 'ascared? Did you ever get wounded?"

After a time, some soldiers who had finished eating left their tables to go outside for a smoke. Unnoticed by anyone, Tad watched a group of six men heading out and when they moved towards a copse of trees, he followed stealthily.

Night had fully descended and with Tad's dark coat not one of the soldiers saw or heard the boy. He shivered a bit and immediately took his hat out of his pocket to put on, pulling down the flaps over his ears.

Tad wondered what fun things the soldiers would talk about tonight. They often told him stories and sometimes they would let him watch their races. Tad knew they wouldn't be racing tonight, it was too cold and dark but maybe he would hear a good story.

The group stopped under the trees and Tad inched closer to the men. No one took notice and Tad listened, hoping to hear of a battle or injuries. The men took their time with their tobacco pouches, two of them had pipes and the others rolled cigarettes.

Tad liked to watched the men smoke. He wondered what it was like to smoke. Especially a fine cigar. He had seen General Grant light up one evening as he left the White House. He picked up a small twig and put it in his mouth and pretended to smoke. One of the men had built a small campfire and two of the soldiers squatted down. Tad moved closer hoping to hear some good stories.

Before he could ask any questions, however, three of the men broke away from the others . . . moving toward Tad.

Tad slipped behind a huge oak tree when he saw them approach. He wasn't sure why he hid, he just did it. The nearby campfire sent shafts of lights and shadows in their direction yet Tad couldn't see the men clearly. He didn't think he'd ever seen or talked to any of them before, however.

* * *

"What we going to do with that money we took off that old Reb?" Alton Thompson, a sergeant from Erie, had a thick black moustache and was a large muscular man.

"Split it up, just like we said," a tall thin soldier named Frank Barnes answered. He was from a small town in northeastern Pennsylvania but no one could remember its name. "Alton, what do you think is the fair way to do that? Split three ways?"

"You must be kidding," said Alton. "I get half and you two can split half."

"Why do you get half?" asked Frank.

"Because I'm the one who done the shooting. Neither of you had the stomach for it."

"I—I just wish I hadn't of seen his eyes when you shot him," said Richard. Richard Scott was short, barrel-chested and extremely timid. He had only attended school through the fourth grade and his speech showed his lack of education. "I—I don' know why you had to kill 'im anyway?"

"Because, Stupid," said Alton, "he wasn't going to let us have that bag of money. He was saving it for his precious son. His Johnny Reb son, off somewhere killing our boys—maybe your brother or mine. You know as well as me, no Reb deserves to live. I don't care if he was an old man or not."

Tad could tell the men were arguing, but their tones were hushed as if to keep the others over by the campfire from overhearing. He just didn't understand all of what they talked about.

"He weren't no soldier." Richard threw his cigarette on the ground and stomped it out. "He was just an old man. We could've jest took the money and rode off. He'd never finded us."

"But Richard, I had such fun watchin' him mess his pants when he knew what I was going to do."

"Well, I dun dee-cided I don' want no part of that money. Do what you want with it." Richard started to move away but Frank caught him by the shoulder.

"Hold on now, Richard. You just calm down and think about what you can do with your share of that money. And you didn't do anything to that old man. It was all me." Frank's tone was placating.

Ned and Willie suddenly came out of the mess tent looking for Tad. He saw them and started to hurry in their direction.

Some noise stopped him. The sound held him where he was as he strained to listen and tried to understand.

He saw Frank pull Richard's arms back behind his back and hold them there.

The other soldiers over by the campfire had already walked back towards the bivouac area and a small gleam of the firelight again reached towards the group who had been arguing.

Alton moved close to Richard and Tad heard a strange gurgling sound.

"I just don't trust that you can keep your mouth shut, Richard. Too bad, you dumb-nut." Alton's arm swung again.

This time Tad saw a dark juice run out of the stout man's chest. In the dark it looked exactly like gravy.

Willie called out. "Tad? Are you out there?"

Alton whirled around as Tad looked to the mess tent.

Ned called out to Willie. "Willie, come help me a moment and then we'll find Tad."

Tad began to run but a strong arm caught him and lifted him up. "Hello, little boy. Where did you come from?"

The man was smelly and rough and his lips moved against Tad's ear. Tad shivered and pointed towards the mess tent.

"And what did you see here, little boy?" Alton's voice was gruff and his bristly whiskers scraped Tad's face. "You didn't see nothing and you didn't hear nothing, did you?"

Tad shook his head but couldn't say a word.

Behind them Tad could still hear the stout man coughing and the thin man grunting but neither were talking.

"Ta . . . add. Tad Lincoln, where are you? Where *did* that boy get off to now?" Ned's tone sounded exasperated. "You'd better stop this nonsense.

You trying to get me and Miss Rosa in trouble?" His voice trailed off. "Willie? You'd better walk out there and see if you can find him. I'll go get a lantern."

The thin man behind them said, "Oh, Jeeezus. That's Tad Lincoln. That's the president's son. Oh Lord, the president's son."

Alton squeezed Tad a bit tighter. "You ain't gonna tell nobody nothing. You unnerstand?" The man placed a blade close to the boy's ear. "I'll kill your mother, your father, and your brother. You hear me, boy?"

Tad couldn't think, couldn't talk, he was shaking so hard.

"You hear me? I'll come into your big white house and I'll kill you all while you sleep if you ever tell a soul what you saw and heard. You understand me, boy?" The man pushed the blade a bit deeper into the boy's neck and Tad felt a pin prick. "Answer me, boy!"

Tad whispered, "Cross my heart. Never tell."

"Good boy." The big man lowered Tad back down to the ground but still held the child's arm tight for a moment. "Don't forget what I said. All your family. I promise. Every one." He let go of the boy and turned back to the other man who was still cursing. "It's going to be okay, Frank. It will be fine now."

Tad went running back towards the tent as quickly as his legs would carry him. He didn't even turn around when a pistol shot rang out. He ran straight through the tent and into Ned's comforting arms.

Ned heard the gunshot but he pushed both boys in the direction of the house. Willie kept trying to turn around but Ned wouldn't let him.

"Just keep going, boys. Keep going. Let the colonel take care of things out here. We need to get you boys to bed. Just keep on."

Tad was glad not to look back. Rosa, after a whispered conversation with Ned, took the boys by the hands and straight up the back stairs to their bedroom.

Before Tad could think about what had happened, he was in his night-shirt and tucked in bed. He was still shaking a little, not from the cold, but from fear.

Willie wanted to talk. "Wonder what was happening? Did you see anything? I wanted to see what going on, didn't you, Tad?"

But Tad was too afraid to say anything. After a time, Willie turned over and went to sleep.

Tad wondered why the big soldier man got so mad. Why did the man put that knife at his neck? He couldn't ask Willie and if he didn't know what he was not supposed to tell them, how could he talk to any of them? Would that man come in here into their house and kill them if he just talked to his family? Tad began sobbing and wiping his eyes. What could he do?

Tabby cat softly leaped up on the bed beside Tad and reached out one paw to pull Tad's hand away from his face, wanting to be petted. "Oh, Tabby. I'm so glad you're here." And the little boy told his cat, Tabby, how something bad had happened out on the south grounds. He whispered how he had followed the men out and that he had hidden and how some men kept talking about a lot of money. One man even talked about killing a Johnny Reb.

"Why did the man get mad about that?" Tad whispered to Tabby. Soldiers always talked about killing Johnny Reb. That was no big secret.

Somehow Tad knew the men were talking about some big, big secret. And Tad just could not for the life of him understand what the secret was. He kept talking softly to Tabby until they both went to sleep.

The next morning Tad didn't want to get up. Willie left after trying to convince his little brother he should get up and eat some breakfast. Tad just ducked his head underneath the quilts and wouldn't answer Willie.

When Willie left the room, Tad got up and used the chamber pot, then locked the bedroom door and went back to bed.

A short time later, Rosa came up and tried to talk to the boy through the door. Tad told her to go away, that he didn't feel well. Later, Ned came and knocked on Tad's door.

"If you're sick, Tad, you need to let Rosa take care of you. We might have to call the doctor."

Tad didn't answer, he just lay in bed and sobbed. He didn't know how to help himself or his family, and he didn't know what to do.

After a while, Tad's father came up and stood outside the door.

"Tad? You are causing your mother and me some trouble here, and I'm sure you don't mean to do that. I think it's time you opened the door."

Tad got up and opened the door. Without saying a word, he gave his father a fierce hug and began putting on his regular clothes.

The president headed downstairs to his duties, but wondered what was going on with his young son.

Mrs. Lincoln spent several minutes asking her son what the problem was, but he kept shaking his head. Mary Lincoln finally threw up her hands in frustration and went back to her bedroom to get dressed for a tea she was to host for the senate wives that afternoon.

Mr. Adams, the school tutor who was teaching Tad his letters, couldn't get the young man to speak and finally said Tad could be dismissed for the day. Whenever anyone spoke to the boy, he would only answer with a "yes sir" or "no ma'am" and went out of his way to go elsewhere.

Willie tried to get Tad to talk for a long time, but didn't make any headway. Finally he played his last card. "Let's go outside and ride my pony," said Willie. The older boy felt sure that would pull Tad out of his doldrums as Tad dearly loved riding Willie's favorite pony, even though Tad's leg stuck straight out since he was so small.

"No, don't," said Tad. He pulled on his brother's arm as if to keep Willie inside, but Willie pulled away and left Tad standing at the side door. Tad wiped away his tears.

Tad spent the remainder of the morning staying away from everyone by ducking under furniture and into dark corners and nooks to hide. He was still terribly worried, but he just did not know what the mean soldier had been so angry about. He only knew he had to keep his family safe by not talking to anyone. He ate the lunch that Rosa made for him, but he wouldn't talk to her. He overheard other staff members as they wondered what was wrong with the boy.

Late in the afternoon, Tad found Tabby and took the cat and hid underneath his father's desk in the Oval Office. The two of them curled up and went to sleep.

A short time after that, Colonel Smith and President Lincoln came into the Oval Office and sat in chairs near the fireplace.

"Did you discover why those two men were fighting last night, Colonel?" asked the president.

"Yes, sir. Fighting over a woman the two of them met the last time we bivouacked here. Seems as though Private Richard Scott made what Private

Frank Barnes called unwanted advances to the lady. They got into fisticuffs that time."

"And it began again last night?" Mr. Lincoln was shaking his head.

Abe Lincoln heard a faint scratching sound under his desk and looking down spied a cat's paw and the shoe of his youngest son. He didn't acknowledge what he'd seen, and the Colonel didn't pause in his report.

"According to their platoon leader, Corporal Alton Thompson, he tried to break up the fight. He says Barnes had pulled a knife on Scott and killed him. When Thompson tried to subdue Barnes, Barnes turned the knife on him and so Thompson had to shoot Barnes."

"A rather sad state of affairs for just an affair of the heart," said the president.

"Yes, sir."

"And you are sure Thompson acted in self-defense?"

"Yes, I believe so, sir. Thompson was only trying to prevent the problem from escalating. Unfortunately by the time he arrived on the scene, it was too late and about all he could do was defend hisself."

"You'll send letters to the family of both boys then, Colonel."

"Yes, sir. But I'm not sure what to say. Quite a sad thing to think you lost a son fighting over a woman."

"Well, I'm sure you'll find the right words, Colonel. You don't have to gloss over the truth but you don't have to be too specific either." The two men stood and Colonel Smith left the room. The president, who had walked part way out with the colonel, turned back, crossed the room and sat back down to watch the fire. In a few minutes, he leaned his head back in the soft chair and closed his eyes.

Tad, holding Tabby in his arms, scooted out from under the desk.

"Come here, son."

Tad started to put Tabby down.

"No," said his father. "Let's just sit down right here on the floor and play with Mr. Tabby." Abraham Lincoln sat down and began teasing Tabby with a bit of string he pulled out of his pocket. "You've had a rather hard day, haven't you, son?"

Tad nodded his head.

"You want to tell me about it?"

Tad shook his head. "I . . . uh, I can't."

"I believe you must have observed something last night that frightened you, am I right? Do you know what *observed* means?"

"No, sir."

"It means to see something. Did you see something last night that was scary?"

Tad nodded his head.

"Will you tell me what you saw?"

Tad shook his head again.

"All right, son. But I will ask you to do something. I'm going to go out the door there and you can tell Tabby what you saw that frightened you. No one but Tabby can hear what you say and after you tell Tabby, maybe you won't be afraid anymore. Will you do that?" He handed Tad the string for Tabby.

Tad thought for a moment then nodded in agreement. And the president walked out of his office.

In only a few short minutes the president overheard the whole story as Tad told everything to his cat. How he saw one man hit another in the chest and how he saw some dark juice run out of the man. Then he told Tabby about the man who had held the knife to the his throat and promised to kill his family.

Abraham Lincoln walked back into the office. "Why don't you go upstairs to your room now, son. I'll be up in a few minutes."

Tad walked slowly upstairs to his bedroom, and Tabby trailed along behind. Tad climbed upon his bed, and the cat curled up beside the boy.

* * *

No wonder the boy isn't talking. He's frightened to death, Mr. Lincoln thought.

He quickly walked back toward the kitchen, found Ned and asked him if he'd mind fetching Colonel Smith. He knew the colonel would handle everything from his end once he knew the full story.

Before long his father came up and sat in a chair near Tad's bed. "Colonel Smith came in to see me a few minutes ago, Tad, and do you know what he told me?"

Tad shook his head.

"After further investigation, the colonel found out how one of his men had done a very bad thing and lied about it. I'm sure you know what happens when people lie, but do you know what happens when soldiers lie to their commanding officer?"

Tad shook his head, but his eyes grew as big as saucers.

"Well, this man, a corporal named Alton Thompson, actually killed a man and now he's in the brig. He will be in prison forever and he will never get to be a soldier again."

"You mean, he will go away from here?" Tad asked.

"He will go away and never come back. My goodness, I just realized you've started talking again. I'm glad of that. Your Mother and I were getting very worried. We kept thinking you were sick or something."

"I'm all right, sir." Tad gave his father a fierce hug. "May I go get my toy cannon? Willie and I want to play soldier."

"Yes, you may. But I don't think you'd better bring those goats inside for a time. Your mother was very, very upset about that." The president leaned over and scratched behind Tabby's ear. "When I read the paper this morning, I saw how a newsman called our Tabby 'First Cat.'"

Tad look puzzled.

"You know, how they sometimes call your mother the First Lady? First Cat. I think it's a most appropriate title, don't you?" Tabby purred and closed his eyes.

Tad didn't answer. He had hurriedly put on his Union soldier uniform and was too busy adjusting his belt. He saluted his father and, without a word, turned and raced downstairs.

The president laughed and Tabby, the First Cat, continued to purr.

Under Hoof
Jeffrey Marks

Humans often notice that General Ulysses Grant had a way with horses, as if he carried on one-sided conversations. Those same people inspect my teeth and hooves, but the prognosticators never bother to look into my eyes. If they did, the fools would know that I could talk to them just as easily.

On more than one occasion during those four noisy years the humans call war, I rescued my favorite rider. He was as fearless against other humans as he was good to me. I couldn't risk falling into the hands of someone who would harness me to plow cotton fields for the rest of my days. I was born for greater things than that. I was the progeny of Lexington, the fastest four-mile thoroughbred in the United States—or what had been the United States.

Most of the animals in the division looked up to me, and not just because I stand seventeen and a half hands high. I'm not sure if it's because I was the mount of the general in chief or because President Lincoln was the only other man permitted to ride me. Most of the animals here were in awe of him, one of the few people to stand as tall as the sleek-coated cavalry horses.

So it wasn't a surprise that a few of the more spirited mounts came for my counsel when Maximillian was taken away. I had been traveling to City Point when the incident occurred, so I didn't know what had happened to Maximillian. His place by the trough was vacant, and none of the others would talk about the events that led to the disappearance.

"Cincinnati, you've got to help. They've taken Maximillian." Bugler was a bit excitable. He was supposed to be a draft horse, but the rumors were that his dam had passed a few late night stall visits with a thoroughbred, producing high-strung Bugler.

"When did this happen?" I looked around, but most of the other mounts had shied away, moving towards the far end of the enclosure to graze, keeping their heads down.

"Two moons ago." Sundance, a haughty black stallion who had been loaned to us by a rich man from the north, had edged forward. "The same night that there was such a fuss by the tents. Then they came and took Max." The steed pranced as he spoke, as if he might gallop off at any second. He was more nervous than in the heat of battle. The rhythmic tapping of his shoes on the grass made me skittish.

I whinnied as I drew my lips back from my teeth. I couldn't handle the choppy manner of this story. I wanted a tale that went like a race, start to finish. I was getting bits and pieces of nothing. "Let's move back to the starting line here. What happened by the tents?"

"No one was sure. There was a lot of yelling and talk, but they were too far away. It might have had something to do with the man who fell asleep by us."

"Describe the sleeping man to me." A picture was starting to form in my mind, and I didn't like it one bit.

Bugler started first. "He was laying on the ground and all. His eyes were closed. He looked like the raccoons."

"What do you mean?" I shot back.

"His eyes had circles, like Dusty." Bugler looked to one of the other horses that had a ring around one eye. I knew that humans weren't born with rings. They got them from fighting and kicking with their front paws.

"And he slept so soundly that the others couldn't wake him up. Even with all the noise. Those mules make a terrible ruckus." Sundance hated the mules who pulled the quartermaster supplies. I could have pointed out that my general started as a quartermaster, but I don't think that would have changed his opinion about the mules.

Bugler cut in. "The men finally carried him back to camp on a stretcher. The poor guy couldn't breathe. They put a cloth over his head and took him away."

That explained more. The horses should have recognized death, but somehow without the sounds of bullets and cannons, they thought that death couldn't occur. Life ended with a boom in these days. Somehow Maximillian's move came as a result of that soldier being killed.

"Where were the guards? Shouldn't they have been watching us?" I was angry to think that the men thought so little of us when we could save them at a moment's notice.

"They took a break. We watched them leave, and then two men came up with the sleeping man. One on each side of him. They were helping him along." Sundance looked away as if he didn't enjoy the memory. "Then they dumped him in the pen."

Sundance closed his eyes and whinnied. "The one man had a white mane that didn't come down in front. The humans call that bald-faced," Sundance said, pleased with himself.

"Bald," I corrected. "And the other?"

"He had a black mane that he kept tucked up under his hat, shifty eyes, and a big Roman nose."

"That's all you remember?" I was disappointed that he couldn't be more precise to help our friend.

"All those humans look alike. What do you expect?"

Certainly they didn't think that a horse could be responsible for the death of a soldier. We weren't bloodthirsty like the men who rode us. When was the last time that the equine kingdom had declared war on each other? With so much bloodshed surrounding us, it was unthinkable that we could contribute to that pile of dead men who lined the roads.

I wasn't sure what the soldiers would do to a horse that killed a man. He would be unfit for duty. No other soldier would saddle up a mount that could be deadly. They'd rather have a horse that obeyed and knew when to run. So much of war was running in one direction or the other. Even so, would Grant, who had been able to tame a beast like York during his West Point days, so easily give up on a good steed?

I foresaw problems in saving our friend. The first was finding out what had really happened to that soldier. I had a cavalry regiment to help me, but I didn't know what they had seen and I wasn't sure that they understood it either. The horses were already showing difficulty in recognizing a killing, if their stories were to be believed. Spotting a killer among all these soldiers would be next to impossible. All those humans looked similar.

It didn't help that no one knew what had happened to Maximillian either. If he was already put down for his supposed crimes, then anything we would do would be for naught. One of the horses needed to do some reconnaissance to find out where our friend was being held captive. If he was still alive, then we had a chance to save him from whatever fate the Army had planned for our companion.

The final problem would be communicating what we learned to the Army. The leaders didn't seem to pay much notice to their horses, as long as we carried them in the right direction. My general would pay attention. He would look into my eyes and somehow he'd know that I knew what had happened to that man—that Maximillian was not a killer.

I trotted off to find out the truth. Sundance had wandered to the other end of the corral as far from the mules as he could get. The half-horses were braying in amusement over something that we didn't understand. Sundance's head stuck through the boards of the fence, straining his long graceful neck to nip at the grass just outside his reach. I tried to be casual as I stopped at the fence. "They should take away a few of the other horses, and I might get enough to eat," said Sundance as he snapped a few blades off and started to chew.

"So you saw the men take Maximillian away?" Perhaps I had a witness to what had happened, though Sundance would prove a hostile one at best. If it wasn't riding or eating, he wanted no part of it. He didn't even bother to pull his head up to look at me.

"We all did. It's not like we've been going anywhere lately."

Sundance had a point. Except for the few advance men going out to find the plow horses from the big homes to our immediate south, we had stayed in the same area for months now. The Virginia landscape near Petersburg was hilly, but we could still see the troops from the South and their men. That definitely limited who could have killed the soldier and left him with us.

"So did you see Maximillian step on the man?"

"Well, it was hard to miss. This man lay in the mud, and Maximillian just stepped on his fetlock as if he wasn't even there." Sundance pulled his head back through the fence, content that he'd managed to eat all the grass he could from this position. He held his head high, letting the wind catch his mane. He looked like a general's horse. I knew that was his aspiration in the Army. He might have been larger than most of the horses, but at seventeen and a half hands, I was the largest in the pen.

"But nobody dies from a broken fetlock." I'd seen too many men break a fetlock from being thrown from a less experienced mount. In fact, the general had been injured, riding another horse. I'd never dream of hurting him. He'd limped for weeks, but still managed to make a tough trek across Tennessee to save another battle. Humans went to doctors when they broke a leg. They didn't shoot themselves when a soldier came up lame. "You didn't see anything else?"

"Well, there were those little pieces of paper that the men play with." Sundance looked around to see if any of the other horses were watching us.

"What papers?"

"You know, they play those games with the pieces of paper and trade money after they put them down on the table. The papers have pictures of men and women on them, and some of the cards have little spots on them."

I nodded. I knew that the General didn't much like for the men to trade money when they played. He said it was bad for morale when someone lost too much of their money. "So the man had some of the papers on him?"

Sundance pulled his lips back from his teeth. "He had seven papers on him, all of them exactly the same. Each one had one spot in the middle of the paper."

I tried to figure out what that could mean. It didn't sound right. Maybe the man had cheated somehow, like when a horse got off to a fast start in a race. The other horses didn't much care for that.

One of the Southern horses whinnied a laugh. They had not been cooperative since our troops had captured their humans. I had to wonder if perhaps they had been involved in killing the soldier. After all, that was the point of war. It would be hard to ask them because they were tetchy about every little thing. They didn't appreciate it at all that the General had a little horse named Jeff Davis, but I wasn't sure that a horse named after the enemy could be taken seriously as a reason for killing. Still, it would be too fun to crack it a good one with the whip and say, "Gee, Jeff Davis." Who wouldn't have fun doing that? I didn't know if the Southern gentlemen had horses named after Mr. Lincoln or not, but it would be a gangly horse with a mind of its own, for sure.

Even if Maximillian had stepped on the man's fetlock, he hadn't killed him—just as I suspected. That meant the man had been dead in the mud before Maximillian carelessly stepped on him. Either he was dead or had been drinking that amber water that made men so silly.

Fortunately, my general took me out for a ride that very afternoon. Usually, he had a specific course for our trips, but today he seemed distracted by something. The reins hung looser than normal and I took the liberty to skirt the camp. My general seemed content to survey the perimeter.

The Virginia countryside didn't look much like what I imagined the rest of the Appalachians looked like this spring. A giant hole pocked a side of the town's defensive line, and the troops had taken the time to tear up railroad tracks. Even during the season of renewal, the ground was muddy and lifeless from the movement of man and beast. Even in the waiting of a siege, my general had to keep busy. He kept at the Rebels from all sides.

We stayed to the rear of the camp, not wanting to be fired upon by the pent-up Southerners. The feeling in camp was that it was only a matter of time until the South had to take the bit and be broken by the North. I wanted my creature comforts back, a nice warm stall and my own bale of hay.

We'd made it to the far end of the camp, when I saw a lone horse tethered to a post. At first, I couldn't make out who it was, but as we trotted closer, I could see the outline of my old friend. He stood alone in the field, tied to a single post. Apparently, bad horses didn't need a guard like humans. Even though Maximillian didn't look up, I felt as if he knew I was there. We'd been in battle before and we had a few too many bullets shot at us not to instinctively know where the other was. I hoped that the sight of one of his brethren would give him hope for a rescue.

I'd been glad to be given the chance to wander the camp this way. When my general wanted to go somewhere, it was futile to argue with him. You followed his command and went. He'd seemed preoccupied today, and I wondered what new strategy would be in place by the end of the week.

When I returned to the pen, my general led me to the water trough where I drank heavily. The March days had been getting warmer by the day with no signs of a mild spring. After he went off to his tent, I went to tell the others that it was time to put our strategy into motion.

The first part of the plan was easy. Since the horses listen to me, I was easily able to get Laramie to feign a loose shoe. Laramie was General Hancock's horse, an Appaloosa who would do anything to fit in with the other horses. He didn't relish his spots like some Appaloosas. He wanted a plain brown coat instead.

His general was due to review the troops that next morning. I'd been carrying Grant when I overheard the command. With Laramie faking a loose shoe, Sundance would have an opportunity to review all the troops and spot the men who had pushed the soldier down in the mud. We'd all had enough loose shoes to fake the symptoms. Laramie did a good act and the quartermaster led the Appaloosa off to the blacksmith while Sundance prepared for his role.

The next morning dawned sunny, and the troops were presented to the generals before the start of another maneuver towards Petersburg. Sundance took his time in looking around. With his mane thrown back and his Arabian nose jutted out, I suspected that he enjoyed the attention. General Hancock made a particular fuss over him, and Sundance took care of the general like a load of eggs. The man couldn't have had a smoother ride if he'd been carried on feather pillows.

I whinnied twice before the horse snapped back to life and remembered his purpose here. His eyes roamed the troops, but with so many men, it would be hard to find a single guilty face in the sea of blue hats and woolen coats. So often they looked alike with their long manes and unkempt fur. The effort was as futile as trying to locate an Appaloosa by the sake of owning spots.

I had begun to despair that we would be able to save our friend Maximillian. I didn't want to see him end up like the other animals who had been hurt in the course of the war and put down. That fate seemed too cruel when I knew him to be innocent. The search seemed fruitless, and I could tell that Sundance had grown weary of trying to find one man amongst so many.

From the corner of my eye, I could see Laramie being led back this way. The smithy would not have found anything wrong with his shoe, and would return him as soon as he could. Laramie had refused to ruin a good shoe, even for the sake of another horse, so their time had been limited.

For all his airs, Sundance was not a pleasant steed for a general. Too often, he fought his rider, thinking that he knew best for the both of them. All of that meant that Laramie would soon be replacing Sundance again and the one chance of spotting the humans would be lost.

Without notice, Sundance began pawing the ground. The general appeared not to notice, but I did. The two men right in front of the general and his steed were just as Sundance had described them. Short, thin, and with face whiskers. Their coats were covered with mud—not proof by any means, but it confirmed the notion that they had deposited that other man in the pen for Maximillian to step on.

This pair were an unsavory lot from the general's staff. Neither was of much authority, but I knew them by reputation. On more than one occasion, the general had called them out for their behavior. I knew they had crossed a line this time.

As we stood there, waiting for the review to finish, I started to form a plan in my mind. I wasn't sure how to convey to the general what I knew to be true. So physical evidence would have to convince him that Maximillian was innocent.

I had to wait until later in the day when Sundance had stopped telling his tale to every four-legged creature in the pen. He'd garnered a lot of interest by carrying the general as well as taking responsibility for saving Maximillian.

In the meantime, I'd spent the day looking for what we would need to set our plan in motion. Finding a used horseshoe was easy. One of the steeds was always pulling off a shoe and coming up lame. I found one at the outside perimeter of the pen, half buried in the mud. I took it in my teeth over to the mules' watering trough and washed it off as best I could. It couldn't be too dirty for what I had in mind.

Next came the matter of the blood. Even though this was war, finding the red sticky fluid was not as easy as you'd think. In the hot Virginia sun, the blood dried into so much more brownish-red mud. We needed it to be fresh when it was applied like ointment. One of the cavalry steeds offered to assist. The poor gelding had been injured in a scouting expedition, his rider killed instantly, and a musket ball in the hind flanks had wounded him. Now I took the horseshoe in my teeth and smeared it into the bullet hole that he had rubbed raw on a tree trunk. The blood smelled thick and salty as I made sure that the stains would not be missed. I hid the shoe by the place where Sundance had been eating grass. No one was likely to go out that far, and most of the lazy soldiers wouldn't walk that far to be discharged. After a few hours in the hot dry summer sun, I knew that the plan was ready. The humans would never call this horseshoe lucky.

We had to use Sundance's despised mules to carry it out. The horses didn't get out of the pen much, but the mules were given more free access to the camp. The contrary creatures were more likely to stand in one place than run away. I explained the situation in detail to two of them, Harry and Jerry. At first, I thought that they might only drop the shoe somewhere outside of our reach, just to be difficult, but finally they agreed that it was a shame that a horse of any type should be blamed for a human crime.

They took the shoe to the camp, and, in a maneuver worthy of my general, they got it in the coat of the blond man who had carried the dead man's body to our pen. Harry had managed to step in some manure on the way to the tent and proceeded to wipe it across the entrance to the man's tent. When the blond man tried to shoo him away, Harry became stubborn and stood his ground. No single man would ever move him. When the man was struggling with Harry, Jerry moved in and slid the horseshoe into the man's pocket.

The only thing left to do was to cause a commotion, but I had no doubt that the mules could do that without trouble. Sure enough, no sooner had they put the shoe in the man's coat than one of them bit clean through the tent ropes. The whole structure tumbled down around them, and the two partners in crime crept away, braying like the asses they were. No one noticed that they were outside of their enclosure in the ensuing melee.

General Grant came running at the sound of the noise and the falling structure. The encampment had experienced a few problems with spies, unwanted people who came to visit. No one could recognize them since humans all looked alike. Everyone was on his toes about the matter.

The little blond man tried to make it seem like nothing was wrong, but under the stern gaze of his commanding officer, he had to put on his uniform. The pocket bulged so much on the one side that even we could see the wool droop from our enclosure.

Grant took a look at the man, and stuffed his hand in the man's pocket. As predicted, my general knew exactly what had happened. The man was led away in shackles to await his fate. He pointed out the other man who had helped him carry the body to the pen, and the guards quickly snatched the other man as well.

It was no time at all before the guards brought Maximillian back to our pen. The horse was practically prancing as they led him in and released him from the lead. He galloped around the perimeter of the pen for a good three minutes before he slowed down enough for anyone to welcome him home.

We never saw the two men again. Some of the animals heard that they ran away, and others heard they were sent off to the big enclosure where bad men are kept.

* * *

Author's note: The horse Cincinnati was presented to Grant after the battle of Chattanooga in late 1863 by a grateful man in St. Louis, Missouri. Cincinnati was his favorite steed for the rest of the war. I can't find any references to Cincinnati after the war, except that Grant retained him. A man once offered Grant $10,000 for the horse, and Grant refused.

Grant was born a natural horseman. By the age of five, he was driving a team of horses to haul lumber to market. In Georgetown where he grew up, he was often asked to break horses that no one else in town could handle.

By the time he reached West Point, he was well-known as an equestrian, and at his graduation, he rode a wild steed named York that nobody else could even touch.

In the Mexican War, he again was recognized for his horsemanship when he rode through enemy lines by riding suspended from the side of the horse, rather than sitting on the horse. By the end of the Civil War, Grant was recognized as one of the best horsemen in America.

The Princess and the Pickle

Carolyn Wheat

The way the dog carried on, you'd think Pickle weighed half a ton. It was true he'd put on a pound or two since they'd moved to the nation's capital. 'A fine figure of a cat' was how he saw himself. After all, these were the days when a man puffed out his chest and let his stomach precede him into a room, proud of what he called his 'corporation.' But the dog scanned Pickle up and down with her doggy brown eyes and then said in a snarky voice, "Good morning, *Piccolomino*," emphasizing the no longer appropriate name he'd acquired as a kitten.

"'Morning, liver-breath," Pickle replied. As if a mere dog could ever hope to match wits with a feline.

"Seen the new princess yet?" The dog, as always, stood uncomfortably close, her long black nose edging into his personal space in a way he'd always found downright disgusting. He knew where that nose had been and he didn't want it anywhere near his nice clean fur.

One more step and it would be claw time. Which the dog understood very well; she backed away prudently when he narrowed his green eyes.

"What princess?" He hated to give the dog the satisfaction, but he felt it his duty to keep a close watch on the premises and a new arrival meant one more charge to protect. Pickle thought of himself as a house detective, not unlike certain pals in Chicago or New York City, only instead of sordid affairs in dingy hotel rooms, he had the honor of guarding the most important house in the entire United States.

Princesses were nothing new to him. He'd seen them at state dinners, the leftovers from which had helped create the Pickle Corporation.

"From England?" He licked an indifferent paw. "From Holland? How long is she staying?" Then he dropped his mask and asked the truly important question. "Will there be a state dinner?"

"Ha," Mrs. Sniffles, for that was the dog's egregious name, replied. "That's all you know about it." With that she walked away. Waddled, actually; she'd sampled at least as many leftovers as he and, being a dachshund, had a Germanic propensity toward plumpness.

*   *   *

Rutherford B. Hayes, nineteenth president of the United States, crumpled the letter into a ball and tossed it into the fireplace, where it lit and crackled into fiery ash.

Pickle's green eyes followed the paper ball's trajectory, but he made no attempt to catch it. A cat of his years and dignity didn't make a fool of himself racing after every little thing that flew through the air, and besides, he could see that it would be in the fire before he could reach it. He closed his eyes and, from his hiding place behind the embroidered fire screen, basked in the glow of the flames.

"Pa, what'd you do that for?" Webb, the president's oldest son and private secretary, looked put out. "That's evidence, that is."

"Evidence of what, Webb?" Hayes sighed deeply and shook his massive head. "Evidence that some people still think I'm not the rightful president?" Having lost the popular vote, Hayes had prevailed in the Electoral College only after a bipartisan commission declared him the victor. Some people and many newspapers still referred to him as 'His Fraudulency.' Well-founded fears of assassination attempts had cancelled the inaugural ball, and Webb never left the White House without a pistol in his belt.

"The letter said 'Remember what happened to Lincoln.'" Webb's eyes narrowed. "That's more than just a disgruntled citizen, that's someone threatening to kill you."

"I can't help but feel sorry for some of these people, Webb," Hayes said in his deep voice. "They lived their entire lives by one set of rules, and now somebody comes along and changes those rules. There's bound to be resistance."

"Pa, you know you did the right thing by signing the Civil Service Act," Webb replied. He ran his slender fingers through straight brown hair, a young man grown older through work and worry. "It had to be done, like lancing a boil. Why, I've heard there were so-called postmasters who never learned to read! Just because a man delivers votes for the Party doesn't mean he ought to have a sinecure for life and you know it."

"I do know it." Hayes took three steps toward the heavy damask drapes, then three steps back, his black boots shining in the firelight. "But I also know people are going to vent their spleen, just like they did when I was first elected."

"Remember the bullet someone fired through our window back in Fremont?" Webb's face was red, his voice filled with the passion of youth. "That was more than just venting spleen, and so is this. You have to tell somebody, get more protection."

Hayes waved a hand at the fire, where the letter had long since burned to ash. "This letter writer's no more dangerous than a barking dog."

Webb Hayes regarded his father with the large, sorrowful brown eyes he'd inherited from his mother. "Pa, just a reminder: some dogs bite."

Pickle's ears, one black, one white, perked up.

Webb was right: the president was in danger. He knew as much as anyone about barking dogs and he was willing to bet that letter writer wasn't just venting spleen.

What was he, Pickle, going to do about it?

* * *

At least there were peacocks.

One peacock, anyway.

They had told Kamkun she was going to a great palace far, far away. Farther away even than Burma. That it was an enormous honor and that she had been chosen because she was the most beautiful of the latest crop of royal princesses.

This, at least, was true. She licked a complacent paw as she contemplated her own perfection.

But as to the rest—where was the palace? Where were the richly colored silks and the gold and the jewels? Where were the white elephants and golden umbrellas and why didn't this Two-Legs who was supposed to be their king wear a crown like her Royal Master Whose Name Was Spoken in Whispers?

His face was furry. This was something she'd never seen before. All the Two-Legs in her country wore skin on their faces and had very little fur. But the big white Two-Legs who was her new master stroked his furry face like a feline; she found that oddly endearing. It was perhaps the only thing she liked about her new home.

That and the peacock.

Not that he was friendly. Far from it; he shrieked and pecked and chased her just like the peacocks back home in Siam. But at least his presence confirmed that she was indeed in some sort of palace. Only a king could own peacocks, so perhaps this furry Two-Legs was a king after all, even though he had only one peacock and his servants didn't prostrate themselves and crawl across the room on their bellies like snakes when they brought him his food.

*   *   *

Her eyes were blue.

Blue.

The president had blue eyes. He'd always found that spooky. Dogs had brown eyes, like The Lady, and of course cats had lovely yellow or green eyes.

No cat he'd ever seen before had blue eyes.

But then she was like no other cat. Small and beautifully proportioned, she had a body as tan as the hunting dogs who lived in the kennel. Her ears and mouth, her tail and paws were the dark, rich brown of Winnie Monroe's exquisite gravy. And her eyes were an extraordinary, otherworldly blue.

They stared through him as if he wasn't there.

"You must be the princess," he said and cursed himself the minute the words were out of his mouth. *Get a grip on yourself. She'll think you're a real rube.*

"I am Siamese, if you please," she said in a low throaty voice that sent a shiver through him. He'd thought he was getting too old for that sort of thing, but her whisky voice brought out the tom in him.

"I am Siamese," she added disdainfully, "if you don't please."

Pickle had heard The Lady talk about Siam. It was a country far, far away with a king who wanted The Lady to stop Americans from selling alcohol to his country. The Lady hated alcohol and refused to serve it in the White House, which was why some people called her Lemonade Lucy.

Pickle wasn't entirely sure what alcohol was, but it sounded a bit like catnip. Personally, he enjoyed a nip now and then, but he could see where some Two-Legs, like some cats, didn't know when to stop.

So the princess was from Siam.

In spite of himself, Pickle was impressed.

"My name is Kamkun," she continued. "It means *gold* in the language of my people."

"I'm—" he hesitated. Should he give his full name and hope she didn't know Italian, or —

"Call me Pickle," he said. "It means—"

"We have pickles in my country," she said with a wistful tone in her voice. Her great blue eyes stared into his. "I miss Siamese food so much. My tongue has not burned once since I have been in this cold, damp place."

Pickle didn't understand why any cat would want her tongue to burn, but before he could say so, Kamkun opened her tiny mouth in a wide yawn and he saw sharp little teeth that would feel just fine on his neck when he—

Oh, no. He'd made a deal with himself a long time ago: no relationships on the job.

* * *

Winnie Monroe, who presided over the White House kitchen with as much authority as Mr. Hayes presided over the country, had never seen a cat like Kamkun before either. More to the point, she'd never heard a cat like Kamkun before.

"Got a mighty big voice for such a little thing," Winnie said to her daughter as they sliced potatoes for tonight's dinner. She was going to try a new recipe from France, a dish called Potatoes Anna, whoever Anna was.

It seemed to her that before coming to Washington, D.C., Mrs. Hayes had been satisfied with Potatoes Winnie, but she supposed that it was important for the First Lady of the land to eat as fine as possible, and if some foreign cook named Anna could make them potatoes, why, then, so could she. She could make almost anything and what she couldn't make herself could be sent over from the massive kitchen of the Willard Hotel, just a block away.

Kamkun rubbed up against Winnie's skirt, alternately purring and meowing the loudest, harshest meow Winnie had ever heard. "Sound like the peacock, and Lord knows, he's enough to scare a body out of bed. Sound like he callin' for help, like someone's out there dyin'."

"Mama, you been sayin' that about Colonel Prior ever since Mrs. Hayes first brought him to Spiegel Grove," Winnie's sixteen-year-old daughter Mary said with a laugh as her knife made an arabesque in the steamy kitchen air. "Ain't you ever gonna get used to that bird?"

"Hm. Ought to take a ax out there and chop off his fool head, then cook him for dinner like they did in them old Roman days. That's what Mr. Rud told me once. They ate them peacocks in Rome, had they tail feathers all spread out on the platter and ate they tongues like delicacies. Serve that noisy bird right."

"Can't get much of a meal out'n a bird's tongue," Mary replied. She dried her hands on a muslin towel and reached for the butter. Kamkun raced over and jumped up on her hind legs, catching her front claws on Mary's apron and crying like a baby.

"Oh, we got ourselves a butter cat here, Mama," Mary said.

"Butter her paws, she'll never run away," Winnie said sagely.

Mary suited action to words, smearing fresh butter on the chocolate-colored paws of the strange, blue-eyed cat. Kamkun yowled joyously and plopped herself smack in the middle of the kitchen, her small pink tongue making short work of the tasty delight.

"Guess Miss Pussy's here to stay for good now," Mary said. She leaned down and petted the sharp, triangle-shaped head. Kamkun closed her eyes and purred appreciatively. Butter and petting—it might almost make up for cold and damp and no gold in sight.

* * *

Pickle had never liked the old tabby. A sour, complaining sort of cat, she came around every so often hoping for a dish of milk from the kitchen, maybe a plate of scraps, and never failed to hiss and claw at Pickle. Once the old tabby managed to draw blood and The Lady nursed him back to health, dabbing peroxide on the wound to draw out the infection.

So the sight of the old tabby lying stiff and still as a board behind the lilac bush ought to have pleased Pickle, or at least left him with a sense of relief. Instead, he sniffed at the corpse of his old enemy, noting how small, how thin, the old cat had been. Pickle could see her ribs under a coat matted by recent rains.

How had the old tabby died? Something strange assailed Pickle's nose; he crept closer to her mouth and recoiled at the strong medicinal smell. Surely no cat would have put something like that in her mouth on purpose.

The old tabby had tried to rid herself of whatever had poisoned her; evidence of vomiting lay in dried puddles around the scene of death. Sardine bones, meat scraps, a bit of bread and milk—what you'd expect a street cat to eat, morsels scraped from the table into a wooden bowl and set outside for the stray.

Then he found the smoked oysters.

Not a dish he'd expect the old tabby to be familiar with; it was posh food, the kind his president served, the kind people ate in fancy hotels and drawing rooms.

Even The Lady, kind-hearted as she was toward animals, never gave the old tabby smoked oysters, yet here they lay, half-digested, purged from the system of the dead feline.

They smelled of more than oyster. The medicinal scent was very strong here, and Pickle realized with a sinking heart that the old tabby had been poisoned. Someone had deliberately tempted the hungry old thing with a savory dish, knowing it would kill her.

Did the killer watch her die? Did he take some perverted pleasure from the suffering of small creatures? Or was there something even more sinister at work, some dark force that must be stopped before—

Before it killed his president? Could the threatening letter writer be planning to poison—

But no—how could anyone get past the guards outside the White House, get into Winnie Monroe's kitchen, and poison food meant for the president? It just wasn't possible.

Unless—Pickle went back over to the oysters, sniffed them again, and remembered the last time he'd had smoked oysters. The president had sent to Willard's Hotel for a trayful of the salty delicacies when Senator Garfield came to visit.

Could poisoned shellfish reach the White House from Willard's?

Pickle wasn't sure. He knew only one thing: this horrible death had taken place on the South Lawn of the White House and was therefore his responsibility. He headed toward a six-story brick building with a pennant on the roof, determined to talk to the one cat in Washington who knew where all the bodies were buried.

* * *

"Mama, come and look at Miss Pussy," Fanny Hayes said, a giggle bursting from her. Normally a serious little miss of ten, she was red-faced from racing down the steps and trying to subdue her laughter at the same time.

Lucy Webb Hayes looked up from her knitting and smiled at her only daughter. "What's that cat gotten into now? Don't tell me she's discovered my needlework again!"

"No, Mama, she's discovered *Hiawatha*," Fanny said, a peal of laughter accompanying her words. "You must come and see—she's so cunning."

"Hiawatha—oh, I hope she isn't tearing up my books." Lucy followed her daughter down the stairs, from the family quarters to the ceremonial rooms. Fanny marched directly into the State Dining Room, where she stopped suddenly and pointed. "Look," she said in a stage whisper.

Lucy looked. On the massive sideboard sat a silver centerpiece, a holdover from the free-spending Grant Administration. The size of a roast pig, it was a fanciful interpretation of Longfellow's Hiawatha. The tray was highly polished silver with a mirror overlay representing the water, on which rested a silver canoe with a magnificent sail the Indians would scarcely have recognized. In the rear of the canoe sat Hiawatha, the Indian hero, an oar in one hand and a weapon in the other, gazing fiercely into the horizon. Around the bottom of the glass 'lake' was a verse from the epic poem: *All alone went Hiawatha through the clear transparent water.*

In the front of the canoe, her eyes closed and her chest rising and falling in a very loud purr, sat Princess Kamkun of Siam, known to the Hayes family as Miss Pussy.

Lucy Hayes let out a whoop of laughter, for a moment looking as young as her child. Her mild brown eyes softened as she gazed at the newest animal member of her household.

"She must be feeling at home," Lucy said. "I'm glad she and Pickle seem to be getting along."

Fanny placed her hand over her heart as if she were in school and declaimed, "'All alone went Hiawatha'—all alone except for Miss Pussy!"

*　*　*

Blackie eyed Pickle with his one good orb, a rheumy yellow object that saw far more than veterinary science thought it could. His other eye had been permanently closed in a fight with the District's most notorious ward heeler, a tough, wiry orange tom known as The Mick. Blackie may have lost an eye, but The Mick, who hadn't been seen since, was reputed to have lost his ninth life.

Presidential cats come and presidential cats go, was Blackie's philosophy. He would be where he'd always been, curled up beside the fire in the front parlor of the Willard Hotel, when the Hayes Administration was over, just as he'd been when Grant first took his oath of office.

Pickle, well aware of the other cat's power and influence, greeted Blackie accordingly. After a few preliminary hisses and snarls just to let the other know he was no pushover, Pickle got down to business.

"I think someone's trying to kill the president," he said glumly. "I'm going to look like a sap if I let that happen, and I don't play the sap for anybody."

"What makes you think so?" Blackie had a way of talking out of the side of his mouth that much impressed Pickle. It wasn't the way a gentleman talked, of course, but it was rather effective.

Pickle explained about the dead tabby. "If someone just liked poisoning cats, and we both know there are sick Two-Legs who do, why would he pay top dollar for smoked oysters? That tabby would have gobbled up tripe just as fast. So I have to think she was poisoned for some other reason, and the only one I can come up with is that it was a test."

"Make sure the poison worked, you mean," Blackie said with a shake of his ebony head. "Hate to think about not being able to trust a smoked oyster. Still, I suppose the old girl died happy."

"No, she didn't," Pickle said shortly. The sad little body had gotten to him all right, and the last thing he wanted was to think about Mr. Rud dying the way the old tabby had died, convulsing and vomiting, helpless and in pain.

"What I hear is that a few people are gunning for your boss," Blackie said. "Word in the parlor is that he's put a lot of good Party people out of work and they don't like it."

"Who doesn't like it enough to put poison in his food?"

Blackie sidled over to Pickle and rubbed up against his face. "I don't name names," he said. "It isn't good for business. But don't worry," he went on, "your boss is safe. After all, how could they get to him? I know for a fact Winnie Monroe doesn't let just anybody into her kitchen."

Pickle stifled a smile; he'd been in the herb garden one morning when Mary Monroe's broom swept an indignant Blackie out into the courtyard.

"If the president wanted to serve something special at a party, say smoked oysters, he'd order them from Willard's, wouldn't he?"

Blackie nodded. "President Grant had so much food delivered to the White House from here, he might as well have sacked his cook."

"So all I have to do is keep an eye out for an oyster delivery," Pickle mused.

"It wouldn't have to be oysters," Blackie pointed out. "It could be our world-famous corned beef and cabbage."

"Presidents don't serve corned beef and cabbage to guests," Pickle retorted. He might not have Blackie's local knowledge, but he *was* a man of the world.

"I hear there's a Russian prince coming to dinner next week," Blackie said, his good eye lighting up. "Russians mean caviar, and caviar means—"

"Caviar has a very strong taste," Pickle reflected. It was a taste he personally loved even more than smoked oysters, but he could see where it might be a good disguise for poison. "Thanks for the tip; I'll keep my eyes open."

* * *

"*Consomme royale*, yes, Ma'am," Winnie Monroe repeated. "Then *petits bouchees a la Cardinale*." The cook made no notes; her writing wasn't up to the foreign names, but the dishes themselves would be perfect. She cooked the way some people played piano: "by ear." All she had to do was taste a dish once and it was hers, down to the most delicate mixture of spices.

"That's where the caviar from Willard's comes in," Lucy Hayes explained. "*Petits bouchees* means 'little mouthfuls' so we'll take puff pastry and fill it with different delicacies, including caviar, smoked salmon, and smoked oysters."

"The fish course is bass, Miz Hayes?" Winnie wore the striped dress of polished cotton that saw her to the Baptist church every Sunday morning.

The menu planning session took two hours, each dish requiring a full discussion of its ingredients and its relationship to the dishes before and after it. State dinners, like all large banquets of the day, were served in 'removes,' and meals were composed like symphonies, with much attention paid to contrasts of taste, color, and richness.

"I'm told the prince adores caviar, and will want a plate of it with lemon and capers, even if it is served as part of another course," Lucy said. She smiled her angelic smile and added, "And Rud might as well have a plate as well. It's not the thing our Ohio constituents might like to hear, but my homespun husband has developed a taste for caviar, too. Why not let him indulge it?"

Why not indeed?

Under ordinary circumstances, Pickle, who sat in his accustomed place behind The Lady's chair, would have purred with delight at the prospect of large mounds of fish eggs making their way into the White House. But with someone out to kill his president, the last thing he wanted were strange foods in Winnie's kitchen—and with Grand Duke Alexis coming from Russia, strange foods were what he was going to get.

*   *   *

It did nothing for Pickle's state of mind that yet another threatening letter came to the president's office that morning. This one was even more explicit, or so Webb thought.

"Pa, it mentions the State Dinner," he said, his voice rising in exasperation. "It says 'he who sits down with the Russian will be clawed as if by a bear.' You have to take this seriously."

The president's light blue eyes lit with inner laughter. "That sounds to me like someone who doesn't much like princes, and I can't say I blame him for that. I'd much rather have a few friends over for Winnie's beef stew than—"

"It goes on to say 'may you choke on your dinner and die. You robbed me of my job and now I'll rob you of yours.'" Webb thrust the letter, written on cheap paper, under his father's nose and waved it back and forth.

Pickle wanted that paper. His inner kitten wanted to claw at it, tear into it, bite it with his teeth. He leapt out from under the oak desk onto the Presidential lap and clawed at it.

"Ow," Webb said, drawing back and taking the letter with him. "He scratched me!"

"You didn't mean to, did you, Mr. Pickle?" The president's slender fingers reached for the sweet spot behind Pickle's bicolored ears. At the soft touch, he melted, flopping down onto his side, showing soft underbelly. Hayes kept his fingers moving over the receptive cat, now tickling his belly, now chucking under his chin, now stroking the sensitive hairs just above his nose.

Pickle writhed with pleasure. How could he let anything happen to a man who knew this much about petting cats?

*   *   *

"A banquet?" Kamkun's blue eyes shone with delight. She looked at him through a palm frond, her front paws folded decorously in front of her. "Oh, I can't wait! Will there be fried wasps? And *nam pla* on everything?"

"Fried wasps?" Pickle swatted a vagrant fly with his paw. "Why would anyone fry a wasp?"

"The Two-Legs in my country love fried wasps," Kamkun replied. "And if I purr very loudly and let them rub my ears, they often feed me some. They're so crunchy and delicious, you can't think!"

The two cats sat at their ease in the Conservatory, which had rapidly become Kamkun's favorite room in the White House. A glassed-in greenhouse with tropical plants, palm trees, and humid heat, it reminded her forcefully of Siam, and she drank in the scent of orchid with a melancholy sigh every time she stepped into its green repose.

"Fried wasps," Pickle repeated, shaking his black and white head. "And what's *nam pla*?"

"Sauce made from fermented fish," the princess said in a sad voice. "And I suppose you *farangs* don't eat that, either."

"Well, I'll admit fish sauce sounds better than fried wasps," replied Pickle, "but I'm not the foreigner here, you are. Besides," he went on in a kinder tone, "you'll like our banquet food, really you will. Canvasback duck, terrapin, oysters, crab cakes, lamb chops—"

"Aren't you forgetting something?"

"Oh, you're right. We're eating French dishes instead of good old American ones. Pity, you'd have loved the canvasback duck."

Kamkun raked Pickle up and down with her cool blue eyes. "Aren't you forgetting that some of that food will be poisoned?"

He hadn't told her, any more than the president had told Mrs. Hayes about the threats on his life. Two more letters had come to the White House, each more explicit than the last, and each consigned to the fire by the president, who had sworn Webb to secrecy.

Yet somehow Kamkun had found out about the danger. Women were like that.

The dinner would take place tonight. Already the famous Hayes china graced the U-shaped table in the state dining room. Already Mrs. Hayes was being prepared by Mary Monroe and a borrowed lady's maid, her long lustrous hair being brushed and her gown aired. Already the deliveries from baker and poulterer, greengrocer and dairyman, had begun to make their way to the kitchen entrance of the White House.

The two cats gazed at one another with glum faces. What could they do to avert the disaster they felt sure was to come?

It was no use trying to communicate with Two-Legs. Pickle and

Kamkun were both aware that no amount of plain, rational speech had the power to penetrate the immense ignorance of the large, ungainly beasts who shared their lives. Oh, Two-Legs were wonderful to play with, and quite intelligent in their way, but limited in understanding.

No, direct action was called for—but what action?

* * *

The Hayes' china was unlike all other presidential dinnerware in that each platter, each plate and bowl, was different. Instead of a single repeating pattern, the Hayes' china bore hand-painted images of American wildlife, particularly the edible sort, so that the fish platter boasted a portrait of a stream with cattails, while each fish plate had a different fish painted on it. Shad, trout, bluefish, perch. Similarly, the game platter showed a hunting scene and the plates themselves were decorated with duck, rail, quail, pheasant, and other game birds. The platters and plates curled up at the corners, like dried parchment; there was even an ice cream platter in the form of a snowshoe.

In the butler's pantry, the showy dishes sat ready to be placed at the dining table. The platters were in the kitchen, ready to be filled and then passed around the table by the footman. Oyster plates rested on a cake of ice so that they would be chilled when the gray Chesapeake pearls were shucked and put in place.

The Willard's Hotel van had already been to the White House four times when the caviar arrived. First had come the smoked oysters, then the smoked salmon, then an extra cask of olives for the *cimbales*.

Pickle huddled under a holly bush on one side of the path, Kamkun under a yew on the other. The horse pulling the van stamped and snorted, swished her big tail at a fly, and generally acted impatient to be on her way.

The deliveryman opened the back door of the van, took out a wooden cask, and hefted it onto his shoulder, then stepped toward the door whistling a tune.

Wood. That was unlucky.

Kamkun yowled her otherworldly howl. Colonel Prior the peacock picked up the cry, sounding for all the world like someone being stabbed to death. The delivery man stopped, wild terror on his Irish face, and muttered something about a banshee. Pickle raced out from under his bush, taking off as if shot from a cannon, rocketing toward the man with the cask, then swerving away at the absolutely last minute.

Just as the deliveryman stepped back to avoid one streaking cat, Kamkun snaked out and positioned herself behind him, tangling herself in his legs. Over he went, landing on his backside with a grunt. The cask fell from his shoulder and rolled down the gentle slope toward the street.

The deliveryman shouted, struggled to his feet, tried to wave at the passing carriage, but it was too late. The carriage wheels slammed into the cask and broke it open. Caviar spilled into the mud and horse-droppings, ruined beyond all saving.

Cat eyed cat with satisfaction. A job well done. No caviar for the prince; no poison for the president.

A stray dog lumbered along, a slow stupid animal Pickle had had occasion to warn off the South Lawn. He stepped toward the cask, sniffed, and opened his big doggy mouth to take a huge—

"Stop!" Pickle yelled. He didn't much like the yellow hound, but he didn't want to see an animal die right in front of him.

It was too late. The lapping sound that traveled from the street to the back door of the White House was a yellow dog snorting up every single fish egg he could put his huge pink tongue around.

"I can't look," moaned Pickle. Kamkun too averted her blue eyes from the appalling sight.

But after five minutes, the dog trotted away, leaving an empty cask, with no sign of poisoning.

"That's not right," Pickle said. "I know the old tabby died suddenly, or else she'd have found a more private place. No cat dies in the open by choice."

"Which means there was nothing wrong with that caviar," Kamkun agreed. "Either we're wrong about the threat to the president, or we're wrong about which food will be tainted."

"All the food has been delivered," Pickle said. "Which means that if there is poison in something, it's in Winnie Monroe's kitchen right this minute."

* * *

Godey's Lady's Book would write that "The First Lady wore an exquisite gown of rich ivory satin trimmed with Duchess lace, embroidered with seed pearls and rosebuds worked in threads of gold. The square Court train finished a skirt trimmed with bias folds of satin arranged horizontally with a fringe of gold and pearls between. Mrs. Hayes wore a silver comb in her lustrous chestnut hair; a pendant with a cameo of the president set in diamonds was her only jewelry. We are told the dress was made by M. A. Connelly of New York and cost $980.00."

Godey's Lady's Book would not record the president's reaction upon being given the bill, nor would it record Lucy's response to the effect that society women spent twice as much on their gowns and paid to have them shipped from Paris. She was well aware that some Washington ladies looked down on her as an Ohio provincial and she was determined, for once in her husband's Presidency, to dress with as much fashion as she could stand.

It was a gown Kamkun longed to climb. It looked positively enchanting to a cat with itchy claws. How wonderful it would feel to ride those horizontal folds right to the Lady's bosom, to rub the sides of her face against the scratchy net, to rip and tear the lace, which had such convenient holes already, as if just waiting for feline attention.

Something in the strange blue eyes—or perhaps it was the way she tilted her brown head up and down, measuring the distance between floor and bustle—told Lucy Hayes what was on her cat's mind.

"Fanny, take that animal somewhere," she said absently as she arranged the silver comb in her hair one more time. "I don't care where, just get her away from me."

"I know—I'll take her to the conservatory."

But Kamkun didn't want to be shut up all night away from the action, not even in her favorite room. She scratched poor Fanny's arm and jumped down, racing toward the state dining room. Surely there she could find a place to hide, to watch out for anything sinister during the dinner.

Besides, that would give her one more glimpse of the sumptuous dress.

* * *

It was unclear whether or not anyone saw the small brown animal in the big silver boat. True, the centerpiece wasn't in the middle of the dining table, but rested instead on a sideboard that wasn't to be used until the dessert course, when the plates decorated with painted fruits would be filled with meringues. True, many diners had their backs to the sideboard, and also true, the cat was uncharacteristically silent during the meal and had her head turned under her paw. But perhaps Grand Duke Alexis merely dismissed the presence of a Siamese cat in a large ugly silver boat as a quaint American custom.

Pickle, meanwhile, was drowning his sorrows in Winnie Monroe's kitchen. The kindhearted cook, who had fed him since he was a kitten, scooped sour cream into a bowl and set it down near the stove for him.

"This was supposed to go into the *bouchees* with the caviar," she said to no one in particular. "Too bad that ruined cask was the last one Willard's had. I shouldn't be giving you no treats, you bad Pickle, you, but you look so sorry for what you done, I guess I can forgive you."

Pickle lapped gratefully at the sour cream, glad to be forgiven even if he didn't feel sorry. Well—he was sorry the caviar hadn't been poisoned, because that meant the threat was still out there, still about to happen, but perhaps this banquet would go just as planned, with the notable absence of fish eggs.

Or perhaps the president was right after all, and the letter writer was just blustering, like a cat hissing at a larger animal.

He'd taken precautions, sniffing every single bit of the Willard's deliveries, making sure that salmon smelt like salmon and oysters like oysters and nothing had been wrong. He not only would have staked his life on it, he *had* staked his life on it, taking little bites of every single delicacy. No medicinal taste. No poison.

He hoped there would be plenty of leftovers.

*   *   *

Removes came, removes went. The bass *de Normande* gave way to *filets de boeuf Richelieu*. Lamb chops with *petits pois* left and *cimbales d'olives* took their place. Every time a new dish reached the table, the diners turned to the guest on their other side and began a new conversation. Discussions across the table would have been not only highly improper but also impossible, due to the large amount of greenery in the way.

Kamkun had no interest in olives. At first, they had intrigued her with their size and greenness. She thought they might be edible, but, no, they'd turned out to be sour and not fishy and not good for anything but batting around Winnie Monroe's nice kitchen floor, which Winnie was not going to permit in any case.

But suddenly a thought struck her. She and Pickle had tested all the food that came from Willard's, all the food that *they* considered food, but the olives—

The olives hadn't interested them.

So they hadn't bothered with them.

But the Two-Legs were about to eat the olives, and if the caviar hadn't been poisoned, then there was a good chance that these cold green balls contained the poison that was meant to kill the president,

Who at that moment was reaching with silver tongs toward the platter John Footman held out toward him, so Kamkun:

Leapt out of the Hiawatha boat with a heartrending cry,

Landed on the table going thirty miles an hour,

Caught her claws on the tablecloth and began dragging it toward the First Lady's lap.

The president dropped the silver tongs back onto the platter.

John Footman jumped back, dropping several olives on the carpet.

Lucy Hayes screamed and covered her expensive dress with her napkin, just as the plate in front of her skated toward the edge of the table.

The Grand Duke looked both alarmed and amused, as though convinced that these quaint Americans used their pets as dinner entertainment on a regular basis.

The wire-strung flower baskets suspended above the table swayed and danced with the movement of the tablecloth. Finger bowls wobbled and dripped onto the tablecloth. Ladies screamed, one shouting something about seeing a rat.

Kamkun yowled again and flung herself toward John, claws out. He stumbled and more olives fell to the floor.

"I'm sorry, Mr. President," he said, sounding near tears, "I can't hold onto this plate with that wildcat comin' after me."

Kamkun turned her attention from the footman to Webb Hayes. Arching her back, she hissed at the olives, as if confronting a deadly enemy. She did this several times, looking up at Webb with her strange blue eyes in between hisses.

"She doesn't seem to like olives," Lucy remarked in a voice that shook with suppressed laughter.

But Webb wasn't laughing. All of a sudden, he reached down and picked up one of the olives, using his napkin to protect his fingers from the green orb.

"I think maybe we should have these tested by a doctor," he said, giving his father a meaningful glance.

The olives were removed and John Footman told to wash his hands very thoroughly with lye soap. Fortunately, no one else at the table had chosen to eat the olives. They were, in fact, known to be a favorite of the president's.

Equally fortunately, none of the Hayes dishes were damaged. Even today, you can go to the Smithsonian Institution and see some of the hand-painted china on display. You can also see Lucy's dress, and if you look very carefully at the netting, you may notice one or two holes that weren't made by the dressmaker, but were put there by a curious cat with itchy claws.

The Hiawatha boat, left over from the Grant Administration, is in a glass case at the White House Visitor's Center. When you see that centerpiece, you might want to think about how that silver boat looked one night in 1877 when a small brown Siamese cat jumped out of it and saved the president's life.

They all lived happily ever after. The Hayes presidency ended after one term, which was what Rutherford B. Hayes promised when he ran for office. The family went back to Spiegel Grove, their house in Ohio, taking Pickle and Kamkun and Colonel Prior with them.

Pickle and Kamkun had litter after litter of the most beautiful kittens, most of whom had their parents' formidable brainpower, but only a few of whom had their mother's extraordinary blue eyes.

Remember the Maine?
by Blanche
edited by Jeanne M. Dams

It is not, certainly, from any vulgar desire for publicity that I venture to set forth my story. My kind have never sought the limelight. Humans, during the more enlightened periods of their history, have understood that we were to be worshipped. In these degraded times we graciously consent to be treated more simply, as the adored darlings of hearth and home rather than as deities.

My name, at least the name by which my humans know me, is Blanche. Not an imaginative name for a white Angora cat of my exquisite beauty and impeccable breeding, true, but my humans are not people of imagination. It is difficult for me to tell you their names, since they change constantly. The female calls the male "The Major" when other humans are present, and "Dearest" when only I am with them. The male calls the female "Ida" or "my dear wife." But other humans call him "Mr. President" and her "Mrs. McKinley."

I think humans enjoy confusion.

They are also remarkably unable to distinguish between important and unimportant matters. Look, for example, at the attention they pay to The Major's parrot, a loud, despicable creature named Pedro. The bird has so little self-respect it permits itself to be kept in a cage and made to perform tricks. For some reason the humans are enchanted by these inane performances and publish accounts of them in the newspapers.

Much is made in these accounts of the fact that Pedro can mimic a kind of human speech. The Major is fond of whistling a tune to Pedro which the bird then completes. (I have heard the humans refer to the tune as "Yankee Doodle." Sometimes they sing words to it, which seem to me to be sillier even than most human speech.)

For of course I understand human speech, and respond to it when I choose to. I can even read their written communications, although I never do so, finding them inexpressibly tedious. I have never bothered to speak as humans do. I leave such clumsy communication to the likes of parrots. Since, however, the humans may wish to have some record of what I am about to relate, I shall dictate it to the oaf, Pedro. I trust that the bird will translate it into human and convey it to a person who is sufficiently intelligent to write it down.

You see, I alone know the secret of the events that took place on that fateful night in February, 1898. . . .

I must explain, first, how I came to be involved in the matter at all. The Major and Ida and I live, along with the pestilential Pedro and a large number of assorted humans to wait on us, in an old house called the White House. (The dwelling is, as one might suspect, white; the name is another example of the paucity of human imagination.)

The White House is not a place I would choose to live, were I not fond of The Major and Ida. The paint is cracked, the wallpaper is peeling, the heating arrangements are woefully inadequate, and the place would be overrun with vermin were it not for my continuous and diligent efforts. Even so prodigious a hunter as I, however, cannot keep all the rats at bay. I do my best, but the house is too big and too old, nearly one hundred years old.

I have heard Ida say that she does not like living here, either, and would rather stay at home in Ohio. The Major sighs when she says this. He wants so much to keep her happy, but she suffers from woefully poor health, and the chilly drafts in the house don't help matters any. I have often wondered why The Major and Ida do not remove themselves to a more comfortable home, since they seem to be wealthy and he seems to be reckoned quite an important man. Humans do behave oddly.

I pay little attention to human events as a rule. However, in a place like the White House, where noisy, clumsy humans come and go at all hours, talk, talk, talking, it is difficult to avoid hearing something of what they say. For many months before that calamitous February day, they had talked of Cuba. It was, I gathered, a place far away where the humans were creating problems.

There is, of course, nothing unusual about that. Humans appear to spend most of their time creating problems. I attribute the failing to lack of sleep. Any cat knows that twenty hours of sleep per day is the acceptable allotment, and that less rest causes one to be irritable, weak, and faulty in judgment. Humans seem to think that a paltry seven or eight hours of sleep is sufficient, and they are stupid enough to take that in a solid stretch instead of in frequent naps.

I must constantly remind myself that it is folly to expect feline wisdom of the creatures, and that they are for the most part good, kind souls who mean well.

It became increasingly apparent, however, that some of the humans in Cuba did not mean very well at all. I heard talk of rioting, of rebellion, and finally, insistently, of war.

I was not at the time sure what "war" meant, though I know now. I could discern that something like a very large catfight was involved, and it didn't sound at all pleasant. I myself have never approved of violence unless it was a matter of self-defense (and I was sure of winning).

That February night was very cold, I remember. Though I ordinarily scorn the use of stealth, I had deemed it prudent that night to evade those humans who were delegated to "put out the cat." After they had given up trying to find me, I made my way silently and invisibly to the bedroom shared by The Major and Ida. They had both retired early, and since I can land on a bed very lightly, Ida never woke when I jumped up and made myself comfortable among her soft, warm bedclothes.

I was dreaming pleasantly of chicken and cream when a rap came at the bedroom, waking us all. Ida was instantly upset; she is far more nervous than any cat I ever knew. The Major soothed her, put on a dressing gown, and left the room, saying he would return soon.

I followed him, of course. My rest had already been disturbed, and I had the normal intelligent feline need for information. (Humans refer to this trait as curiosity and joke about it being fatal to cats. *Au contraire*. The desire to be well-informed, far from being fatal, is essential for self-preservation.)

The news that had summoned The Major from his bed that cold February night was that something called the *Maine* had exploded in that place called Cuba.

To save time, I will tell you what I know now, that the *Maine* was a ship of the kind humans call a battleship. A ship is a device that enables humans to travel on water without getting wet, one of their more sensible inventions, actually. A battleship, though, seems in some way to be useful in waging war, which is not sensible. The humans, in their odd way, set great store by these huge ships, and everyone that February night was extremely upset that one had been destroyed.

Most of their distress appeared to be prompted by the fact that many humans inside this ship had been drowned when it exploded. I could understand that part. I am unhappy every time I hear of a litter of kittens being drowned, even when I didn't know the little creatures or their mother. The death of others of one's own kind is always painful. Being a reasonable cat, however, I have never lost sleep over such a sad event. The Major lost a great deal of sleep that night and in the nights to come.

Ida lost sleep, too, and began to suffer even more from her fainting spells and nervous prostration. (That is what the humans call her ailments. I do not fully understand, since cats do not suffer from such complaints.) She was not easy to live with during those days, but The Major was always gentle with her, and so was I. A cat has a duty to the lower species.

I began, nevertheless, to suffer from nerves myself during those worrisome days and weeks. The Major, it appeared, was required to take some action about the destruction of the *Maine*, and he could not decide what to do. The decision seemed to turn on discovering the cause of the explosion. Some said it must have happened accidentally. Others were quite sure it was caused by some humans called the Spanish. Nobody seemed to like them very much, and this matter called war apparently hung in the balance.

Male humans with very large feet and very loud voices and very smelly cigars swarmed over the White House like ill-tempered bees for hours every day and far into the night. I could spend very little time with The Major for fear of being trampled underfoot or getting my coat covered with ashes. Ida, prostrate in bed much of the time, became peevish and pushed me away. I tried to bear these indignities with the graciousness of a true feline, but it became more and more difficult, and one night in March I had had enough. Eluding attention from the human attendants, I escaped to the cellars of the White House for a little harmless recreation.

There were plenty of mice. I chased a few for pure pleasure, the satisfaction of muscles working at their peak, the delight of a sprint, the sensuous feel of squirming fur under my claws. I had dispatched one particularly fat mouse for a snack and was washing my whiskers when I became aware of a nasty, rank smell. I turned to see, in a dark corner, a pair of glowing red eyes and the tip of a thin, moth-eaten tail.

I crouched and lashed my tail and was waggling my hindquarters for a spring when the rat spoke.

"That's right, cat. Kill me—if you can. I might bite you, you know, and you might be the one to die."

I don't bandy words with rats. My tail lashed faster.

"You might even be able to do it, I suppose. You're a bit fat from living soft, but you're youngish yet and still almost fast enough."

I dug in my back claws and waggled once to set them firmly.

"But don't you want to hear why you shouldn't kill me just yet? I know something you'd like to know."

The last was spoken in a maddening, jeering sing-song that nearly launched my spring. But there was a look in the rat's eye that stopped me for a moment.

All rats are liars. Remember that, if you ever have any dealings with them. But they do have a sort of low cunning, and they do travel extensively. Every now and then one will have something interesting to say, though they usually demand a bribe.

"Move one whisker and you're dead," I said in a low growl, "and tell me what you know before I decide to make rat hash of you." (There is no point in speaking politely to a rat. One must use the language the filthy creatures understand, distasteful as it may be.)

"Oh, no, my fine feline. You know it doesn't work quite that way. I'm hungry. Lead me to the kitchen and I'll decide whether to tell you or not."

A long period of negotiation might have ensued. Rats enjoy negotiation; it gives them so many opportunities for treachery.

I was not in the mood. Before the rat even guessed what was happening my left paw flashed out and pinned his tail to the floor while my right dug into the nape of his neck.

"Tell."

He thrashed about and squealed and whined, but he couldn't free himself, gnash his filthy yellow teeth though he might. He tired quickly. I thought he was probably telling the truth about his hunger; he was thin and not as fit as he might have been.

At last, sullenly, he gave in. "Bully!" he said furiously. "You're like all of them. Think because you're bigger you can boss us little guys around."

"I can," I said calmly. "Tell."

"Not until you let me go."

"Do you know," I said thoughtfully, "if I dug my claws in just a little deeper I think I might hit your spinal cord. Let me see, now . . ."

"It's about the *Maine*!" said the rat in a loud squeal.

That gave me pause. I took no personal interest in the *Maine*, but I knew it was important to The Major. Certainly the wretched ship and what happened to it had disrupted my home for weeks. Any information that might return life to normal was welcome, but I didn't care to show my interest to the rat.

"Oh. That." I yawned elaborately, making sure the rat got a good view of my sharpest teeth, and let my eyes half-close.

The rat shivered, but recovered himself quickly. "Let me go and I'll tell you what your boss has been wanting to know ever since the ship blew up."

I opened one eye. "First of all, I have no 'boss.' Second, I have no intention of letting you go. I'll rest for a little and then finish my job." I yawned again.

That completed the rat's demoralization. He must have been very hungry indeed. He slumped under my paw. "All right, all right! But I want a good piece of cheese for this!"

I looked the other way.

"I know who blew up the *Maine*, cat! Now are you going to listen, or aren't you?"

I snorted (delicately, as became a cat of breeding). "How would you know a thing like that, when very important humans like The Major do not know?"

"Because I have a cousin who had shipped aboard her, and got out just before she blew up, that's how! She finally boarded a ship that was headed for Washington, and she just got here."

It is well known that rats, possessing no sense of loyalty and a keen sense of danger, will desert a ship that is in difficulties. The rat's story was almost plausible. "Go on," I said.

"Hah! Thought that'd get you! Don't you want to know what Murgatroyd told me?"

"*Who?*"

"My cousin Murgatroyd, and my name is Marmaduke, and you don't need to be rude about it, either. I don't have to tell you anything, you know."

"You do if you want that cheese." I let one claw penetrate his tail a millimeter deeper, and gradually, peevishly, he told his story.

Murgatroyd (heavens, what a name!) or Marmaduke himself had embroidered the story heavily, but shorn of its extraneous detail, it was serious and of great interest. Murgatroyd claimed to have seen and heard male humans aboard the *Maine* shortly before the explosion. They were in a part of the ship where the crew almost never ventured (never having been in a ship, I did not understand exactly where), and they were speaking a form of human speech that Murgatroyd had insisted was called Spanish.

Well, of course, that word caught my attention. Hadn't my humans been arguing for weeks about whether these Spanish humans had caused the explosion? And wasn't this an indication that perhaps they had?

I took Marmaduke over the details again and again, until he began to whine, and then (much against my better judgment) I allowed him his freedom. He insisted that I show him the kitchen and find him some cheese. I reluctantly led him upstairs, but that was as far as I would go. I knew that if the cook saw him, I would be given short rations for a week, and I certainly wasn't willing to risk our being seen together.

Besides, I had a great deal to think about. I had information The Major needed badly, but how was I to convey it to him?

Cats communicate in many ways, most of them infinitely subtle. The lift of a whisker, the widening of an eye, the angle of a tail, all these convey volumes to other cats. With humans we are reduced to cruder means, principally the meow and the purr. With effort, we can educate our housekeepers to understand the meanings of various vocalizations, though even the most intelligent humans fail to understand nuances.

Certainly it never occurs to them that a cat might have something of grave importance to communicate to them. I might go to The Major and Ida and meow until I was hoarse, and they would offer me cream, or pet me, or send for one of their minions to let me out.

I was in a dilemma.

Having seen the rat headed in the direction of the larder, I padded upstairs to a quiet corner in an unoccupied bedroom and lay down to think things out. I find concentrated thought to be exhausting, so I settled down for a refreshing nap. And when I woke I was indeed refreshed and had conceived a plan.

The execution of my plan had to wait until daylight when the Major would wake. I find it inexplicable that humans almost always spend the most alert and productive hours, those just before dawn, in sleep. However, a cat must learn to adjust. I took my place on The Major's desk and napped until he appeared, well after sunrise.

He was not pleased to find me there, lying on his papers, but he was gentle with me, as always. He stroked me, spoke to me kindly, and attempted to lift me off the papers.

I became heavier and clung.

"Blanche, my dear. Those papers are important. Be a good kitty and let me have them."

I adhered.

His tone became sharper. "Blanche! Off! At once!"

I stared into his eyes, trying with all my might to convey thoughts to his unreceptive mind. I might as well have tried to communicate with the desk. He became more and more angry, and at last I had to give up out of sheer pity. The man was in a pathetic state, dark circles under his eyes, lines in his face, his hair turning grayer by the minute.

It was obvious that he was in no state to deal with what he perceived as a disobedient animal. I sat up, gave my whiskers a swipe with my paw to indicate that my actions reflected my own decisions and were not a response to coercion, and jumped off the desk. I made sure, however, that my claws swept one of the papers to the ground with me.

It was a message from the Spanish commission that had investigated the explosion and claimed it an accidental occurrence. My claws had virtually shredded it.

The Major is not unintelligent, as humans go. I had been quite sure that he would understand, when I clawed the document, that the information it contained was not to be trusted.

But no. I had failed to take into consideration his lack of imagination. He merely looked sadly at it, and at me, put it back on the desk, and sank into reverie until interrupted by several of his "advisors," come to trouble and harass him.

I retreated to a quiet spot to reconsider.

It would be tedious to relate all the ploys and subterfuges I attempted. From the subtle to the obvious (or what I thought was obvious), I tried them all. I clawed the place marked "Spain" on the big map in The Major's office. I hissed and spat at the Spanish Ambassador every time he came to call. I even contemplated committing an indiscretion on the Ambassador's silk hat as it lay on the cloakroom shelf, but there are some lengths to which a well-bred cat will not go.

I discussed the matter with Pedro, who is the rudest and most conceited creature it has ever been my misfortune to encounter. He simply mimicked me, squawking with laughter, and actually fell off his perch at the idea that I could have important information.

In the end I was forced to employ the extreme, the forbidden tactic. I was loath to do so for many reasons. Not only was I fond of The Major, I had my self-respect to think of, and my impeccable reputation, not to mention my (relatively) comfortable home, though that last was the least important consideration. A cat as beautiful as I need have no worries about obtaining devoted housekeepers.

But, once having made my decision, I launched my plan with determination. I had to choose my moment very carefully. For several days I watched The Major's moods as he agonized over a decision that would mean war. I listened to his advisors. I needed to find him in exactly the right temper if I was to anger him sufficiently to force his action.

At last the day came. It was a lovely day in April. The temperature was unseasonably warm; shrubs and fruit trees perfumed the air with their blossoms. The Major's mood was dark, however. His advisors had been pressing him for a decision and he could not decide. He hated war with all his being, but he also hated tyranny, and he knew a decision must be made soon.

I waited until a small horde of angry men left his office and then strolled in. He did not see me when I jumped lightly to his desk. His head was in his hands; a document from the Spanish ministry lay under his hands.

I would never have a better opportunity. Moving very quietly, I sidled close to him, took aim, and bit his hand.

There! I have said it! Yes, I bit a man for whom I felt great affection and not a little pity. I used the last means at my command to try to force his understanding and rouse his anger.

He yelped and looked up, but I had of course jumped down and hidden where I could watch him. He sat for a moment, feeling in his pocket for a handkerchief and watching his blood drip onto the letter from Spain. I saw him wrap the cloth around his hand. An expression of great sadness came over his face. "*Et tu*, Blanche?" he whispered. I did not understand all the words, but I understood his perception of betrayal. And then he looked at the letter again.

His face changed again. It grew dark red. His breathing came quickly. He picked up his other hand and with it rang a bell on his desk. Rang it violently. Then, with his injured hand, he slowly and deliberately crumpled the letter from Spain into a ball and threw it furiously against the wall.

If Pedro does his job, and any humans ever do read this account, they will know what happened next. The Major wrote the war message and sent it to Congress, and a few days later we were at war with Spain. The war was brief, and we, of course, won it.

Now, two years later, there is little doubt, according to The Major's advisors, that he will continue to live in this White House for some time to come. For the people love him, and that fact is apparently tied somehow to his continuing residence here. That is, in a way, a pity, for I would vastly prefer a quieter, less crowded domicile. Ida seems pleased at last, however, and that makes my life (and The Major's) easier.

I realize, as I recall what I have said in these remarks, that I have perhaps offended humans who may someday read my revelations. Please be assured that I meant no offense. Humans cannot help their limitations, and may in time, if they devote themselves to the study of cats, overcome some of their handicaps.

Particularly if they pay attention to what their cats are trying to tell them.

Editor's note: I do not intend to reveal the complex process by which this manuscript fell into my hands. I believe it to be genuine and truthful, as far as it goes, though Blanche's comment that all rats are liars was perhaps more perspicacious than her decision to trust Marmaduke's word. Recent historical research indicates that the *Maine* almost certainly exploded accidentally, without the aid of the Spanish. However, we weren't there, and Murgatroyd was, and who's to say?

We know now, of course, that The Major, as Blanche called him, was indeed fated to win a second term in the White House, but would serve only a few months of that term before being assassinated in Buffalo, New York. I trust that Ida and Blanche (though perhaps not Pedro, who was very much The Major's pet) enjoyed the remainder of their days in Canton, Ohio, in the home to which The Major had so much wanted to retire.

The Secret Staff

Janet Pack

Eli. That's what the five Roosevelt children, known as the White House Crew, and the Tyrant himself all called me. I came to the president's interior staff early in his administration, and noticed the need for a coordinator of his Secret Staff. From this height I was always able to observe and comment on what I saw happening.

Not that President Theodore Roosevelt ever paid serious attention to me, except in a few circumstances when I proved my worth. He always had his own opinions, presented boisterously in his high-pitched, rapid-fire voice that drowned out many quieter ones. The cadre I picked for each special operation therefore had to rely on actions instead of words. Sometimes those were subtle, other times blatant. We were very much taken for granted, our innate capabilities dismissed or ignored.

But that was all right. Despite his pushy tone and his Big Stick attitude, TR was a kindly rough-and-tumble gentleman who wished the best for his country. We supported him unilaterally with our widely diverse talents. The Tyrant never admitted that he had a secret White House force behind the scenes dedicated to furthering his policies while he ruled there.

Sometimes it was damned difficult to coordinate those talents—it took all my strength and wit, let me tell you!

Yes, there were even occasions when we needed to apply pressure to influence foreign policy. The Secret Staff really shone during those capers, and the president listened to me during such times. I suppose it's all right to tell this story now after so many years, especially since most of the main characters have passed on, including TR himself. I'm the only witness left. It was not one of our more glamorous exploits, although we managed to garner total success after much effort. Despite the . . . well, the embarrassing debacle near its end, we did manage to enhance this situation, mainly due to my quick thinking and the lightning reflexes of my crack force.

It happened over a period of time during the end of 1902 and in 1903, at the height of the argument over where to locate that big ditch down south.

Everybody and his dog knew a canal was needed to transfer shipping from the Atlantic side to the Pacific without going the long way 'round South America's inaptly named Cape of Good Hope. It was the argument of *where* that became so important and tied up some of the most influential brains of the time in divisive detail. Some dullards, including most of the United States Congress, wanted it pushed through the middle of the jungle in a country called Nicaragua. Stupid. That required miles more digging through terrain close to an active volcano. The Nicaraguan government thought they had Congress's votes tied up.

(Snort.) Anybody with a sunflower seed worth of sense looking at a map can see that Nicaragua wasn't the prime choice. But there were too many political games being played here for some people to see the trees for the jungle.

Our beloved Tyrant had a crystal vision of this whole situation. He wished the canal dug in a tiny place called Panama, which at the time belonged to the somewhat antagonistic South American country Colombia. The route was more direct, hence the costs were considerably less, and the distance required fewer locks which lowered or raised the level of water from one ocean to the other. Any fool could see the location was perfect. Colombia, however, didn't want to give up land rights for the canal without large compensation for their so-called loss, and feared the presence of a stronger government than theirs in Central America. That country threatened to withdraw from the negotiations, hoping to leave the United States in a position bad enough to concede to its demands.

TR called a series of secret White House meetings, mostly between himself and Secretary of State John Hay, who was a good friend of mine.

Before the first discussion, John came to where I sat in the president's private library. "Good evening, Eli," he said, even though it was late at night. (TR tended to keep long hours.) "It's a pleasure to see you again."

"'Evening, Mr. Secretary," I returned from my corner.

Hay chuckled and turned as Roosevelt burst into the room. He was always bursting into rooms. "John, you're here. Good, good. Let's get started."

"I'm assuming this is about Panama."

"Right. Perhaps the three of us can get some new ideas going."

"Three?" Hay glanced at me sidelong, questioning my presence wordlessly.

"Glad to help if I can," I said clearly.

The Tyrant indicated a chair to Hay, threw his bulk into another nearby, and grinned toothily. "We need to keep these discussions as quiet as possible."

"You know you can rely on my discretion, Theodore."

"Always, John. What are your feelings on the matter?"

"It's a difficult situation." Hay arranged himself more comfortably. I cocked my head and both ears their direction, determined not to miss a word. "We've got a Congress fixed on the idea of digging the canal in Nicaragua, and deteriorating discussions with the Colombians over Panama. The Colombian ambassador has left, leaving his aide, that short man with the bristling moustache, to negotiate. Quite an insult. I don't like him—he's not trustworthy. I think we'll have to do . . . something."

"I had hoped it wouldn't come to that, John." TR looked in my direction and stared through me. I'm good at being almost invisible when the need arises. Tonight even the normally dynamic Tyrant looked a little tired, the flame of his bright-flaring energy dimmed by the pressing situation. "It would be much better if we could get Congress to favor Panama, and Colombia to be realistic about their demands for the rights to the land. That greedy government sent another set of new requirements just a few hours ago. We've already given them a fair offer, but they seem to want the moon as well. The French, as former rulers there, have been very generous offering assets. They've also been helpful, as you know."

The president slapped an open hand against his chair arm in frustration. "We're so close, yet still so far away from finalizing the canal."

"Push Colombia a little more, Theodore."

"I've already pushed them as far as they'll go, you know that." The president removed his pince-nez and scrubbed a hand across his weak eyes. "Anything more will start a war. And I don't want that. It looks bad enough to have two sizable Western Hemisphere countries feuding over a tiny strip of land that barely shows on a map." He sighed gustily. "If the consequences weren't so huge for this country as well as the rest of the world, I'd give up the struggle."

"Then what are your suggestions?"

"I'm completely out of those right now. I hoped you'd bring some, John." But the Secretary of State was silent, one long finger resting beneath his lips in a characteristic position of deep thought.

"Riots." The word sprang from my throat and dropped into the silent room, startling both august men. They stared at me. I nodded encouragingly.

"Of course," said Roosevelt, savoring the idea. "That's an excellent proposal, Eli. An excellent proposal! We start protests against Colombia in Panama. Panama eventually declares independence. That way, I can deal with a new country sympathetic to the United States. John, do we know anyone in Panama who can help foment this?"

"I think I've got a couple of names, Theodore." Hay took a piece of paper from his pocket and began jotting reminders to himself with a pencil stub belonging to the Roosevelt children, which he'd found on a nearby table. "Philippe Bunau-Varilla of that French company, and William Nelson Cromwell from the Panama Railroad leap to mind. I've been in touch with both men recently. And may I suggest that we involve the Secretary of War and the Attorney General in any further discussions?"

The president nodded, excitement making his energy level surge back to normal heights. "Involving Elihu Root and Philander Knox is an excellent idea. I propose that we five meet again tomorrow night. Bring the names of anyone else in Panama who you think might help."

Hay rose and looked hard at TR as he reached for the doorknob. "Five of us, Theodore? You mean four, surely."

"Absolutely not, John." The Tyrant rose also, beaming one of his million-kilowatt smiles that eclipsed the library's lamps. "Eli's included, of course. He's one of us. In on this from the beginning. You must admit, he's already made a sterling suggestion neither of us invented."

Smiling and shaking his head, the Secretary of State tucked the piece of paper in his outside jacket pocket and left the room.

It was that piece of paper that started the internal problem. John couldn't find it the next day. I immediately put the covert team of the Secret Staff on alert, mobilizing half of them. They reported back to me one by one several hours later. Even Emily Spinach, the most willing to investigate every nook and cranny, found nothing. She did, however, manage to startle the Secretary of State when he got to his desk and pulled open a drawer: he found her inexpressive eyes in that incredibly green face staring at him from among his papers.

I suspected rats. The wild ones, not the pets. With Washington, D.C., a thriving port city, you never knew who or what might come off the cargo ships in the harbor. I knew there'd been some foreign types sneaking in, especially lately. I now tried to find out if some of them were infiltrating from Colombia. Skip and Jack, always interested in testing dishes intended for the White House tables, offered to spend some time wagging tails and listening in the kitchens. Quick little Tom Quartz, ever the adventurer, went with them to ferry the pair's messages. I also sent Algonquin trotting away to alert my Special Forces team. Their leader came to see me.

The rat terrier and I faced each other, his bright brown eyes looking steadily into my black ones. He found it difficult to sit still for more than thirty seconds at a time, the nature of that beast. The ratters were always on the go, always pushing for an advantage, especially after someone decided to name the breed after the president and they became somewhat vain about the honor. I vouchsafed only what he and his troop had to know. In this situation, I had to keep the upper hand.

"What's the status of foreign rats in the White House?" I asked bluntly.

"Well, sir, there are a few." His pink tongue flicked over his glossy white canines as if tasting warm blood. "But we're taking care of 'em, the lads an' me."

"Any of them foreign?"

He nodded, cocking his head and lifting his ears. "Somethin' up?"

Bright boy. "Yes. I suspect Colombians will try and infiltrate the White House. If they haven't already, they will soon."

"Ah, it's about that big ditch, ain't it? Had my ears full o' that lately. The talk's all over this place."

"You're likely to hear much more. And John Hay's lost a piece of paper, which holds notes suggesting some plans we hatched last night and a couple of names. It was folded in the middle and tucked into his jacket pocket. If it's seen by the wrong people, especially someone high in the Colombian government . . ." I left the implication hanging.

The ratter nodded, his backside rising from the floor and wriggling with the excitement of imminent activity. "So you want us to take care o' the foreigners, and get that paper back."

"Return it to me, or destroy it. If you destroy it, let me know. Security regarding this must be absolute. I don't want a whisper of TR's plans to leak beyond the White House. You can send me messages by Algonquin and Tom Quartz. Don't use either of the Deweys, Father O'Grady, or Bishop Doan—the guinea pigs are all untrustable, too easily distracted." I gave the terrier a short nod. "Be off, and good luck."

"Yes, Sir!" The ratter sat up and snapped me a salute. "Me an' the lads'll get right on it! We'll have the thief and that paper back afore you can wag your tail three times." He scampered out of the room at full bounce, claws slipping against the polished wooden floor.

I sighed. Despite the terrier's optimism, I had a feeling that this was going to be a long and involved campaign, culminating in a dynamic contest of wills. I hoped the Tyrant was ready for this, and that he had his Big Stick ready. He might need it.

* * *

TR was still trying to break in his new French ambassador. Jean Jules Jusserand was a distinguished-looking man with a short trimmed gray beard and an intelligent expression, always elegantly dressed. When *monsieur le diplomate* arrived for morning meetings, the Tyrant often insisted on hiking as they talked. This activity besmirched the ambassador's lovely clothing and shoes with local mud, grasses, and occasional burrs. I think TR drove him a little crazy, but the Frenchman persevered despite a necessary increase in his clothing budget. Monsieur Jusserand became a regular visitor at the White House, especially as events in Panama entered their final phases.

I assigned Sailor Boy the Chesapeake retriever and sometimes Manchu, Alice's elegant little spaniel, to these perambulatory meetings. Both had excellent memories, and brought me much good information. Pete occasionally accompanied the hikers, but he had no ear for languages. He missed much detail since the meat of the discussion swayed back and forth from American English, which he understood, to French, which he did not. I encouraged him to take lessons, but the bull terrier didn't seem to own the aptitude for learning more than half a dozen French words, most of which were unsuitable for polite conversation.

Sessions between John Hay, Elihu Root, Philander Knox, TR, and myself became commonplace. We worked very hard at changing minds in Congress to favor a canal across Panama. That became easier after I saw a one-centavo Nicaraguan stamp, and suggested to John that he mention these to Philippe Bunau-Varilla. A savvy man, Philippe immediately realized the significance of the artwork, which featured the volcano called Mt. Momotombo disgorging impressive amounts of lava. He immediately sent one of the stamps to every member of Congress in a letter.

That achieved wonderful results. Upon seeing Mt. Momotombo in full belch, and remembering how close the volcano was to the proposed Nicaraguan canal, most congressmen immediately changed their minds to favor the Panama route. That was another success for TR.

Even though it was worth little now, I was still determined to find out who had stolen John Hay's piece of paper and alerted the Colombians regarding our Panamanian sympathizers. To that end, I met several more times with the leader of the White House rat terriers. The first two incidents were frustrating affairs—in their zeal to eradicate all vermin detrimental to the president's cause, they managed to kill two and injure another so badly she was unable to provide information. The head terrier hung his head and apologized profusely.

They finally did capture a couple of the foreign riffraff without thoroughly damaging them first. Through an interpreter, we learned that the information, perhaps memorized from the paper, had been passed from the White House confines, but was not part of general Colombian knowledge.

Yet not a single captive divulged the name of the thief. Perhaps they didn't know. I needed to deal with more pressing matters, but I couldn't forget those two niggling details: who had stolen the note, and how had he or she slipped the information out of the White House? There had to be a connection. To make sure I had time for everything I needed to do, I enlisted the aid of Alan, the kleptomaniac raccoon who was an expert at juggling several things at once in his dexterous paws.

The normally slow grind of foreign policy began to tilt toward Panamanian independence. A major White House reception loomed on the near horizon, bringing most of the players in this situation together for the first and only time. Reading the final guest list one day over TR's shoulder, I shivered.

The Nicaraguan ambassador, the Colombian ambassador's aide, Philippe Bunau-Varilla, William Nelson Cromwell, French ambassador Jusserand, Senator Spooner, and Senator Hanna, among others. "Theodore," I said, "are you certain?" All these people in the same room on the same night might produce a volatile situation.

The president chuckled. "Yes, Eli, it should be very interesting. I think we'll learn a great deal from all of them circulating together. There might be a few sparks, but most of them are professionals in their various capacities, and I expect them to act as such. I'll have security everywhere." He grinned at me. "Might as well make this a night to remember!"

The next day I was roused early by the feeling of someone staring at me. I shook off sleep, and discovered young Tom Quartz. The gray kitten eyed me sidelong from his big gold orbs, and acted nervous.

"What is it, Tom? A message from our special tasters in the kitchens?"

"No. I've been having a talk with Josiah the Badger. He said I'd better tell you about . . . uh, that I'm involved in . . . well, that I—"

"Come on, come on, young Quartz," I encouraged. "If you talked with Josiah, who's a grouchy old rug with feet at each corner, you certainly can't find me as formidable!"

The half-grown kitten turned in a quick circle, his tail making agitated loops in the air. "All right. I'm the one who took the paper out of John Hay's pocket. I mean, it fell out. But I didn't mean to steal it! I didn't know the writing was anything important. It was just a folded piece of paper, and

I played with it for awhile. Kittens do that, you know," he finished.

Finally, reliable information! "What happened to it after you played with the note?" I asked gently. "Where did you leave it?"

"I was out in the hallway beyond the Tyrant's private library pouncing on a dustball the cleaning staff missed when you were having that first meeting," Tom admitted. "When John Hay came out, I sprang at him. He brushed a hand out to fend me off, then he petted me, and that's when the note dropped out of his pocket. He didn't notice. It must have been about to fall out anyway, or he hit it with his hand. I played with it awhile, batting it around, then Dewey, Jr. came by. He nosed it, picked it up in his teeth, and waddled away. You know how the guinea pigs are when they get out of their cages—he was acting stunned and stupid. I whacked at his stub-tail trying to get him to play with me, then I tried to stop him to get the paper back, but he just bit down on it harder and carried it off." He flicked his whiskers and crouched. There's nothing more miserable looking than an embarrassed cat, I reflected, unless it's a soggy bird.

"That's all I know," Tom continued. "When I heard you were looking for it, I thought you'd be awfully angry." He glanced up again. "Are you?"

"I just wish you'd come to me sooner, young Tom," I soothed. "It would have saved me several weeks wrapped in a tornado of thinking to find out what happened to it. Now I only have one question left: who shifted the information on that scrap to the Colombians? Oh, you're dismissed, Tom. You're not the main culprit in this theft."

"Thank you. Thank you!" The kitten, relieved, spun on silent pads and bounded for the door.

"Wait. I want you at the White House reception in a few weeks. Most of the Secret Staff that's been working on this matter needs to be there. Pass the word."

"Yes, sir."

A swish of tail was the only salute he ever gave me. I allowed him to leave without a reprimand.

Tension at the White House increased as time for the reception drew nearer. The invitations had been sent: everyone accepted, unwilling to miss what might prove an extraordinary confrontation. I had to reassign Skip and Jack from the kitchens to the outdoor hiking meetings because both were getting fat. Sailor Boy happily took over their kitchen duties. The rat terriers increased their patrols. Manchu paced the halls with stately tread, perky ears cocked for any intriguing tidbits of information. Emily Spinach took charge of getting the legless cadre and the lizards out of their cages and into odd places that might offer pertinent details. Algonquin couldn't always get into the White House, but he managed to make the most of the times he did, poking his long brown and white nose through doors only he and Alan could jiggle open. And Tom Quartz was everywhere, earnestly desiring to make up for not telling me about the fate of John Hay's note.

The day of the reception opened with pewter skies and drizzle. All the White House staffs on all levels had been engaged in fevered preparations since early hours: cleaning, cooking, and decorating finally finished, followed by a rush of the governmental folk to bedrooms to don dress clothing and find the one shoe that always goes missing during such times. TR and John Hay appeared early, followed soon by Elihu Root and Philander Knox, both with beautifully bedecked partners on their arms. William Howard Taft soon made his ponderous way into the room, greeting the other men warmly. Senator Mark Hanna, who'd supported the president's original Panamanian canal idea proposed in 1902, arrived with his wife.

French ambassador Monsieur Jusserand, accompanied by his elegant lady, and the Colombian ambassador's aide exited their vehicles and entered the White House at nearly the same time. I didn't personally see this, but Manchu told me Jusserand was wearing a small secretive smile after exchanging bows and pleasantries with the assistant of his South American counterpart. Philippe Bunau-Varilla entered a bit later, soon followed by William Nelson Cromwell. The room swirled with movement: some of the most important men in the Western Hemisphere danced the dance of diplomatic conversation, highlighted by their ladies in gorgeous satins, laces, silks, and chiffons. The president beamed at each newcomer, shook hands, bowed, and played the perfect host.

All the major players had arrived, I thought to myself from my perch in the corner. Now we'd see what would happen as the catalytic TR stirred the pot. There was an interesting feeling in the atmosphere—I suspected something was going to happen.

I stationed Manchu, Sailor Boy, Jack, and Pete to circulate in the room.

Tom Quartz was there too, gleefully running sorties after the hems of women's dresses and the pendulous ends of men's tail coats from beneath the refreshment table, at the same time keeping eyes and ears alert. Algonquin was too conspicuous to be inside the whole time, but he pranced through with the Tyrant's sons Archie and Quentin on his back twice just to not feel left out. Emily Spinach put in an appearance laced through TR's daughter Alice's curls. The rat terriers guarded every door and patrolled the outside hallway. Alan wandered through once (large gatherings are not to his interest), and tried to wash a shrimp in the punch bowl until I hissed at him.

The night's hours increased. I kept watchful eyes on everything I could see, and received regular reports from my Secret Staff. All seemed to be going well. After a sketchy greeting, the Colombian ambassador's aide, the man with the bristling black mustache, kept to the opposite side of the room from Monsieur Bunau-Varilla, who, it was lately rumored, was likely to be named as the first Panamanian ambassador to the United States if that tiny country could triumph in its independence.

And it would, I thought with satisfaction. Panama, a little bitty country with a big canal. Things were going the Tyrant's way. That was good, because when TR was unhappy, everyone in the White House was unhappy.

A facet of color along the floor caught my attention. It was hard to spot scooting beneath the excellent cover of ladies' long skirts, showing brightly against short patches of dark hardwood floors as it streaked toward a corner of the reception room. I squinted, first with one eye, then with the other, thinking it might be one of the lizards bringing me information. Recognition hit me moments later.

"Haitian boa!" I screeched. "Insider spy! Stop the boa!"

Five dogs and a small gray cat leapt into motion from various parts of the room. The heads of guests turned, all eyes following the sudden flights of my White House Secret Staffers. I fluttered into the air, determined to see better to direct my troops, but I found clear sight was thwarted by men's floor-length pantlegs and women's swirling skirts. The dogs and cat fared no better from their lower levels—their vision was as impaired as mine. They were racing blindly toward the area over which I circled. Desperately, I tried to figure out a way to tell them what to do.

Discovered, the boa squiggled at top speed toward two men standing near one another. I caught sight of its copper- and butter-colored body before losing it again amid the profusion of human lower limbs. I adjusted my flight to match the snake's path, and hoped the beast wouldn't take refuge in the petticoats of one of the ladies between me and the door. We'd never extricate him then!

It didn't. The boa apparently knew it couldn't make it out of the room on its own. I flew closer, stirring women's hair with the tips of my wings, causing startled comments from several. The last vision I had of the snake was its glossy tail disappearing beneath the hem of the formal trousers of the Colombian ambassador's aide.

"The aide!" I hollered to my group, then realized they needed clarification. "It's with the Colombian ambassador's aide!"

The headlong rushes of Skip, Jack, and Manchu abruptly changed direction at my yell. Several guests teetered and protested, trying to balance drinks or plates of delicacies as the dogs turned and raced by. Sailor Boy had gotten trapped by an admiring group and was delayed. By this time, Tom Quartz was nearly at the scene and seemed to have the correct personage targeted.

Pete the bull terrier, who actually had a shorter distance to cover than anyone else, arrived first. I saw him stop and tilt his head in confusion. Not the brightest light of his litter, he'd always been, uh, well, excitable. It suddenly hit me that dear old Pete hadn't been the best choice for this operation. Nor did he really know the importance of what was going on.

I gasped in dismay and realization. The bull terrier hadn't seen the snake's tail, and had no idea where the reptile was.

"Pete!" I shouted, hoping he'd look up. He only shook his head as if he had ear mites, and squinted at the two men standing near him.

Then it happened. Monsieur Jean Jules Jusserand made a neat quarter-turn and stepped back, excusing himself from the conversation he'd been involved in to get coffee. He trod upon Pete's paw. The bull terrier reacted typically to the pain—he snapped open his jaws and closed them upon his assailant's calf.

"*Nom d'un chien!*" Monsieur Jusserand exclaimed.

I nearly pitched headlong into the silk bodice of Mrs. Hanna's gown, faint with mortification that stilled my wingbeats and shortened my breath. With great effort, I worked to control my consciousness: necessity finally thawed my dysfunction. I flared my wings and began flapping madly, gaining altitude while I surveyed the current situation.

Pete still had Monsieur Jusserand in his grip. Wisely, the French ambassador was standing still and not panicking. The two were now encircled by a knot of hopeful helpful humans trying with bribes of canapés, petting, and verbal persuasion to make the canine let go. TR, alerted to the situation by his secretary, created a wake through governmental luminaries as he strode vigorously across the room.

Tom Quartz, that little dynamo, was still in motion. With a prodigious leap, he reached all sixteen tiny crescent claws to full extension and aimed for the elegant trousers of the Colombian ambassador's aide. Tom wasn't large, but his impact near a sensitive part of the man's anatomy was startling. The South American's eruption of expletive-laced Spanish was much more colorful than the Frenchman's.

"Get the boa!" I cried from above.

Tom hung on with his back legs and quickly patted the ambassador's aide with his front paws one at a time, at the same time avoiding the man's hands trying to pry him from the trousers. The kitten whacked at something beneath the fabric, then climbed backward three steps. The ambassador's aide wriggled and slapped at the cat. Tom whacked again harder, then dropped to the floor. His face disappeared under the gray-striped fabric for a moment, then reappeared, his teeth wrapped firmly around the tail of the copper and butter colored snake.

The Colombian dignitary cursed again, this time in amazement at seeing a small reptile's back end emerge from his evening wear. His eyes rolled up in his head, his knees buckled, and he crashed to the floor, preceded by a full china plate and goblet of red wine.

Just our luck that the boa picked the one man in the room deathly afraid of snakes.

Tom pulled on the boa's tail with every ounce of his strength, backed up a short step, and pulled again. The firmly-anchored snake didn't budge.

"That's my brave kitten," I encouraged as reinforcements—Sailor Boy, Skip, and Jack—arrived. "Hold on, Tom!" At a nod from me, Jack continued on to where Pete and Monsieur Jusserand stood at impasse.

"No, no, it is just a small bruise," the French ambassador reassured humans surrounding him. "He is not hurting me." How the man managed to look dignified with a bull terrier connected to his leg was a tribute to his professionalism.

The president arrived to help Monsieur Jusserand, apologizing profusely. Kneeling beside Pete, TR persuaded the dog to let go after a few more minutes, and handed him over to his secretary to take upstairs. Still confused but pleased by all the attention he'd garnered, convinced that he'd done something good although he didn't know what, the white dog trotted happily out of the reception to the family's private quarters upstairs. The Tyrant sent for his doctor to administer first aid to the French ambassador. Limping not at all and protesting his infirmity, Monsieur Jusserand nonetheless succumbed to verbal pressure and retired to a nearby room with the physician.

Secretary of War Elihu Root put himself in charge of reviving the Colombian ambassador's aide, and of negotiating with the Haitian boa wrapped around the dignitary's left knee. Elihu passed the snake to a nearby Marine to hold for questioning by my Secret Staff. I put Emily Spinach and Alan in charge of guarding him. Root eventually assisted the aide to his shaky feet; they too retired to another room. As they passed, the Colombian spouted a constant fuming stream of Spanish mixed with a little English. Mr. Root nodded interest, but his eyes sparkled with lively humor at the aide's plight.

Let's face it, he would've been in real trouble if that reptile had been a viper instead!

"Come down, Eli." John Hay stood below me, touching his shoulder. Gratefully fluttering my tired wings, I landed. "So what was this, an inside job?"

I bobbed my head.

"Ah," he said, "I think I understand. The Colombians wanted to discredit the president, so they sent that boa in a roundabout way to TR's oldest son Quentin last year. You probably didn't suspect anyone who'd been here for that long a time—you concentrated at first on foreign rats, correct?"

He had the right of it. I nodded more quickly this time.

"Until I lost that piece of paper. Silly, that. I should have checked my pockets and backtracked that night. Anyway, you started asking the right questions then, and deployed most of TR's Secret Staff, except for the guinea pigs of course. Your group's been listening and searching for the culprit since. And tonight we found it.

"Good work, Eli." I preened under his praise. John and I watched as Skip allowed Tom Quartz to leap onto his back. Escorted by Attorney General Philander Knox and a Marine honor guard, proudly attended by Jack and Manchu, the triumphant gray kitten rode out of the reception in style.

"And now," said Hay, "it's time for *you* to rest."

He took me to my regular perch in the president's private library. I fell asleep immediately, blanketed by the Secretary of State's approbation and the knowledge of a job well done. Except for Pete biting Monsieur Jusserand, of course. That fact plagued my dreams. What would the Tyrant do with the poor dumb bull terrier?

Word came the next day. Pete was "banished" to Sagamore Hill, the Roosevelt family estate. Skip, Jack, and Manchu visited him on a regular basis. With all that acreage to guard and a big house to patrol, the white dog didn't miss his Washington, D.C., duties one bit.

Tom Quartz was the White House hero. He walked around for two weeks with his nose *and* his tail in the air, which irritated the rat terriers to no end. After that, Tom returned to ambushing passing ankles and pouncing on nearly anything moving. Only in quiet moments and in his dreams could I tell he recalled that night—the corners of his mouth turned a little farther upward than before.

Monsieur Jusserand's bruise healed perfectly. He always recalled the incident with gracious humor, often referring to the night of the reception as "the evening of the dog."

The Colombian ambassador's aide did not have as good a sense of humor as the Frenchman. He resigned his position soon after the reception and returned to his home country, claiming he couldn't abide "that cowboy in the White House who lets his pets run loose during formal functions." We got along just fine without him.

During the closing months of 1903, my Secret Staffers celebrated the fruition of the events our efforts helped shape. Panama won its independence from Colombia (with a little help from TR's white ship naval force), and Congress approved the canal at the narrowest part of the isthmus. Digging began almost immediately. Skip and Jack begged to go help, but I needed their talents at the White House.

After all, the president's Secret Staff had to be ready to go into action at any moment.

Author's note: Theodore Roosevelt and his children lived with the largest menagerie of any residents of the White House. Eli was a blue macaw, and there was another parrot (whose name I couldn't find) in the family. Sailor Boy was a Chesapeake retriever, Jack a terrier, and Skip a mongrel hound. Tom Quartz was described by TR in a letter to his son Kermit as ". . . the cunningest kitten I've ever seen." Emily Spinach was a green garden snake. Alan was a raccoon, Josiah the very long-lived badger, and Algonquin a "calico" brown and white pony. The rest of the list includes Bleistein, the president's favorite riding horse, and other equines named Renown, Roswell, Rusty, Jocko, Root, Grey, Dawn, Wyoming, Yangenka, General, and Judge. Dewey Senior, Dewey Junior, Bob Evans, Bishop Doan, and Father O'Grady were guinea pigs. There was also a lion, a hyena, a wildcat, a coyote, a zebra, a barn owl, five bears, lizards, pet rats, and roosters in residence.

The author wishes to thank The Theodore Roosevelt Society for providing pertinent details, Stephen Moon for research, and Thomas L. Hise for loaning me his computer and internet resources when mine decided to argue. Thanks also to Bruce A. Heard for French translations and encouragement, and to Jean Rabe for critiques and unflagging optimism.

Trouble A-Bruin

Esther Friesner

If you ask me, there is only one great mystery in this tired old world, and that's you humans. For sheer out-and-out cussedness you can't be beat with a stick, and when it comes to turning the straightest piece of road into a snarl of ins, outs, detours, and dead end alleyways, you stand alone, which is probably just as well seeing as how you smell funny.

I will give you a case in point concerning how you can turn what's plain as a bowl of milk into a puzzlement. I reckon I'm the one to tell it best, seeing as how it happened to me and also I was the only one fit to sort matters out and solve it in the end.

I left the great state of Oklahoma behind bars and arrived in our nation's fair capital, Washington Dee of Cee, accompanied by a brass band and speeches from several high officials. I would say that in that respect, things kind of fell out reverse-like from what is the usual course of events for most people. But then, I am not a congressman. I am a bear. Maybe having my own fur coat from the get-go was an encouragement for me to take the moral high road as opposed to getting into politics. I couldn't say.

What I could and do say is that I never did see the like of the reception that was awaiting me when the large van in which I was travelling reached its destination. The van was being driven by the downright honorable Colonel B. R. Rearson, who was also the gentleman who had effected my capture back home in Oklahoma. Although I was a mite put out by his having snatched me from the golden bosom of my cubhood memories, I did keep it in my heart to be thankful that the feller had not opted to shoot me, as well he might have done. If there's anyone who cares to debate the matter with me—*Resolved: That it is better to live on your knees than lie on your stomach as a bearskin rug*—then I am willing to oblige and will defend the affirmative.

Besides, bears don't have knees as such.

In the course of our journey from Oklahoma, I overheard more than a little concerning my ultimate fate. Apparently I was to be Colonel Rearson's small token of esteem for our own president of these here United States, Mr. Calvin Coolidge. I have no idea where he got the notion that a bear makes a suitable gift, but I gave up trying to figure out the whys and wherefors behind what people do even before I was entirely out of my cub days.

Being as how I was intended as a presidential offering, I was to be given the full Hollywood treatment, part of which entailed Colonel Rearson's having enlisted the Oklahoma City Brass Band being a part of our entourage all the way to Washington. Now as you may know, one of my fellow Sooners, Mister Will Rogers, has likewise taken the path from obscurity to celebrity upon which I found my paws in those days. Only in his case I do not think he needed to be trapped, hogtied, stuck into a cage, and shipped off forcibly to meet his Destiny. On the other hand, I know very little about the inner workings of Show Business and I could be wrong.

I had due and just cause to recall Mister Will Rogers many times over the course of my subsequent adventures in Washington. (The similarities between us are manifold. My ancestors too had a little Cherokee in them, but only in times when the fishing wasn't good.) As I hear tell, he is a fine one for using the workings of the government of these United States as humorous grist for his own personal entertainment mill. My own exposure to current events and governmental doings had been severely limited up until that point in my life. When I was back in Oklahoma I did not read the newspapers unless some careless camper had used 'em to wrap his trail provisions in. Then I devoured them.

So I was more than a little ill-prepared for the Destiny awaiting me at the end of the trail. The truck transporting my cage wove through streets that were busier than a stove-in anthill. Everywhere I looked, I saw multitudes of people and vehicles, both groups with about as much sense behind their comings and goings as a bunch of armadillos fed full of loco weed.

(If I have as yet neglected to mention that Colonel Rearson swapped his van for a flatbed truck just before we entered the precincts of Washington Dee of Cee proper, the better to give the people an eyeful of his gift for Mr. Coolidge, I hope you'll forgive me. That is certainly more than I will do for the Colonel and his bright idea to put me out for public viewing that way.)

Pretty soon we pulled to a halt near a large, white building that stood opposite a nice enough park. That park was the first scrap of greenery I had seen since my unjust incarceration back home and it stirred up some mighty powerful longings in me. I did not have the leisure to indulge myself in yearning after tall trees and verdant fields or even—thank heavens!—to go in for off-the-paw poetry, for just then the air was filled with a godawful fractious bray, clash and clamor that came nigh to making me jump out of my bear skin. It was the sound of the Oklahoma City Brass Band, launching itself upon the seas of music with about as much hope of reaching the far side of the piece currently under torture as the Titanic.

With trumpets blaring and cymbals banging away, the band began to move and my truck followed suit. Now there *was* guards enough, flanking our cavalcade, but Washington Dee of Cee is a city like any other and all cities teem with idlers and ne'er-do-wells and unruly children. The only difference is that in Washington, they are mostly locked up safe in Congress. Unfortunately for me, our government had missed recruiting all of them, and so the assorted riff-raff fell into line along the streets, following the progress of my cage, hooting and a-hollering and throwing fruit and peanuts, and in general carrying on fierce. I didn't so much mind the refreshments themselves, but I considered the service an affront to my dignity. I tell you, I was plumb grateful when we passed through the great iron fence surrounding the large white house and reached our destination.

I should have known better. That was when the speeches began.

Now bears are not much for speechifying. We tend to turn a deaf ear, sometimes two, to all the palaver you two-legged folk produce. We do not see the point of it. Oh, I know that it does have a purpose, said purpose being communication, but it strikes me that nine times out of ten there is not so much communication as obfuscation behind the words that come spouting out of your mouths just like a badly capped gusher.

That was why I was not so much listening as half-listening-mostly-dozing when Colonel Rearson, purporting to represent the great state of Oklahoma (and all who dwelled therein) got on his high horse and busted through the starting gate. Lord, how he did go on! I might've got me a fairly good leg up on my winter hibernation with the soothing drone of his words like a lullaby in my ear, except all of a sudden that son-of-a-senator cheated and said something *interesting*.

Of course it was about me. I said it was something *interesting*, didn't I? I already knew that I was to be a gift to the president, thanks to having eavesdropped on the Colonel during the course of our trip here, but this speech of his added one important fact to my existing knowledge that just about took the grin off the coyote: I was to be a *very particular* kind of a gift to the president.

I was a pet.

Friends, I am not an erudite ursine. I only know what I eat in the newspapers. But I do know this: If the Lord God Jehovah had meant for us bears to be pets, He would not have equipped us with claws and teeth and appetites and instincts that tend toward the devourment of anything smaller and slower than ourselves. Dogs and cats and birds and fish and such may get along under one roof, but once you add a bear to the mix, you will be looking at a whole passel of devastation and a large bill for the cleaning of blood stains out of carpets. We just can't help it. It's how we are.

From my place inside the cage, I shifted my gaze to the president. I hoped he was a man of sense enough to say that there was no way a bear could be kept as a pet, even in a house as big as this'n, with such a nice park just across the street from it, but I also hoped he was a man of compassion enough *not* to say that this being the case, Colonel Rearson might as well shoot me and be done with it.

It was hard to tell how Mr. Coolidge was taking the news of my being his new pet. He was not the sort of a man to wear his heart on his sleeve nor to play his cards anywhere but close to his vest if he chose to play them at all. The grave shall yield up its dead sooner than the face of Silent Cal shall yield up so much as a twitch that might let a body guess his thoughts.

I studied and I *studied* on that man, and I came away from it none the wiser.

That's a bad thing, for a bear. We like to know which way the wind blows, just in case it's blowing from the back door of a bakery.

Well sir, once Colonel Rearson was done with his speechifying—at last—Mister Coolidge got up on his feet. He came over to my cage, he looked in at me, he nodded once, as if to say I'd come up to his standards for everything a bear ought to be (which did make me quietly proud) and then he said, "Thank you very much." There may have been some few other words tossed in there, but not a whole lot. Silent Cal didn't run off at the mouth, as a rule. There was some applause, and some cheering, and the band whupped the bejeezus out of another tune, and a team of burly men wearing work shirts and overalls put their shoulders into it and wheeled my cage inside the big white house, and that was that.

More or less.

Mr. Coolidge followed the cage inside the house, still studying me. Despite how rumbly and bumpy the ride was, I returned his gaze as steady as I could. I don't know what it was about him, but I took a real shine to the man. Maybe it was on account of how we bears believe in less talk and more action and so did he.

"That's a fine figure of a bear, isn't it, sir," said a young man who was walking along at the president's elbow. I liked the look of him too. He was the clean-cut, well-scrubbed type, not a hair out of place, neatly dressed, all spit and polish and not a whole lot of baloney behind it (thought more than a little pomade). Besides, he admired me.

"He is," Mister Coolidge replied. "Interesting color."

"The delegation from Oklahoma said he's a cinnamon bear," the young man explained. "Not the sort of thing you see every day."

"Not in the White House." By this time we had rolled my cage onto a freight elevator. Everyone looked mighty surprised when the president followed me onto it.

"Mister President, the boys and I will take it from here," the young man said, looking a little concerned. "You don't need to worry about it."

"I'm not," Mr. Coolidge said. "This is my bear. I'm giving him to the National Zoo."

"I know, sir," the young man said. "I made all the arrangements as soon as we found out he was en route. They really should have been here to pick him up today, but there was some delay in readying the creature's enclosure. They'll be around to fetch him to the zoo tomorrow. In the meanwhile—"

"I know. You told me. He's my bear," the president repeated. "As long as he is under my roof, I am responsible for his welfare." The elevator came to a stop and the doors opened again. The president stepped out and said: "Mister Grimbold, gentlemen, follow me."

The young man and the fellers hauling my cage exchanged a peculiar look, but they did as they were told. By now we were in the soft and tasty underbelly of the big white house, and let me tell you, it was even bigger from the inside, if you can believe that. The president led the way, which was clearly not what the young man—Mr. Grimbold, I presumed—had been planning on. Still, what could he do but go along with it? I did not know whether to watch the passing scene or the ever-growing expression of perplexitude on young Mr. Grimbold's face as we went on our merry way.

At last we reached a room somewhere deep within the bowels of the building. Here the president himself opened a great oak door and indicated we was to pass on through. By this time Mr. Grimbold's face had gone whiter than a deer's behind, if you don't mind my saying so. You would've thought that the inside of that room contained some horrible revelation involving blood and guts and all the sort of stuff that usually causes human beings to fly into a panic (unless they are the ones who have caused the spillage of the aforesaid blood and guts).

But no, all that I could see in this room was another cage, though it was much larger than the one in which Colonel Rearson had transported me from Oklahoma, and made out of wooden slats rather than iron bars. It was nicely furnished with a thick mattress, a small wooden trough full of water, and a feeding bowl the contents of which were giving off a highly tempting aroma. (We bears—and myself in particular—have excellent noses for food.) What in tarnation was there about such a sight to cause a healthy young man like Mr. Grimbold so much apparent distress? I don't mind telling you that I found this to be kind of odd.

"When did *this* come to be here?" he demanded.

The president didn't address this question, but it didn't take an education to figure out the answer: Most likely he'd had someone build this here set-up for me as soon as he heard I was coming. Probably had it done last-minute, when them Zoo folks told him they'd be a tad late taking me to my new home, and never did see the need to tell this excitable young man about it.

"Put him in there 'til morning," the president said.

While the fellers who'd been hauling my cage set to obeying Silent Cal's order, young Mr. Grimbold commenced to raising a ruckus about it. I will not trouble you with the full text of his oratory concerning my overnight accommodations. All that's needful for anyone to know is that he was ag'in' 'em. (Besides, I was not paying any closer attention to Mr. Grimbold's speech than I had to Colonel Rearson's; not when there was a big ol' bowl full of meat and potatoes and fruit and the like calling my name. Soon as they got the two cage doors lined up and open, I was through 'em like a shot and chowing down with a will.)

"Sir, this is a *most* unsatisfactory situation!" he concluded.

The president heard him out, then glanced in my direction. "Apparently the bear disagrees," he said. And with that, he left the premises.

By the time I finished up my supper, the only person left in the room with me was Mr. Grimbold. The fellers who'd supplied the muscle for moving my iron cage had followed the president out, leaving the cage behind, but he'd lingered. I wondered why, and then I wondered how come he was wearing a Sunday-go-to-funeral look on his face like that.

I found out the reason soon enough. There was a timid little knock at the door and then it opened up just a mite. "Yoo-hoo," called a voice as soft and sweet as a marshmallow (which are my weakness). "Horatio? Are you in here? It's only me."

And with that the door opened all the way and a pretty little lady dressed up fancier than a month of Sundays came sashaying in. I never had seen the like of her before, though now I know that she was a prime specimen of that type of human female they call a "flapper." This was a pretty good name, because from what I've since learned, this kind of woman usually does not stop flapping her jaw for two minutes together.

"Oh, Horatio, what's *that?*" the little lady squealed when she saw me.

She rushed right into Mr. Horatio Grimbold's arms and cuddled up close enough to tell what he'd had for lunch last Tuesday.

"Don't be afraid, Maisie darling," he told her. "It's only a bear. He's in a cage, see? He can't hurt you."

I have to say, I took some umbrage at his remarks. First off, there ain't nothing so *only* about a bear. We may look soft and cuddly, and you folks may put your young'ns to bed with cute little toy versions of us, but it's a fool forgets that we're born wild, with all the right and privileges and appetites appertaining thereto.

"Horatio, he's *adorable*—" (I did take a shine to her when I heard her say that.) "—but he's in *our* room! What is he doing in *our* room?" She sounded mighty grieved.

"It's only for tonight," Mr. Horatio Grimbold said, and I never did hear a man speak so plaintive to a woman in all my born days. A blind bat could see that he was in love with her. *Deep* in love. *Stupid* deep in love. "You can imagine how I felt when Mr. Coolidge brought him in here! I was half out of my mind with fear that you'd be early, waiting for me, and how would I explain *that* to the president? But it's all right now: He's gone and no one else will be coming down to this part of the White House cellars—not until morning, anyway. We can find someplace else, though, if the bear being here makes you nervous. The White House basement is full of rooms where no one ever goes. We don't have to meet in this one all the time."

"Yes, we do," she replied, toying with his necktie and batting those spider-leg eyelashes of hers. "Or are you going to get me *all* the keys to the White House?"

She said that all playful-like, but he goggled like a beached fish at her words. "Maisie, you haven't told anyone about the key?" he asked earnestly, grabbing her by the arms.

"Of course not, silly," she said, and she giggled. "I know I'm not supposed to have it, but isn't it nicer that I do? That way I can come in here any old time I like and wait for my sweet li'l gumdrop to get done working for that mean ol' pwesident and be wif his Maisie-Waisey. Don't oo' wike being wiv um's Maisie-Waisey?"

That was when he kissed her. I don't much see the reason why you humans mush your mouths together that way, but I suppose if you do, it's not my place to object. Besides, it made her shut up all that sticky baby-talk. When he finally let her breathe again, he said, "Maisie, I did a terrible thing, giving you that key. True, it only gave you access to a very limited area of the White House cellars, but the longer we tryst here, the more chance there is of discovery."

"Oh, Horatio," she sighed, laying her curly blond head against his chest. "You don't have to worry about that. My uncle doesn't suspect a thing."

"I wasn't talking about your uncle," he replied. "But since you mentioned him—" He cleared his throat a time or two, like a man who's either got a fishbone lodged deep or else has got something momentous to say. "Maisie, my beloved—" he finally managed to cough up. "Maisie, my own, I think it's about time I met this strict old boogeyman uncle of yours. After all, I'll need to speak with him, to tell him that my intentions toward you are strictly honorable, and to ask him for your hand in—"

"My hand?" Maisie interrupted him. Her eyes lit up brighter than the noonday sun. "You mean—you mean you want to—to *marry* me?"

Mr. Horatio Grimbold did not answer; not with words, anyhow. He just laid his lips to hers and commenced to kissing that little flapper-gal so hard and so tender and so thorough that when he finally called it quits it was a wonder that either one of 'em had lips to call their own.

"Oh!" was all Maisie could say, though she sorta gasped it more than said it.

"Yes," Mr. Grimbold replied, sounding as determined as all get-out. "I love you and I want to marry you. After all these weeks of clandestine meetings, is that so hard to believe? Don't you realize how much I love you? Enough to have endangered my career here in President Coolidge's service by—"

She laid her little hand over his mouth before he could say another word. "Oh, Horatio, I know how much you love me," she said, kinda mournful. "What I don't think I—I mean *you* realize is how much I love you." She reached to her neck and pulled at the flimsy little silver chain she wore there. When she was done reeling it up out of the depths of her bosom, I caught sight of the key dangling there. "When you showed me the secret door to this part of the White House cellars and gave me this key, you more than proved your love for me. Now I'm going to prove mine for you by giving it back and . . . and"—her voice broked right pitiful to hear—"and never seeing you again!"

She flung the little key at that fine young man and wheeled around, ready to cut and run, 'cept he laid a-hold of her wrist and stopped her. "Maisie, what are you doing?" he cried. "If this is about your uncle's unseemly prejudice against government employees—"

"No! No!" she exclaimed. "Don't ask me to explain. Our love was not meant to be!" And with that she wrenched herself free and dashed out of the room, with him hotfooting it after.

I was alone.

No, actually, I was not. I was accompanied by a puzzlement big enough to stymie half a dozen bears and a passel of coyotes besides.

Now humans have always been mostly a mystery to us critters. Hardly a thing the two-legged varmints does but it looks mighty strange to us. But this—! I'll tell you, the goings-on between Maisie and Mr. Grimbold which I had just witnessed was the purest puzzlement. You see, a bear's got a good nose. Ain't much we *can't* smell, if we put our minds it, and I'll swear up, down and sideways that there was a powerful scent of Wanting coming off both those young'ns when they looked at one another. *Wanting,* that's strong medicine. Strongest in all the world. You can't stand against it, not if you've got the strength of a flash flood or the staying power of a mountain. It's the one thing we *do* have in common with humans, so there's no mystery attached to it: We bears understand Wanting just fine.

So with all that Wanting, why'd she run away? Could it be I'd scented it wrong? I took a deep snort of the air in that cellar room, just to double-check. Nope. It was Wanting, all right; maybe even WANTING. The place was thick with the smell of it.

Wanting . . . and something more.

I sniffed, trying to sort out the new scent from the smell of Wanting. I sniffed again, deeper, to make certain I was not letting my own yearnings affect my senses. But no, there it was, plain to smell even if I'd only had half a working nostril (which was thankfully not the case):

Oh, joy.

Oh, rapture.

Oh, my paws, pelt, and palpitating heart, I smelled *honey!*

Friends, let me tell you a little something about bears and honey: We are right fond of it. That's what humans say, anyhow. Well sir, they don't know the half of it. It's like saying they're "right fond" of gold or oil or any of that other useless truck they're always tearing up the earth to get at. At least honey is something a body can eat, and no one can eat honey like a bear. When we smell it, we want it, and that's almost as strong as Wanting it, and when a bear Wants something, ain't nothing going to stand between him and it, no sirree. I'll tell you, once I got a snootful of that sweet, sweet honey smell, all thoughts of the mystery of Mr. Grimbold and Maisie just plumb flew out of my head then and there.

Of course I was still stuck in that cage.

The great state of Oklahoma was not settled by folks who was quitters, but they could all take lessons in grit and determination from a bear. Soon as I caught wind of the honey-smell, I commenced to worrying the bars of my cage something powerful. I concentrated on the door, of course, not being a fool. It was made out of wood, like the rest of the cage, with an iron latch that was bolted into the timber. Whoever'd designed it must've been told that it wasn't meant to hold me for long.

They didn't know the half of that. I couldn't break the latch its own self, but ramming it a few times with my head and giving it a couple- three hefty swats with my paw, and the wood holding the latch in place was toothpicks.

Once I was at liberty, I followed the scent of honey. The room I'd been stowed in was only one of many, and there wasn't a soul in sight. I got the feeling that night had fallen in the world beyond those walls—we bears have got a sharp sense for such things—not that the time of day mattered much to me. Thinking back, I reckon it was a good thing it was nighttime, else I likely would've run into some folks.

It didn't take me long for my nose to find what I was after, only it wasn't exactly honey as I was expecting it to be. My goal lay in a little room not too far from the place I'd started, only instead of it hiding a hive or a honeycomb or even a passel of jars full of that sweet, golden goo, it was stacked with barrels. It didn't take much for me to realize that them barrels was where the honey smell was coming from, except now that I was up close to 'em, I noticed there was something else to that smell besides honey. I couldn't quite put my paw on what, so I chose to put my paw through instead. Through the top of one of those barrels, that is.

I will tell you what, I never did figure out what that barrel was full of. It was a mystery, right enough. It sloshed around like water, it smelled like honey, and it tasted— Well sir, it tasted *strong*. I took a lick of it and I liked what I sampled, so I commenced to lapping it up pretty quick, in spite of how it burned some on the way down. And do you know what? Someone must've left a whole hive full of bees in that honey-flavored water because no sooner did I finish off that first barrel and start in on the next but my head was buzzing with 'em. I drained about six of those barrels and wound up feeling frolicsome as a springtime cub. Then I drained three more and got all mopey, thinking about the great state of Oklahoma which I would see no more, so then I figured I needed a little pick-me-up to get out of that somber mood and that was how I came to drink up the contents of sixty-twelve more barrels (to be honest, I kinda lost count) before tumbling over in a dark corner of the little room and falling sound asleep.

I couldn't say how long I was asleep. I only know I woke up to the sound of human voices raised in one wowser of an argument.

"Gimme one reason why I shouldn't kill him, Maisie," one of 'em said. It sounded rough and low-down and mean.

I lifted up my head. This took more effort than usual. I felt like I was toting a load of rocks in my skull, and a whole swarm of them barrel-bees. It didn't put me in a charitable frame of mind.

What I saw when I finally did manage to raise my eyes above the row of barrels what was hiding me from view was that nice young Mr. Grimbold, and his puzzlesome gal Maisie, and the feller who'd just spoke. I can't say I took a liking to him. He had a face like a squooshed spider, a body like a weasel, a voice like wildcat caught in a butter churn, but more to the point of my not liking him, he had a gun. It wasn't no rifle—just a pitiful little snip of a pistol—but I still took exception.

"Please, Frankie, let us go," Maisie was pleading with that gun-toting weasel. "Tie us up, gag us, do whatever you like. That'll give you plenty of time to get the stuff out of here and onto the truck. That's all you wanted, anyway, wasn't it? A place to store the stuff until it was safe to get it out of town?"

"That 'stuff' you're talking about like it was any old batch of bathtub gin is my dear mother's recipe for authentic Polish mead," Frankie told her. "It's my *heritage*, goddammit! And the whole point of hiding the shipment here—aside from it being the one place the G-men'd never dream of looking—was to keep it safe. Well, guess what? It ain't safe! When I come in here, I found about a dozen barrels broke into. Know what I think, Maisie? I think you're double-crossing me. I think you're in cahoots with some other mug and the two of you's siphoning off my hard-made hooch so you can sell it one your own! Hell, maybe it's even this guy." He indicated Mr. Grimbold. "Could be he's not as stupid as he looks."

"How dare you suggest such a thing!" Mr. Grimbold replied, indignant. "*I* went to *Yale*!"

"Yeah, and I went to Harvard," Frankie sneered.

"That would explain your present illicit manner of making a living." Mr. Grimbold was taking him serious, where even a bear like me could tell the little weasel was only funning. I guess that does not say much for Harvard *or* Yale. "It also explains why Maisie fled my proposal of marriage. Clearly you have her in your evil thrall. Release her at once, or I'll— I'll—"

"Or you'll what?" Frankie countered. "Bleed?" He waved the gun at Maisie. "Stand aside, doll. I gotta deal with the witness. Then we can take it on the lam."

"No," Maisie said, and she got even closer to Mr. Grimbold, which I did not think possible. "I'm not going with you, Frankie. I'm staying here and sharing Horatio's fate."

"Huh?" Frankie looked like she'd just clouted him in the ear with a baseball bat. "Since when?"

"Since I'm in love," Maisie shot back at him. (I do wish the girl hadn't got such a shrill voice. It knifed through my aching head something fierce.) She turned to Mr. Grimbold. "Oh, Horatio, I confess: I was working with Frankie. I—I enticed your affections like some common Jezebel, then I made up that whole silly story about my uncle to get you to let me into the White House. Frankie's been making mead, just starting out small-time, trying to make a name for himself as a bootlegger. He doesn't have a network or warehouses or anything."

"Hey!" Frankie objected. "Stop making me sound like some penny-ante stooge to your boyfriend! Everyone has to start small."

"Say no more, Maisie," Mr. Grimbold said. He looked about as pained as if he'd stepped in a wolf trap, but he was trying to put a brave face on a bad situation. "I quite understand how you and your . . . *associate* have used me."

"But Horatio!" Maisie cried. "That was before I realized that I—that I love you! That I really, truly love you!" And with that she attached her face to his in a display of partiality that left Frankie the weasel grinding his teeth in rage.

"All right, break it up!" the little stoat commanded. He gestured pretty free with his gun. "So you love him, huh, Maisie? Then you won't mind dying with him. But first he's gonna help me load up what's left of this shipment onto the truck, and fast."

"And why would I consent to help you, you fiend, when you have already sworn our deaths?"

"'Cause there's more'n one way to die, College Man." Frankie reached his free hand into one pocket of his saggy suit and pulled out a big knife. "You'll help me, or you'll stand there and see what I do to your girlfriend with *this*."

And he raised the blade high and thunked it down hard right in the center of the nearest barrel.

Now I could've told that little man that those barrels was not intended to take so much abuse. If'n he hadn't made 'em himself, he'd bought 'em off someone who snookered him good, using low-grade wood for the job. One blow with the knife and the top of the barrel stove in. Heck, the whole dang barrel flew apart, honey-water splashing everywhere.

Everywhere included me. Me included my eyes. I don't mind telling you, that stuff did burn some going down my gullet, but that was nothing as compared to how bad it burned when it hit my eyes. I rose up with a roar that even scared the tarnation out of *me*. I was hurting, I was angry, and I was hosting what felt like ten thousand red-hot splinters inside my skull. I can't say as I could put a name to everything I was feeling at the moment, but I can tell you this:

I was not in a mood to be trifled with.

Unfortunately, that was exactly what Frankie decided to do. I heard his little pistol go off about three, four times, I heard the bullets go zinging past my ears, and I heard Maisie scream and hit the floor with a mighty loud thud for such a little lady. At the same time, I saw Mr. Grimbold take full advantage of the situation, because before Frankie could take another shot at me, that fine young man launched himself on the weasel and tackled him, bringing him crashing to the floor. The gun went skittering away, in between the broke-up barrels. As for the knife, the little man took a desperate slash at Mr. Grimbold that drew blood. The young man hollered in pain and threw himself back, away from the blade. I understood that, right enough: It was pure instinct at work, the same pure instinct that made Frankie the weasel drop that selfsame knife in a panic and go hotfooting it right out the door.

Funny thing, instinct. It's what makes the sight of a running piece of meat sort of *speak* to a bear. And you know what it's saying? It's saying: *Catch me! Catch me! I'm delicious, nutritious, and for all you know I've got a valuable free prize inside!* So while Mr. Grimbold clutched his bleeding arm, using some mighty foul language as he did so, I took off at a full gallop after Frankie.

It was about four hours later that I was apprehended in yet another corner of that subterraneous portion of the big white building. I was asleep on a pile of potato sacks, enjoying a nice nap on a full stomach. By that time it must've been next day, because I gathered from the converstion around me that the folks who'd throwed a net over me and conducted me back to my original cage was from the National Zoo.

As my cage was being wheeled out to where a truck was waiting, I caught sight of the president, Mr. Grimbold, Maisie, and several other official-looking types. No one looked particularly happy. Mr. Grimbold had a bandaged arm and a shamed-but-noble look on his face; Maisie just looked shamed.

One of the official fellers was talking to the president. "Sir," he said. "This animal is dangerous. We really ought to have him destroyed." (I felt my heart drop like a rock down into my paws, I don't mind telling you.)

"No," said the president.

"But sir, if he's tasted human flesh—!"

"Evidence?"

"The bootlegger's gone," that official bear-destroying jackass argued. "Vanished! And when we found the bear his stomach was bulging as if he'd just eaten—"

"Bones? Bloodstains?"

"Er . . . He probably ate everything."

Mr. Coolidge just snorted. "Ridiculous."

"In that case, where is the man who—?"

Silent Cal turned to one of the other official-looking fellers. "Roadblocks?" he inquired.

"Already in place, sir," the second feller said. "There's also a citywide manhunt on. I wouldn't be surprised if we flushed him out before the end of the day. And I've spoken to the people from the National Zoo. It's completely impossible for a bear to consume an entire human being and not leave *something* behind. Near as they can figure, the animal filled his belly by foraging through the White House kitchens."

The president nodded, satisfied. Then he turned to Mr. Grimbold and Maisie. "Love her?" he asked.

Mr. Grimbold put his arms around Maisie and held her close. "Despite all that this woman has put me through, sir, I would be lying if I denied it. I have decided to forgive her for her past and to marry her nonetheless."

Mr. Coolidge gave him a funny look, but then he shrugged and turned to Maisie. "Love him?" he asked.

She nodded so brisk that I thought she'd wear out her neck. "I do, and to prove it I'll do anything I can to help bring Frankie to justice. I should never have fallen in with him, but I had read too many sensational novels, seen too many inappropriate motion pictures, and I fear they ruined me. I was a young, impressionable girl when we first met, a sophomore at Vassar College—"

"Vassar?" This time Silent Cal rolled his eyes. "Figures." He looked back at Mr. Grimbold. "Marry her."

"Oh, I will, sir! And thank you! Thank—"

"You're fired."

"—you." Mr. Grimbold's enthusiasm waned right sharp. He looked like a flat tire, but that was when Maisie gave him a big ol' bear hug and said:

"Never mind, darling, we'll be all right. My daddy owns a fortune in stocks in U.S. Steel. You'll never need to work again."

It was all very moving, and I mean that literally, 'cause my cage was well underway to being shifted onto the waiting truck. Just as the National Zoo folks got it secured and was about to drive off, Silent Cal motioned for them to stop. He climbed aboard and peered into the cage.

"Well, friend," he said to me. "It appears that we have you to thank for saving the White House from becoming a way station for bootleggers right under our noses. You should get a medal, or at least a detective's badge. However, you'd have to promise not to eat any of the criminals you caught. Last night notwithstanding, I don't think you can be trusted to do that."

Well shucks, if I'd had the gift of human speech, I could've told the president that there never was any cause to fear me on that account. Can't say as I've ever taken much of a shine to criminals, and you know what I always say:

I never et a man I didn't like.

Izzy's Shoe-In

P. N. Elrod

At five-foot-nothing in her flats, Izzy DeLeon was the tallest of the troop of Girl Scouts milling around her. At twenty-one, she was the oldest by ten years, but trusted that her green uniform would provide all the cover required for her invasion of the White House. There was safety in numbers, and she counted four full troops gathered by the iron gates awaiting admittance to the grounds. In a hundred girls the chances of her being spotted as the cuckoo in the nest were small—if she kept moving.

It worked well; she circulated unobtrusively until the adults called for order and they smartly marched toward the sweeping curved steps to the South Portico. There they stood under the big awnings, scant protection against the summer sun. Izzy felt the oppressive heat sucking the energy from her. The others were lively as birds. A gap-toothed girl of eleven gave Izzy a curious stare. For an instant she wondered if she'd missed a spot when scrubbing her face clean of makeup. Would a lingering hint of powder or lip rouge betray her?

The girl said, "That's a lot of badges."

Izzy glanced down at her shoulder sash, which was covered with a number of merit badges, all of which held little meaning to her. Where she'd grown up you didn't earn such things, you learned those skills to survive. "I guess so," she admitted, pitching her voice high.

"You got a cold?" the girl asked sharply. The troops were here to sing patriotic songs to the president and first lady. Any Scout with a cold would be unwelcome in the chorus.

Shaking her head vehemently, Izzy then shrugged. "I talk funny, but sing just fine. My mom told me."

The girl did not look convinced and edged away. Good. The less contact the better. Izzy had flattened her chest with bandaging, thrust her size seven feet into size six shoes, and bitten her nails down to look right for the part. The uniform offered perfect protection from the adults, but not kids. One observant little girl could raise the alarm and bring an arrest, and Izzy doubted her editor would be sympathetic enough to bail her out.

Stick to fashion stories, Isabelle. You're female, write female stuff, he'd say, then send her off to a flower show or some other dullness.

Teeth grinding, she dutifully cranked out copy since that was her job, but craved more exciting, germane, *interesting* things to write. She'd not fought her way out of the lazy swamps of Florida, earned a scholarship, and worked hand over fist for a journalism degree merely to make a living. Izzy planned to be more than a reporter; she would be a world-famous writer, destined for honors, applause, and the respect of her peers . . . if she could just get away from daffodil festivals.

The only way to prove herself worthy of an assignment with real meat to it was to go hunting for one. But strangely, in the heart of Washington, D.C., in the swirl of politics and the passionate vituperations resulting from the clash of one party against another, that proved frustratingly difficult. Requests to interview a senator or congressman always landed her in a parlor with their wives, sipping tea. While she managed to make enough copy to please her editor, those encounters had no national importance. The few wives who would speak to her were concerned with matters like raising children in the public eye or promoting their favorite charity and, in one case, sharing a special fudge recipe. Laudable, but not what Izzy wanted.

But when Herbert Hoover took office, she mounted a more active campaign on the White House itself. Even if she was fobbed off to Mrs. Hoover, Izzy would count *that* as a victory. Lou Henry Hoover was extremely well-educated and had traveled around the world with her engineer husband. She spoke five languages fluently, had received medals from other countries for her charity work, survived the Boxer Rebellion—surely *she* would have tales to share with the American public with real weight to them.

But after five months of sending in regular requests, it became more clear with each polite refusal (carefully typed on White House stationery and personally signed by the first lady) that though a gracious hostess, Mrs. Hoover shunned the spotlight. She was inordinately modest about her many accomplishments.

Unless . . . it had to do with the Girl Scouts. Having served as their national president, and raising membership from ten thousand to over a million girls, she was always ready to talk about them—and entertain them. Thus Izzy hatched her idea to get inside the great sanctum. A routine interview with one of the Scout mistresses sparked things. The woman had proudly mentioned her troop's upcoming visit to the White House and the whole scheme burst upon Izzy's mind in a flash brilliant enough to impress even Edison.

She bought the largest-sized green uniform available at a local department store, a tight fit but manageable. With the connivance of a slightly-misled janitor at the local Girl Scout Little House (she bitterly claimed her baby sister had forgotten *everything*), Izzy got the Scouts' schedule and managed to blend in with the crowd of girls. There had been a few hair-raising moments when she thought one or another of the Scout mistresses had spotted her, but nothing came of it. As she'd hoped, each must have thought her to be with a different troop. Now she was only yards from the great oval of the Blue Room. Even coming this far would make a story, but to finally get inside . . . there . . . she spotted movement beyond the sheer curtains of the French doors: people shifting about in the shaded interior.

The girls were restless with curiosity, some jumping up to better see. Izzy missed Mrs. Hoover's entrance; had she opened the doors for herself, or did one of her four secretaries do the honors, or was it a servant? Details like that made interesting color.

Mrs. Hoover greeted the Scout leaders and welcomed everyone. Wearing a cotton dress with a green tint similar to the uniforms and a friendly smile, she had pronounced eyebrows and a firm mouth, and the smile softened her looks, made her more homey. She preceded them, leading the way through the Blue Room to a wide, pillar-studded hall, taking their giddy, shuffling parade to the right. They ended up in the vast East Room where their concert would take place. They all milled through.

Though told to be quiet and respectful of the surroundings, the girls gave in to enthusiasm, squealing at the wide echoing indoor space and impressive decor, which included a grand piano. It was irresistible.

Izzy hung back as much as she dared, torn between the desire to hear everything Mrs. Hoover might utter and the need to check out forbidden areas. Her chance came when a dozen girls surged toward the piano. The room resonated with loud and inexpert renderings—no, make that random *pounding* upon the presidential keys, much to the delight of the rest. More squeals, screams, and laughter followed. Control was quickly restored, but by then Izzy had slipped unobtrusively through a door at the southern end while the servants and Secret Service man were distracted.

She was in the Green Room, and it was thankfully empty. She counted herself very lucky that it was unlocked, but part of the Scouts' visit was to include a tour of the public areas. It must have been left open in anticipation of that. Faced with a choice of five doors, she picked the opposite left, which brought her back to the Blue Room. Some people were talking at the northernmost end of its oval, but no one paid attention as she hurried across and breached the entry to the Red Room.

It was empty, lighted only by the hot summer sunshine pouring through the open windows. Izzy found herself breathless more from excitement than the muggy afternoon heat. She'd hardly hoped to make it this far. If nothing else she would have an excellent piece about the lack of security within the house. Wouldn't that bowl everyone over? The nation's president vulnerable in the most famous house in America . . . of course he wasn't *in* this part at the moment, but there was a principle at stake here, and under the byline of Isabelle DeLeon, Izzy would triumphantly shout it forth.

She wanted more to shout about, though, and to do that required gaining the private quarters in the floors above. What little she knew of the public areas led her to believe access could be made through first the State, then the Family dining rooms. Heart in throat, she set forth.

*   *   *

As with many situations in life, it is far easier to land oneself into a predicament than to make a successful extraction from its coils. Thus did Izzy find herself crouched down behind a bamboo chair surrounded by potted palm trees in a sunlit room that should have been an upstairs hall. This wasn't on the diagram Izzy had gotten from one of her contacts, a maid who had worked here during the Coolidge administration.

Mrs. Hoover had been inordinately busy redecorating the family's private quarters, and she possessed firm, if exotic ideas on how to go about it. The fan-shaped floor-to-ceiling window at the far end washed the room with light, mitigated only slightly by an enormous bird cage full of frantically chirping canaries. Palms, ferns and other plants loomed everywhere, bamboo furniture rested comfortably on a rattan rug, oriental vases dotted tables and shelves. It would have been a most pleasant place to relax under any other circumstances, but Izzy in her overly tight shoes and constricting, hot uniform was anything but comfortable. She was supposed to be gathering news to report, not hiding like a fugitive.

She had just been sneaking into what she thought was the president's own bedroom when a bell abruptly sounded, making three sharp rings. Not knowing if it was a fire drill or a burglar alarm, Izzy let instinct take charge and ran quick as scat down the hall, diving for the nearest cover. For the last half hour she had to hold perfectly still, which was becoming more difficult with the cramps shooting up her legs from her outraged feet. She pushed the pain aside, though, for the president himself sat within spitting distance of her hiding place. He and another man were in deep conversation, and though close, Izzy had to strain to hear them. President Hoover was infamous for mumbling into his tie, and she only caught bits and pieces of their talk.

"You'll want to watch yourself, Allan," he said. "I've warned them time and again that buying on margin will lead to trouble. I hope you'll advise your school friends not to take any such risks on the market."

The reply was lost to her; the other man was busy with the canaries, and their noise and flapping swallowed his words. Izzy couldn't believe her luck. Not only was she overhearing the president, but a private chat between the president and his son, Allan. Wasn't he supposed to be at Harvard? He must have come home for a summer visit.

"—really can't say about much of anything, or they'll think you're trying to influence the market through me," he said over his shoulder. Izzy could barely make out his form through the palm fronds. He looked to be as tall as his father, nearly six feet, and would probably fill out into the same strong huskiness.

The president lighted a large cigar, releasing a cloud of blue smoke. "I know. We must never misuse this office, or even appear to misuse it. It only fuels those Democrat-controlled rags. The way they natter on, you'd think *I* was the Communist. The things I'm accused of is beyond tolerance. Lies, all of it rubbish and lies."

"Don't pay any mind to them," said Allan. "They're always going to be whipping up something out of nothing to sell more papers. Criticism is the best way to do it. You'd think those blasted reporters had better things to do with their time—like going after that bootlegging Kennedy clan."

Both men chuckled.

Izzy set her mouth, used to the not-so-subtle, ongoing, and endless fencing match that existed between politicians and the press. Each needed the other much the same as a rhinoceros needed a tick bird. Well, she was anything but some hack reporter. She was after a *real* story, and this was it: the Hoovers at home, a warm, caring family of true public servants with a disliking for Democrats, Communists . . . and a predilection for canaries.

And dogs. Uh-oh. Izzy froze even more, if that was possible, as a couple of completely gigantic police dogs bounded into the room, one dark, the other white. Allan and his father greeted them, but some kind of altercation broke out with the animals, requiring sharp commands from both men to restore order.

"They just don't mix," said Mr. Hoover. "Better get those two out of here."

"The dogs?"

"Yes, the dogs, at least they know how to obey a command. They work better with the help around here than your herd."

Allan laughed and set about removing the dogs, calling for King Tut and Snowboy to make a quick exit. They reluctantly complied. Izzy breathed soft relief; she'd been terrified the dogs would sense her presence.

"I don't know how you manage to keep those things from eating everything in sight," Hoover admonished. He muttered something else.

"They're not so much trouble," said Allan. "You should be around when I toss them raw chicken. Mother would stop complaining about how fast you eat."

"Just mind that they don't scare the servants."

"If I ever see any. Every time a bell goes off around here they're popping into closets like jack-in-the boxes in reverse. I wish you'd get over your dislike of dealing with them. They're only just people after all."

His father mumbled something in which the word *privacy* figured, and Allan Hoover chuckled.

So that explained the ringing alarm and why she'd not seen anyone. Izzy had no need to take notes, this was too completely extraordinary to forget.

"How did your downstairs concert go?" Allan asked.

"Fine, fine. Cheered your mother up. She does enjoy seeing all those bright faces. I think she'd like to be president of them again, given the chance, but she knows she can do more from here than any other place. Oh, get off, you overgrown newt! Look at that. He's trying to eat my shoe!"

Allan laughed again, what a cheerful sort he was, and there was a dragging sound followed by a strange hissing. "You behave yourself. You want the Secret Service to shoot you?"

Izzy didn't think he was addressing his father, so there must have been someone or something else in the room, perhaps another dog. But what kind of a mutt hissed?

There was a knock. Mr. Hoover bade them enter, though there was no real door, just a gap in a series of partitions meant to create a space removed from the hall. Like the rest of the room there was a heavy Oriental influence to the panels, reflecting the family's travels in China.

A man came in, tall, dark suit, grim and hasty manner. "Mr. President, we think there may be an intruder in the house."

"What? Another one?" Mr. Hoover sounded more annoyed than disturbed at the prospect. Izzy held her breath.

"Yes, sir. We're doing a room-by-room search, but for your own safety it has been suggested that you remove to your office. We've checked and cleared it."

"I was going back to work regardless," said the president. "It never stops, unless Mrs. Hoover insists on a pause for me."

Allan murmured agreement. "I suppose all those Scouts will be gone by now. Mother will want to tell one of us about it. Shall I volunteer?"

"By all means, but she'll have you stuffing envelopes with her secretaries if you're not nimble enough to escape."

"I don't mind. This way I can keep an eye on her."

His father said something to the effect that Mrs. Hoover was more than capable of keeping an eye on herself. Neither of them seemed too concerned about the intruder, which Izzy took for a favorable sign. If by horrible chance she got caught they might laugh it off. Might. She didn't think so. Not really. One of the men must have hit a signal button, for a moment later three rings sounded and they all left.

And not a moment too soon. Izzy flopped flat on the floor, stretching her legs in agony, and unsuccessfully stifled a sneeze caused by the haze of cigar smoke. It came out as a kind of truncated squeak that closed up her ears. She worked her jaw until her hearing popped back to normal, then rubbed her abused shank muscles until she felt the pins and needles of returning circulation. She was tempted to remove her painful shoes before they permanently crippled her toes, but didn't dare as she'd never force them back on again. Since quitting her backwoods home for the city her feet had grown soft, used to the protection of shiny leather and fashionable heels. Her days of running barefoot through grass and swamp were long over.

She noticed an odd slithery sound, like something moving roughly over the rug. Peeking above the chair she looked accusingly at the canaries. They seemed agitated yet at the same time were oddly silent. What a mess they made, feathers and seed husks everywhere. But enough of them; Izzy had to figure a way out of this place. The Secret Service itself was on to her presence, though Lord knew how they found it out. Perhaps one of the people in the Blue Room mentioned seeing a straying Girl Scout wandering around. How could they deem that to be a threat to the president? No matter. She had her story; it was past time to skedaddle.

Her legs mostly functional again, she slowly rose from behind the plants, heading toward the opening to look at the rest of the hall.

Drat. *Now* there were servants moving around, one of them anyway. How to sneak past him? The longer she waited, the worse it would get. Maybe her Scout cover would hold. If she worked herself into some tears and pretended she'd gotten lost from her troop . . . what was the troop leader's name? Monahan or Houlihan? Not important, the White House staff would hardly know the difference. Bluff, bluff, bluff until blue in the face, then run like crazy, that was the way to get a story.

The butler was out of sight. Good, she could slip downstairs and only have to haul out the lost little girl ruse as a last resort.

She eased from behind the partition . . .

. . . And came face-to-face with an extremely surprised-looking man wearing dark livery. He *had* been on the other side of the hall and somehow silently moved up on her. Izzy hadn't wanted to test herself so soon. She'd not even gotten her tears in place.

He never gave her the chance. Before she could move or speak he hauled one arm back and smartly slammed his fist against the side of her head.

Light lanced behind her eyes and she dropped straight down, face in the rug, utterly unable to move.

Izzy never quite lost consciousness, but lay quite breathless and stunned. Instead of raising a hue and cry at discovering the intruder, the servant bolted off. She managed to crack one eyelid enough to mark his retreating feet. Oh, God, now she was in for it. Was trespassing at the White House a federal crime? She should have researched that. Maybe she could write a series about women in prison. Was there a women's federal prison?

Think, Isabelle. They'd not clapped the irons on yet, nor had he sounded the alarm. She could hide in a closet until the ringing in her skull died down. Ow-ow-owwwww. What a bully, hitting a helpless little Girl Scout. If she laid eyes on him again she'd show him a thing or three. . . .

Ring-ring.

That hadn't come from inside her head. The president must be on his way back. Being found sprawled over the hall rug was too ignominious to be endured. She'd go back to her hiding place. Maybe later she could duck into a bedroom, knot sheets together, and escape out a window after dark. . . .

Footsteps. Coming her way.

She managed to get to her knees, and crept past the partitions to her spot behind the palms. She was dizzy, and her head hurt miserably.

Flat on the floor again. How had that happened? Oh, her feet hurt, her head, ouch-ouch; she'd better get a bonus for this one, if she ever got away. Quiet, she had to be very, very quiet.

She put her back to a wall, drawing her knees up, the easier to cradle her pounding head. The president's lingering cigar smoke made her sick to her stomach. Adding to the misery was another smell mingling with the smoke, a strangely familiar musk, redolent of the swamp. There must be some stagnant water in one of the vases, left forgotten after the removal of its flowers. Phew, what a stink.

Two more people seemed to be in the room. Allan Hoover and a woman in the midst of expressing her irritation. Izzy recognized the first lady's voice.

"It's ridiculous," she said. "How can we not be safe in our own home surrounded by guards?"

"They're just being cautious, Mother. Once they've combed the house you can get back to work."

"I've much too much to do to leave it for long. There's mail to answer, dinner invitations to send, and those calling cards will want a reply."

"You don't have to respond to them all."

"Allan, that's not at all proper or polite. Those people took the trouble to come and leave their cards, the least we can do is show our appreciation. This is their house, too."

"I think many leave a card just to get your autograph on the house stationery."

"You have a poor opinion of the people of this country."

"The people are just fine, it's the politicians we want to watch out for."

"Oh, Allan." But there was affection in her tone. "Just let your father hear that."

"I'm certain he would agree."

Despite her nausea, Izzy still took mental notes, albeit with the suspicion that she could just possibly be dreaming. A bang on the head might do terrible things to one's brain, creating hallucinations. Had she imagined that butler? Where had he gotten himself?

"Have they cleared this floor yet?" Mrs. Hoover asked.

Allan went to the opening. "They're still looking around. It shouldn't be too long."

"Please tell them to hurry. There aren't that many places to search. Certainly no closets to speak of." That sounded like a pet grievance of hers. A house this huge with no closets? Unthinkable.

"Not yet, anyway. Any day now I expect you to start tearing into the walls."

"The place needs shaking up. Never did I see such a drab old barn in my life. I don't know how Mrs. Coolidge stood it, and she was always so ill here. Poor thing should have gotten more sunshine. That would have set her right. Always worked well for you two boys."

"Yes, Mother." Allan left, calling to someone in the distance, then went off.

He was gone for longer than the first lady had patience to wait. Izzy heard Mrs. Hoover give an audible sigh, then follow her son.

Izzy wondered if now would be the best time to show herself. After hearing a mother's affectionate talk with her son, Izzy began to realize how she might feel having an uninvited stranger eavesdropping in *her* house. This had gone too far. Time to stop no matter the consequences. They might go light on her. Surely if Mrs. Hoover heard a personal appeal to her well-known humanitarian instincts, along with a groveling apology. . . .

But Izzy couldn't do that. The bash in the head was confusing her. Good heavens, she was tougher than this. She could stick it out a little longer. Besides, this was likely the safest place to hide. She'd wait, escape, and then apologize. Anonymously. From a distance. Chicago, maybe. She could do stories on Al Capone. Unless they fobbed her off to Mrs. Capone . . .

Izzy blinked herself alert to the present, not the future. Yes, she could stick it out, but this seemed to be a favorite gathering spot for the family; what else might she overhear? Personal talk was the bread and butter of the yellow press, but she had higher standards than that. Human interest was acceptable, but one had to draw a line. And what if the dogs were brought in again? They'd been distracted earlier, but sooner or later they'd sniff her out. Perhaps they wouldn't eat her—she'd been raised with coon hounds and knew how to stall excited canines until help arrived—but avoiding the circus would be best for all concerned.

Conscience wanted her to do otherwise, though. Common sense said that throwing herself on the first lady's mercy would be better than explaining things to the Secret Service. Those fellows were uncommonly grim. All right, well and good. Isabelle DeLeon, formerly a member of the Washington press would emerge, confess, and apologize. Besides, it would put everyone's mind at rest about the so-called intruder. No bomb-throwing Bolsheviks, no Communists, just one diminutive reporter with more enthusiasm than wisdom.

Decision made, Izzy unsteadily emerged from her bolt hole. At least now she could get rid of these awful shoes, though on second thought it might not be the right sort of behavior to display before this well-bred crowd. She didn't think Mrs. Hoover would approve of people walking about in socks.

Smothering a groan for her feet and head, Izzy started toward the opening. Mrs. Hoover was in conversation with others from the sound of things. Servants, perhaps? Though from that bell-ringing earlier the clear-the-halls signal applied to her as well as her husband.

Then Izzy saw that darn butler again. Where had he come from? What in heaven's name had he been doing waiting around in this room the whole time she'd wrestled with her conscience? Now he'd spoil everything by giving away her presence before she was ready. She had to get to Mrs. Hoover first.

Izzy shot forward, beating him to the hall, then halted cold in her tracks, frozen with absolute shock. Just ahead of her, moving at a quick pace for its size, was an honest-to-God *alligator*. It couldn't have been hallucination, not with that stagnant water smell. How in heaven's name had it gotten *here*?

The answer could wait. It was heading straight for the first lady, long mouth gaping wide, and she seemed quite unaware of its threat.

Without thinking, Izzy launched bodily toward the thing. It was nearly as long as she was tall, but she knew how to deal with the varmints. She and her brothers had pulled more than one of them out of the hen house. If you were strong enough you could grab the tail and haul backwards, and if quick enough, jump clear before the head whipped around to bite off anything important. Izzy was quick, but lacked the muscle power for heavy hauling.

Instead, she landed on the reptile in a flying tackle, pushing down hard with all of her ninety-nine pounds and clamping her small hands onto its snout. The beast had a fearsome bite, but first it had to get its jaws open. Preventing that took surprisingly little effort. However, the rest of its body was pure muscle, especially the tail. She wrapped her legs around the gator just as it bucked and rolled, twisting with outrage. Izzy knew she would tire before it did and unashamedly shouted for help, hoping the Secret Service would shoot only it and not her.

"Run, Mrs. Hoover!" she put in for good measure. "I've got it! Run!"

Mrs. Hoover did not run, and in fact looked remarkably calm about the whole business, calling for her son. "Allan, will you please remove this reptile from that poor girl?"

The gator had other ideas and twisted again, violently thrashing until it was on top. She tried to hold it firm, but its great head began to get away from her, which could be deadly. She felt the shape of the teeth under her fingers; one slash from those in the right place would cut to the bone and beyond.

Then a man stepped into her field of view, made a successful grab at the snout, and pulled the thing right from her. He danced backward with it, nearly blundering into a Secret Service agent brandishing a gun.

"Shoot it!" Izzy yelled.

"No!" the man yelled back. He was Allan Hoover and seemed much taller from Izzy's low vantage point. In very quick order he had the gator under control. He charged toward the partitioned end of the hall, and released the thing, skipping away in time to avoid getting whacked by the tail. Her brothers couldn't have done better. Young Hoover puffed, grinned, and shook his rumpled suit back into place.

"He's going to be mad for awhile," he said. "We better stay out of that area until he settles down."

"Allan, I think it's time you put that monster in a zoo."

"Oh, Mother, he's not even half grown yet. He behaves so long as people don't surprise him." He glowered down at Izzy, but failed at truly intimidating her. After wrestling with an alligator she didn't think very much else would.

Goodness, but he was handsomer than his photos. His cleft chin was more pronounced than his father's, and he had his mother's forthright eyebrows. All in all, an impressive combination.

"Don't go scaring the girl," said Mrs. Hoover. "She's been through enough."

"I'm all right," Izzy ventured. She started to pick herself up—how many hours had she been on the floor today?—but the agent with the gun came forward.

"Don't move," he ordered, sighting down its short muzzle at her.

Izzy had no intention of arguing with him, but Mrs. Hoover did. "Do put that away, Mr. Borden. I'll take care of this."

"Sorry, ma'am. Orders."

"I said to put that away." She did not raise her voice, but there was a note in it that would brook no argument. She wasn't used to repeating herself, this was her house, and in domestic matters she was in full charge of it. All that in half a dozen words combined with a slight lifting of her chin. Light flickered off her eyeglass lenses, concealing some of her expression, but none of her dynamism. The agent wavered. "Use your head, Mr. Borden, this little girl thought she was saving me from being eaten alive. Isn't that right, dear?"

Izzy nodded. Could her disheveled Scout disguise be working? Probably not. Mrs. Hoover seemed the type not to miss much. Allan Hoover had begun to smile. Or was that a smirk? Going suddenly red, Izzy yanked her skirt down to a more socially acceptable level.

"But, ma'am . . ." agent Borden looked very unhappy, reluctant to abandon his protective instincts.

"Report it to the appropriate party," said Mrs. Hoover. "In the meantime, I'll look into this. Allan, she seems in need of help."

Allan readily stepped forward and assisted Izzy to her feet. Ow, they were still in agony, and she was still sick; the aftermath of the fight left her shaking from unused adrenaline.

"Are you injured?" he asked, supporting her.

"The gator didn't hurt me, it was that butler who hit me in the head."

"What butler?"

"One of the butlers or footmen or someone socked me one in the noggin," she said. "Then he ran off."

Allan looked at the agent. "I think she's seen your intruder, Mr. Borden."

"Where?" Borden demanded.

Izzy waved toward the sun room. "He was in there a minute ago."

"The Palm Court?"

This time Mrs. Hoover did not demure. When Borden gestured decisively toward the other end of the hall and some stairs, she went without a word. Allan, also silent, followed, helping Izzy limp along. She was too slow for him, though, so he swept her up just like that and carried her down. She was too surprised to protest. Besides, it was very *nice* to be in the strong arms of a handsome young man, made her glad she wasn't really a Girl Scout.

Borden shouted, and a number of men in dark suits bounded upstairs. At the lower landing several more surrounded the Hoovers, leading them away. Someone had forgotten to ring the signal bells to warn of the first lady's approach. Two maids carrying linens were caught flatfooted by the quick-moving parade and hurriedly ducked around a corner. Izzy hoped they wouldn't get into trouble. That would hardly be fair.

They finally came to something resembling a sitting room, but without windows and only one door. Izzy wondered if it might have originally been a storage cupboard converted to a waiting area. Borden shut them in with one of his men and rushed outside to see to other duties.

Allan set Izzy down on one of the chairs. It must have been a leftover from Lincoln's day, it had the look, and she became conscious that she was not only disheveled, but smelled strongly of alligator. Ugh.

"Felling better?" he asked.

"Very much," she lied. "Thank you, and I owe you both a huge apology."

"Why don't you tell us your name first?" suggested Mrs. Hoover, taking a chair opposite. "Then you can explain the details behind your apology. Are you or have you ever been a Girl Scout?"

Izzy winced, having collected the instant impression that the first lady would be as rankled by the misuse of this uniform as any military man upon seeing an undeserving civilian masquerading in full officer's kit. Wrestling another alligator would be preferable to this particular accounting, that or getting shot by the Secret Service. She could make a run for it. The man by the door would cut her down point-blank . . . but no. Izzy had already resolved to bare all, but for that butler spoiling things.

Besides, these shoes made running *quite* impossible.

She offered a weak smile, squirmed, gave her name, and began talking, starting with her desire to get an interview to her impersonation idea, to her misinterpretation of the gator's intentions. It was explained to that the beast had indeed been looking for food, but seeking out Allan to give it some, not to make a meal of the first lady.

"Father will be none too pleased," Allan said, referring to the business of the interview and the eavesdropping. Izzy had apologized frequently and sincerely.

"He won't be the only one," agreed Mrs. Hoover. "However, Miss DeLeon exhibited a remarkable turn of wit and nerve to get so far, and then to leap so boldly upon that great reptile . . ."

Allan's smile returned briefly. "That *was* smooth. Miss DeLeon, you're the only female I've ever met who wasn't terrified to shrieking at the very sight of my pets. That puts you ahead of a number of men, too."

"Pets?" she squeaked. While growing up Izzy had had to put up with occasional gator incursions. They were a sometimes dangerous nuisance and more often than not turned into the family's dinner depending on who had the gun that day, but certainly nothing you'd want to keep as a pet. A coon hound was much more practical. "You have more than one?"

"I've a matched set. A Mr. Cornell Woolley gave them to me a few years ago when we lived on S Street. They were whizzer. I was the only boy in the whole town with my very own alligators."

From that perspective his enthusiasm for the distinction was understandable. Mrs. Hoover's expression was reserved, but it was clear she was holding back her private opinion concerning Mr. Woolley's questionable generosity. "Allan still keeps them in the bathtubs at night. It's a wonder we have any servants left."

Allan seemed used to this particular observation. "They're better than the Marines. In all that time on S Street, were we ever worried over burglars?"

"No, just finding ourselves short of a cook some morning, whether she departed in the night of her own accord or had been untimely consumed. But we are losing the point. What are we to do with you, Miss DeLeon?"

Izzy had a number of proposals, all of which ended with her being free to leave the grounds, never to return. She would gratefully totter home, tender her resignation to the paper, and hop the first train to Chicago where things were safer. So far as she knew, no gators roamed free in the houses of the rich and *refined* there. And after this debacle, interviewing Al

Capone would be far less fatiguing or perilous. But Izzy never got the chance to voice her ideas; Borden returned.

"Are we free to leave?" Mrs. Hoover asked him.

"Sorry, ma'am, no."

"You've still not found him?"

"We have and we haven't."

She raised her brows, inquiring.

"We made a search of the house and rounded up every man in servant clothing. Some are new to the general staff, but all are known to each other and the house usher. If this miss would make an identification of the culprit we can clear it up right away."

"I only got a glimpse," said Izzy.

"Miss, you are in very serious trouble. The best way to ameliorate things is to cooperate with us."

"At least give it a try," said Allan. "Shall I carry you again?"

If his mother hadn't been looking on with a shrewd eye Izzy might have taken him up on that. "I can manage now." Biting back the shoe discomfort, she stood, but had a genuine need to lean on his arm.

They went to a wide hall, the equivalent of the one on the floor above, but with majestic pillars marching down its length. What a grand impression it must make on visiting heads of state. Izzy felt a swell of pride to have her country represented in such a beautiful manner. Between the pillars on one side nearly twenty men in servant livery were gathered, looking remarkably alike except for the dark faces of the Negroes. With a jar, Izzy noticed that to a man, they were all exactly the same height.

"The one who hit me was white," she whispered to Borden.

At a word from him the ranks were thinned. The men dismissed from the line-up—for that was what it looked like—were slow to leave, obviously curious to know what was going on. Mrs. Hoover took off her glasses and twirled them. They instantly departed.

"Which one?" asked Borden.

Izzy checked each remaining face, none were remotely familiar. In a fit of inspiration she examined their trouser knees for signs of crawling around. Last she inspected their shoes, and finally shook her head. "I'm sorry, but he's not here. The man I saw had old, worn-down heels. He'd polished his shoes, but there was too much scuffing to cover up the damage."

"Good eye for detail," said Allan. "Miss DeLeon should be working for you. Well, if he's not here, then he's still upstairs. Is my father is safe?"

"Yes, Mr. Hoover. I doubled the number of men around him. They're alert for trouble."

"The man may still be on the same floor," said Mrs. Hoover. "Just in a very good hiding place. I trust you looked under the beds in the family quarters?"

"Yes, Mrs. Hoover." Borden seemed unpiqued at having so basic a point raised. "We will check all over again."

"The windows are wide open with this heat. Perhaps he made an exit by that means."

"From so high up?" asked Izzy, then remembered she'd planned a similar escape using knotted sheets. "It could be possible that . . ."

"What?"

"Well, something Mr. Hoover said about not having burglars at your previous residence. I'd been hiding a very long time in that sunny room."

"The Palm Court?"

"Yes, and the alligators were there the whole while?"

Allan nodded. "They like to sun themselves. It scares the canaries, though."

"I think they scared more than the birds. If this man got up to the Palm Court, hid himself, then realized he was sharing his bushwhacking blind with a pair of gators—"

"He'd have been too terrified himself to move. Oh, this is smooth! I think you have it. Mr. Borden, let's go hunting."

"Sir, I can't allow you to—"

"Bother that, follow me!"

Allan bounded up the stairs, Borden and his men hastened after, and sore feet or no, Izzy charged too, since no one told her to stay put. Mrs. Hoover called after her son, but to no avail. Perhaps he'd been so quick to go in order to prevent parental restraint.

Izzy had to hang onto the hand rail at the top; she wasn't quite up to her best yet, but wanted a prime location to watch.

Borden reclaimed enough of his authority to compel young Hoover to hang back a sensible distance. Two men were doing their best to stand in front of him while Borden and two others made their way cautiously toward the dividing panels.

"Don't shoot my alligators," said Allan in a very low voice, pitched to carry only a few feet.

Borden gave no sign of acknowledgment, his whole attention focused on listening. All Izzy heard were the birds, singing and flapping in their big cage. She inched forward. Just inside the Palm Court lay one of the gators. Its tail toward them, its head was partly turned. Evidently it was aware of Borden's presence. He hesitated. Though protecting the president required flinging himself between his charge and assailants, dealing with a testy alligator was likely not a normal part of his job duties.

Getting an idea, Izzy took off her shoes. Oh, dear lord, that felt good, but she couldn't pause to enjoy the exquisite relief. She said *psst*. Borden turned. She motioned for him to move to one side. He got her intent and stepped clear. Izzy had the eye and arm for throwing things, and the official Girl Scout footwear was a very sturdy, heavy item, built for tough use. Izzy made use of it by a hard and, as it turned out, accurate throw at the gator's head.

The gator snapped irritably at the object as it bounced off its flat skull. Izzy threw the remaining shoe, this time so it landed past the snout. The thing scrabbled after, snapping it up like a prize.

With the way clear, Borden and his men entered the court, guns ready. Izzy held her breath and could tell Allan did the same. No one moved for a moment, then Borden emerged, disappointment on his face.

"No one's there, sir," he said to Allan.

"My alligator." Allan moved past them. "If he swallows that shoe it could kill him."

Saving the gator was not Borden's concern, but Izzy felt a touch of responsibility. She followed Allan into the Palm Court. It was bright and hot compared to the dim hall, the light dazzling her. Allan was on his knees straddling his pet's back. As if from long practice, he grabbed the alligator's jaws and pulled them apart like a lion tamer.

"Would you retrieve your shoe, Miss DeLeon?" he asked.

Izzy didn't like to risk getting her arm bitten off if his grip slipped, but she couldn't flinch now. The shoe was hanging halfway out, anyway. She snagged it up and backed away.

"Watch out, there's the other one," Allan advised.

Turning, Izzy saw the second gator approaching from the other side of the room, attracted by the activity. "Maybe you'd better feed them," she said.

"Yes, then they might forgive me for all the abuse they've been through." Allan released his hold and jumped back. "Perhaps we can—" He stopped, staring at something behind Izzy. She whirled. A man was clambering through the open window. He had firm hold of a thick, knotted rope that extended upward. Apparently he'd just climbed down from the roof.

Without thinking, Izzy aimed and threw again. Her official Scout shoe smashed square into the side of his head. Allan yelled for help, then tackled the reeling man. Secret Service agents rushed in; there was a mad scuffle for about four seconds, then everything went quiet. The man was lying face to the floor and handcuffed. Allan Hoover, puffing a bit, stood.

"Whizzer," he said, grinning down. "Who are you?"

"I have an appointment with the president," the man stated. He was muffled, his mouth partly imbedded in the rattan rug.

"I think not. People with appointments don't lurk, and *you* were lurking."

"I was trying to get away from those monsters! Kept me from my duty half the day!"

"For that they will get extra chicken. Sounds like his pot is cracked, Mr. Borden."

"We'll find out for certain, sir." Borden, who had been part of the rescue mob, now supervised the man's removal. "This miss needs to come along, too." He put a hand on Izzy's arm.

Allan Hoover removed it. "I'll vouch for her, Mr. Borden."

"But, sir, she—"

"I know, but Mother and I will look into it. I'm satisfied she meant no harm. On the contrary, she and my alligators have endeavored to do your job."

"I'll have to make a report, sir."

"Fine, fine, I'm sure it will be very entertaining. Come, Miss DeLeon.

Let's get your other shoe before my pets eat it."

In the hall, Izzy padded along, shoes in hand. Mrs. Hoover waited by the lower landing, staring after the agents as they led the intruder away. He was speaking very loud and rapidly about his missed appointment with the president.

"Dear me, if he'd just left a calling card he'd have gotten an invitation to one of our receptions," she said. She looked at Izzy. "Well, Miss DeLeon, what are we to do with you? As a staunch supporter of the Constitution I cannot curtail freedom of speech as represented by the press, but—"

Izzy raised a conciliatory hand. "Not to worry, Mrs. Hoover. This is a heck of a—I mean a great story, but I'd rather forget it ever happened. I promise to respect your privacy and that of your family for as long as I live. My word of honor as a not-quite Girl Scout."

Mrs. Hoover blinked a few times, digesting this, and looked at Allan, who nodded. "Then your word is good enough for me, Miss DeLeon. I think you should leave now, but I will expect you back here this evening. We serve dinner at eight sharp."

Izzy felt a case of shock coming on.

"That is, if you're up to it?"

"I . . . yes! I'll be here!" No bump on the head would keep her away.

"Very good. Allan, see that she gets a ride. Good day, Miss DeLeon." Mrs. Hoover left them.

"Dinner," Izzy breathed. Had she heard right?

Allan shrugged. "My parents never eat alone unless it's their anniversary. This is Mother's way of thanking you for your help and providing you with a *safe* story to write. Wait 'til my father hears this."

Oh, this was wonderful . . . terrific . . . *whizzer.* "Dinner at the White House!" Saying it aloud made it more real.

"You'll enjoy it. Can't say that I always do." He took her arm, leading her gently off. "Don't quote me, but this old barn has always given me the willies." So said a man who kept alligators for pets. He gestured back up toward them. "Seems to agree with those two, though."

Fala and the Ghost of Bulows Minde

Kate Grilley

"Morning, Lady!"

Maubi called to me from his Hot to Trot roach coach parked in its usual spot on the waterfront overlooking the peacock-hued Caribbean Sea. "I got coconut ice cream today. Cranked it myself last night with coconut fresh from my granddaddy's trees."

While Maubi scooped a triple-dip cone for me, shamelessly exploiting my weakness for his homemade ice cream, he added, "Those be the very coconut palms President Franklin Delano Roosevelt saw when he and his little dog Fala come to this Caribbean island on the same July day many years ago."

"It was today? July 8th?" I asked. "Was that when your granddaddy won the prize for the best looking homestead?"

Maubi grinned. "You be hearing my stories too many times, Miss Kelly. But here's one you never hear tell about when President Roosevelt was here. Settle yourself on that stool."

I pulled up a backless stool to Maubi's serving counter. He handed me a paper napkin to wipe the ice cream dribbles from my chin, then pulled up his own stool inside the van to ease the weight on his bum left leg before he began his tale.

"This story come to me for true from my grandmama Alveena. She say that when President Roosevelt first take charge in Washington, D.C., times in St. Croix were very hard. While this island was Danish, sugar cane was the big crop. Everybody make money from sugar. But when prohibition become law in 1920, three short years after the Stars and Stripes go up the Fort Christiansvaern flagpole, the rum factory shut down and planters stop growing cane. Cane workers like my granddaddy had no jobs and hungry children to feed. When President Hoover come to the Virgin Islands in 1931 he call these islands 'the poorhouse of the Caribbean.' By the time prohibition ended in 1933, most of the sugar estates had been abandoned and the cane fields gone back to bush. My granddaddy found a little job here, a little job there to make ends meet. Alveena, always handy in the kitchen, took steady work as the cook at Government House."

Maubi paused to pour a cup of ice water for each of us. "President Roosevelt was a doing man. He got the homestead program going for the former cane workers so everybody could have a little something. Granddaddy took all the money he and Alveena had saved and bought a plot of homestead land. First he built a two-room wooden house, then he started planting. They had a big vegetable garden, lots of fruit trees, some avocado pear and coconut palm, a little plot of sugar cane, a few chickens, a couple cows and some goats. Mistress Eleanor Roosevelt come from Washington to check out St. Croix in March, then Alveena hear at Government House that the president himself was coming here by ship in early July. While granddaddy worked the land and spruced up the homestead house for the president's inspection, Alveena was busy at Government House planning the big lunch. But when the governor decided to have the lunch at Bulows Minde instead of Government House, Alveena was troubled."

"Bulows Minde is a beautiful estate in the hills west of Christiansted with a wonderful view of the harbor," I said. "It's always cool and comfortable even when Government House is stifling. Why would having the lunch there bother Alveena?"

Maubi answered with a twinkle in his eye. "Because of Miss Anna."

I waited for Maubi to elaborate.

"Miss Anna was Von Scholten's mistress."

Ah, I thought, remembering that Von Scholten was the Danish crown-appointed governor who proclaimed from the Government House steps in Christiansted on July 3, 1848, "All unfree in the Danish West Indian Islands are from this day free." Overcome by exhaustion, ten days after the proclamation Von Scholten quietly departed by schooner on the predawn tide to join his wife and daughters in Denmark, leaving his beloved country home at Bulows Minde in the care of his housekeeper and unofficial first lady, Anna Heegaard, who never stopped hoping for his return to St. Croix. Von Scholten died in Denmark in 1854. Anne Heegaard died at Bulows Minde in 1859, but was buried on nearby Estate Aldersville owned by her family. Though her marble grave marker is now on the grounds of the Whim Plantation museum, the exact location of her remains is unknown.

"On July 8th, the day the president was to arrive from St. Thomas on the U.S.S. Houston, Alveena woke long before dawn. Taking great care not to wake my granddaddy or any of their five children, she quickly dressed and slipped out of the homestead house. Pausing only to take up the gunny sack she hid in the bush the night before, she hitched up the donkey cart and headed for Bulows Minde, arriving there as the little smile of the waning moon was rising over the east end hills."

Maubi stopped for a gulp of water. I moved my stool closer to the serving counter and leaned forward. "Go on," I said, "what happened?"

"Alveena take the gunny sack from the cart and go to the flower garden surrounding the place where the lunch would be served. Next to the low stone wall separating the garden from the terrace, she first poke tiny pieces of green glass, no bigger than peas, in the ground. While she worked she suddenly feel a chill around her, but the air was still. She sniffed. And smelled jasmine. But no jasmine ever grew at Bulows Minde."

"'Miss Anna,' Alveena say in her no-nonsense voice, planting her hands on her hips, 'it's no use you making a fuss. We got important people coming here today. President Roosevelt and his sons Franklin Junior and John, the governor and gentlemen of the colonial council and their ladies. The president wants to make t'ings better for the people your governor set free a hundred years ago. You stop your foolishness this instant and go back to your resting place. You can watch the harbor for your governor another time.'"

Maubi continued in his own voice. "The air warmed and the smell of jasmine disappeared. Alveena planted the last of green glass, then climbed over the low stone wall to the terrace where she arranged conch shells along the wall just so."

"Maubi, I know about green glass warding off jumbies, the spirits of the dead, and throwing salt on the skin of a jumbie so it can't harm you," I said, thinking of the time Maubi insisted I put empty Heineken bottles top down in the ground around my house, making my own yard look like something out of the Emerald City in *The Wizard of Oz*. "But I never heard about jumbies and conch shells."

"You rest a conch shell open side up, the jumbie hop in quick and hide. But you turn it over, the jumbie be trapped and can't make trouble with you. Alveena turned the shells over, sticking fresh cut red hibiscus in the end of each for decoration. She then went to the kitchen to fire up the wood burning ovens to cook the food that would be served to the president."

I made a mental note about conch shells as Maubi continued. "By nine o'clock that morning everyone was waiting at the dock for the president to arrive. School children were all dressed in clean white middy tops like Navy sailors wear, waving American flags on sticks, ready to sing the song they made up to welcome the president. The few cars on the island were polished like mirrors, gassed up and ready to take the president's party on a tour over the newly paved Centerline road. But when the president finally arrived the children were so excited to see Fala they forgot the words to their song. That year every child ask Santa Claus for a little Fala dog."

"I've read about Fala," I said. "Fala was a black Scottish terrier, a gift to the president from his cousin, Margaret Suckley. The president adored that dog and made a famous speech about Fala in 1944 that helped win the fourth-term election. When Fala was a puppy everyone loved him so much they fed him constantly, making him sick. The president gave strict orders that he was to be the only one who ever fed Fala."

"For true," Maubi said, nodding. "But the president didn't reckon with Miss Anna, a very determined woman who also loved little dogs."

"This I've got to hear," I said.

"When the morning tour was over, the cars arrived at Bulows Minde for lunch. Everything went fine, the president was laughing and making jokes, until Alveena bring out the big silver tray with dishes of coconut ice cream for dessert. Master John, the president's son, picked one of the conch shells off the wall and started to blow on it like he was Louis Armstrong his own self. Alveena went to reach for the salt, but it was too late. Fala stiffened, his ears pricked up, he barked once, then his tail began to wag. Flip, flip, flip. Faster than a hummingbird wing. It wag so hard that little dog shook like he took a chill. The president stopped his story telling and stared at the garden. Turning to the governor's wife, he asked 'do I smell jasmine?'"

"What did she say?" I asked.

"The governor's wife was a well-known gardener and had taken Mistress Roosevelt all around the Government House garden, telling her about every plant. If the lady say yes, someone would surely point out there was no jasmine to be seen. If she say no, the president would think her a fool. The scent of jasmine was growing stronger. Alveena act quick and help the governor's wife by dropping the silver tray right there on the terrace. In the confusion, Fala slipped his leash and bounded over the stone wall into the garden. He performed the tricks the president taught him, rolled over and over on the grass, then sat up waiting to be petted. But Fala wasn't looking at the president or anyone on the terrace.

"'Fala! Come!'" said President Roosevelt in his own no-nonsense voice.

"Fala barked, held up his paw in the air like a little gentleman, then turned, hopped back on the terrace and ran into the main house," said Maubi. "Inside music began to play on the very piano Von Scholten bought for Miss Anna. The governor's wife fainted. Everyone say it was because of the July heat, but Alveena knew it was because the lady was scared of jumbies. Master John ran into the house after Fala. When he come back with the little black dog tucked under his arm, he said there was nobody in the house but Fala who was eating a scrap of meat on the car-pet next to the piano."

"That's easy to explain," I said. "Fala must have gotten it from the kitchen."

Maubi shook his head. "The kitchen was in a separate building away from the main house. One more t'ing. The reporters traveling with the president couldn't take one picture at Bulows Minde."

"Why not?"

"Their cameras went bust. But that afternoon at my granddaddy's place, when the president give him the plaque for the best looking homestead, they work just fine."

Maubi carefully took a framed photo off the wall of Hot to Trot and handed it to me like it was a holy relic. Seated in the back of an open car, with that famous grin illuminating his face, was President Roosevelt holding his little dog Fala. Clustered around the car were Maubi's granddaddy clutching the award the president had just presented to him, his grandmama Alveena, Maubi's father and his brothers and sisters. The picture was signed by President Franklin Delano Roosevelt with a paw print added for Fala.

"When President Roosevelt died in 1945, Alveena went up to Bulows Minde. No one was there, but she say she hear crying. She also say it could have been the wind in the tamarind trees playing tricks with her ears. But when Fala pass in 1952, Alveena went back to the terrace at Bulows Minde. There in the moonlight she know for true she hear piano music coming from the main house, and a little dog barking. Until she pass herself, every year Alveena go and leave a beef bone on the terrace for Fala."

Maubi rubbed his stiff leg. "The last time I work construction was at Bulows Minde. I was on the roof when I smell jasmine, and feel a hand at my back. When I come to on the ground, with my leg broke in three places, my face was wet and tingly like a little dog was licking it."

"Maubi, now you're pulling my leg," I said with a smile.

Maubi winked. "Then you tell me how we come to find beef bones in the garden at Bulows Minde. For true, Miss Kelly. I dug up those bones myself. They were buried next to pieces of green glass no bigger than peas."

Dr. Couch Saves a President:
A Doctor Franklin Couch and Frankie Story

 Nancy Pickard

What was your favorite Christmas, Grandpa?"

"The first one you were here on earth, Frankie. There was another one that sticks in my mind, as well, though. I remember that Christmas of 1945, and not only because the War had ended only a few months earlier."

"What war, Grandpa?"

"World War II, Frankie. The big one. The one that was supposed to be the war to end all wars."

"Why wasn't it, Grandpa?"

"Because some people," the retired veterinarian told his ten-year-old granddaughter, with a rueful smile, "apparently didn't get the message. You can lead a horse to water, as the old saying goes, but you can't make him drink. Or, what makes more sense in this instance, I suppose, is that you can drain the pond, but that won't keep a horse from getting thirsty."

"What does that mean? I don't get that, Grandpa."

"No, of course, you don't. You're much too smart to 'get that,' Frankie, and do you want to know why I say that about you?"

When she nodded eagerly, he assured her, "It's because sometimes I'm too clever to make a lick of sense. That's why. And you are smart enough to recognize that, which means you are very smart indeed. What I actually meant, and said so poorly, is that people will always be people, Frankie, and they'll argue and fuss 'til the end of time, most likely."

An expression of reminiscence crossed his eighty-year-old face. It was a look his grandchild happily recognized as the precursor to one of his stories that she loved so much. The nice thing about the stories her grandfather told her was that since he had been a veterinarian all of his working life there were always animals in them. He knew stories about cats, birds, horses, all kinds of creatures, and she loved that. In her Grandpa's stories, bad things sometimes happened to bad people—and even to good people—but nothing bad ever happened to an animal. Frankie loved that, too, and she trusted him never ever to break that habit. If her granddad was telling her a story, she knew it was safe to relax completely, because he would never tell her anything upsetting about an animal. Even if something bad *seemed* to happen to an animal in one of his stories, Frankie knew it would always turn out all right.

At the age of ten, she was already set on the course of her life: a vet, that's what she wanted more than anything in the world to be, just like Dr. Franklin Couch who was known as Dr. Frank throughout much of Independence, Missouri. She was named for him, of course; besides a name, they also shared the same color of light hazel eyes, and people told her he'd been skinny as a rail when he was her age, just like her. Now, of course, he was big and tall, though stooped, and comfortable to sit upon. Her father called Frankie's grandfather—his father-in-law—"imposing." People treated him with respect, as if he had earned the right to be known as somebody who had made important contributions to their community. Some people even seemed to be awed by him, partly because of his size, partly because of his serious demeanor. Dr. Frank tended only to relax around animals and small children. Frankie wasn't awed, and she wasn't quite sure what "imposing" meant, but if that's what her grandfather was, then she hoped that one day she'd be an imposing person, too.

Knowing all this, the little girl snuggled into his lap—her favorite spot in all the world for listening—and prepared to be entertained. Sure enough, the very next words out of his mouth were as magical to her as Once Upon a Time.

"There was one time, Frankie," he began, looking as if he were peering down a telescope backward into his life, "when I was so clever I actually saved the marriage of a president of the United States."

"No! Really, Grandpa?"

"Yes, really. Well, that's probably a bit of an exaggeration to say I saved it. Just a bit. It probably would have survived, no matter what I did. Actually, if you want to know the truth, their marriage probably wasn't even in big trouble, but I do believe that I helped a president get back into the good graces of his lady. His First Lady, you might say."

"There you go again," his granddaughter teased him.

"There I go again doing what?"

"Being clever, Grandpa!"

He laughed, and he wished for the millionth time that his wife were still alive to adore this perfect child, as he did. He cleared his throat and prepared to take her back to a snowy Christmas after the War.

"We'd had far too much to eat at Christmas dinner that day, Frankie. Your grandmother's homemade yeast rolls! Oh, my, I could eat a dozen of them with butter and jam. And her pumpkin pie with whipped cream! I wish you could remember how much you loved pumpkin pie the first time you ate it when you were only one year old. Well. That night, I felt that I needed to walk off all that rich food, no matter how bad the weather was. And, besides, I was a little worried about something that night. I thought a brisk walk, some fresh air, and a little time to myself might help me figure out what to do about it."

"What were you worried about, Grandpa?"

"I'll get to that, my dear. But first, let me set the scene for you. As I said, it was Christmas Day. December 25, 1945. The weather was so bad over most of the country that every commercial airplane was grounded that day. Can you imagine? All the planes grounded for Christmas? Thousands of travelers were stuck in airports all across the country, when all they wanted to do was to get home to their families to eat turkey and stuffing and mashed potatoes and gravy."

Frankie looked a bit doubtful at this news. "They had airplanes back then, Grandpa?"

Dr. Frank suppressed the smile that wanted to twinkle in his eyes. "Yes, we did, as unlikely as that must sound to you, my dear."

"But not computers."

"Oh, goodness no, in those days a laptop was what you're sitting on."

She looked puzzled only for an instant before she giggled.

"I put on an extra pair of socks," her grandpa continued, "and my high galoshes, and a muffler to go around my neck, and I buttoned up my over-coat and put on gloves and a hat. Men wore hats in those days, Frankie, and not those flimsy backward baseball caps, either. Real hats made of fine brushed fabric, with jaunty creases and brims. There was nothing like it when you tipped your hat to a pretty lady, nothing like it at all." He sighed and smiled to himself, but didn't linger in the memory. "At any rate, I'll wager it was near ten degrees that night, cold as a rattlesnake's nose, and the snow was easily up to my shins when I set out.

"The sidewalks of Independence had been shoveled earlier, but the streets were almost impassable for cars.

"It was nearly light as day, Frankie, because of the snow."

"I love that," she sighed. "The way it stays light at night when it snows."

"Yes, that's quite wonderful, I agree. And of course, the moon and the streetlights helped, as well. So I had no trouble making my solitary way down the sidewalks. I set out to the east, not really thinking of where I was going. I was lost in my own thoughts. So I was taken quite by surprise a few blocks later when I heard the sound of footsteps crunching in the snow, and not just one set, either, but several, Frankie. I looked up and was quite startled to see a small group of men approaching me."

Her eyes grew big. "Were they robbers? Were you scared?"

"I was a little nervous, Frankie, because they all wore black overcoats and black gloves and hats and they looked a bit like gangsters coming toward me in the snow. And what was especially odd was that they were spread all across the street. There were two on the sidewalk across from where I was walking. There was one, walking behind the others, in the very middle of the snowy street. I seem to recall two others, but they all seemed to revolve around one man who walked alone, just as I was doing."

"Was he the main gangster, Grandpa?"

"That crossed my mind, Frankie, until I looked at the street sign and saw where I was. This won't mean anything to you, but I found that I had turned the corner onto North Delaware Street. This was a neighborhood of fine old homes, Frankie. And in the middle of North Delaware there was one big white house that was quite famous, not just in Independence, but all around the world. It was the owner of that house who was walking toward me at that instant."

"Who, Grandpa, who was it?"

"First, I'll tell you who his companions were, and then I think you'll guess who he was. The other men were Secret Service agents, Frankie. Do you know what the Secret Service is, and whom they are sworn to protect with their lives?"

"The president of the United States!"

"Brilliant child. Yes, that's exactly right. I don't suppose you'd know who this president I'm speaking of was, do you?"

She shook her head, looking apologetic.

"That's all right, that won't come in school for a while."

"Which one was it, Grandpa?"

"It was Harry S (ed. note: S has no period because it was not short for a real name. The only middle name Truman was given was an "S".) Truman, the Man From Independence, the twenty-third president of the United States."

"Wowie zowie."

"Quite so. I couldn't have put it better myself."

She giggled at the idea of hearing her grandfather say wowie zowie.

"Did they have guns, Grandpa?"

"I'm sure they did, Frankie. Can't say that I saw any of them, luckily. They spotted me coming down the street long before I became aware of them. The moment I looked up, one of them called out, "Hold up. Stop right there!""

The child in his lap shivered. "That's scary."

"It was a bit, I have to agree, Frankie. I was so surprised. And, as you wisely pointed out, they did look rather like a gang of men. Lucky for me, about the time they might have pulled their guns, the president himself recognized me."

"Gosh, Grandpa."

"That's what I thought. Gosh! Saved by the president."

"What did he say to you?"

"Well, first he said, " 'Is that Dr. Couch? Is that you, Dr. Couch? What are you doing out walking so late? I thought I was the only man in Missouri who was crazy enough to go for a walk in this weather.' ""

"What did you say?"

"I said, 'Yes, Mr. President, I am as crazy as you are.'"

His granddaughter looked shocked, but she giggled. "You said that to a president of the United States?"

"Well, I knew he had a sense of humor."

"How did you know him?"

"Everybody knew him. He knew me because I was active in local politics in those days, and we were both Democrats."

"Did he take his pets to see you?"

"President Truman wasn't much of an animal person, Frankie. I'm sorry to have to say that about any man, but it's the truth. Fortunately, he had other qualities to recommend him. His daughter Margaret had an Irish Setter named Mike who lived for a while in the White House, I believe, but by and large the Trumans weren't overrun with pets. Not like you and me, Frankie."

"We're overrun," she agreed happily, thinking of her two miniature long-haired dachshunds, her pair of parakeets, and her cat.

"Completely furred and feathered," her grandfather concurred with great contentment. "Well, the president and his men came walking on toward me, Frankie, and those Secret Service fellows looked at me pretty darned suspiciously. I stood right where I was, ankle deep in fresh snow, with my hands out in the open so they could see I wasn't holding any weapons.

"'Good evening, Mr. President,' I said, as he got close enough for me to see his face under his hat. He was wearing eyeglasses, those metal framed ones you always see in pictures of him. Mr. Truman wasn't a handsome man, Frankie, nor was he of a large stature. In fact, he was quite a bit shorter than I, but he gave you the impression of meeting you eye to eye no matter how tall you were. He carried himself with a quiet confidence that the whole nation found reassuring in those days of recovery from the war.

"On this particular night, I was definitely reassured when he told his men, 'Relax. This young man is Franklin Couch. He's one of the best damned veterinarians in Missouri, fellas. The only thing he's ever shot is rabies vaccine into a dog's behind.' The president was a plainspoken man, Frankie, even a bit coarse at times. He said what he thought, but he usually thought before he said it, and you can't ask for much more than that, can you?"

"I don't know," she replied, thoughtfully.

Her grandfather laughed with delight. "He'd have liked you, Frankie. You're honest, just like him. That night, he asked me right out why was I out walking in the snow. Ate too much, I told him. Got a few things on my mind. 'Like what?' he wanted to know, and I didn't mind him asking, because he seemed genuinely interested in whatever might be concerning me. It was cold standing there in the snow under a streetlamp with the president, but I felt privileged to do it. I told him straight out that I was puzzled over some thefts at my home."

" 'A thief in this neighborhood?' he asked me, looking stern.

" 'I believe so,' I had to tell him.

" 'What has he taken from you?'

" 'Dog food, Mr. President.'

" 'Dog food!'

" 'I know it sounds a small thing, sir, but it worries me a great deal for some reason, probably more than it should. I'm embarrassed even to say this to you, what with all the great worries you have on your shoulders at this time, and I don't know why this has me so upset. You see, I keep a couple of large tins of manufactured dog food—pellets—stored on our back porch where we can go to dip bowls of them for our own dogs for dinner. Last night, I finally noticed that the quantity has decreased much faster than can be accounted for by the amount I feed our animals.'

" 'Somebody's sneaking onto your porch and pilfering dog food?'

" 'It appears so, Mr. President.'

" 'Lay a trap,' he advised me, quick as anything, as if he were commanding a platoon. 'Position yourself out of sight so you can see how he comes up to do it.'

" 'This is a pretty great thing for me,' I told him then, 'to get to take tactical advice from the man who just won the war.'

" 'The war I need to win is on my own home front.'

" 'Pardon me, Mr. President?'

"He looked around as if he didn't want his Secret Service men to hear. Tactfully, they had turned their backs, but I figured they heard everything he said and he must have known that, too. I could see in the light cast up by the snow that the president looked aggravated and tired. 'It seems I can win a world war, Dr. Couch. I can deal with ol' Joe Stalin, I can handle those damned Republicans on the Hill, I can even fire a general if I have to, but I can't keep my own wife happy. You married, Doctor?'

" 'Yes, sir.'

" 'She ever tell you she wishes you did any line of work but what you do?'

" 'Well, my wife has never actually said that, Mr. President, and I think she actually loves my patients almost more than I do, but once or twice when it's taken me out of the house in the middle of the night, I'm pretty sure she wished I was a plumber.'

" 'That would take you out in the middle of the night, too.'

" 'You're right about that, Mr. President. I'll remind her.'

" 'Mrs. Truman is mad as hell at me for becoming president.'

" 'I'm sorry to hear that, sir.'

" 'Not half as sorry as I am, young man. I don't know what to do about it. She was happy being a senator's wife, but she got mad as a wet hen when I said I'd run for vice president. She said to me, why would you want to do that? Because my president asked me to, I told her. Well, you don't have to say yes, was her answer to that. And then when President Roosevelt up and died, and that made me president, why I thought she'd leave me right then and there and hightail it right back here to live with her mother. She's mad at me right now because the Washington, D.C., press corps is mad at her. Bess is a very private person, you see. She doesn't believe that other people have the right to turn her into something she isn't, and I'm all for that. I love her just the way she is and I always will. But she doesn't love my job just the way it is, and I don't think she ever will. I came home from running the world today, only to find that my own wife thinks I'm about as welcome as mud on her shoe.'

"Frankie, it was clear to me that the president of the United States was just a husband, too, and he was about to explode with frustration. Everybody knew that Bess Truman was a reluctant First Lady. She never wanted that job and she wasn't very good at it, at least not yet as far as anybody could see. I could understand how that might cause friction on the home front. But I'll confess I felt pretty flabbergasted to be standing out there in the snow on Christmas Night hearing the president confess his marital woes to me."

"What did you say to him, Grandpa?"

"Nothing, Frankie. Not that night, anyway. I just said, 'That's a rough one, Mr. President. I hope it works out all right for both of you.' He said, 'This is just between us men, of course,' and I assured him that it was. I like to think that he knew I could keep secrets, Frankie, but the truth is there's no way he could have known that. I like to think he was just a good judge of character, but that's probably flattering myself too much. I think he trusted me because he thought, if you can't trust a veterinarian then who can you trust? And I think he also trusted me because I was a staunch Democrat. Harry Truman had a very high regard for diehard Democrats."

"What if you'd been a Publican?"

Her grandfather feigned an aghast look. "Why he'd have set those Secret Service men onto me, quick as a fox."

"Really, Grandpa?"

"No." He smiled. "But he might have walked on by."

"How did it save his marriage when you didn't say anything?"

"We're coming to that part, Frankie, but first I have to tell you how I didn't catch the thief that night."

"You didn't? Not even after the . . . tactical . . . advice?"

"Oh, I followed the advice, but I wasn't much of a soldier, I'm afraid. You wouldn't want to put me on guard duty, Frankie, not if you valued what you wanted me to save. I sat up by the window, all right, but I fell asleep in my chair. When I woke up and went out onto the porch I saw at once that the thief had been there again."

"Oh, no!"

"You'd have thought our dogs might have barked, but they slept through it, too."

"It must have been a very quiet thief."

"That was part of his secret, Frankie, you've hit the nail on half of its head, all right."

"What did you do then?"

"I got up and went to work and that night I took another walk."

"Was the president taking a walk, too?"

"Yes, he was, and I'll admit that I was hoping he would. I was concerned for him, about how things were going at home for him by then. And I kind of wanted to tell him that my thief had struck again, see if he had any other suggestions for me. I was embarrassed to tell him that I'd dozed off at my post, but it wasn't every day that a man got to seek military advice from a commander in chief, so I wasn't going to let a little thing like feeling mortified stand in my way."

"Good for you, Grandpa."

He paused, feeling touched by this accolade that she'd bestowed on him. As a prize for them both, he reached over into his candy bowl, plucked out a Hershey Kiss for himself and two for her. As they both unwrapped the silver foil and then companionably chewed the chocolate, he told her what had happened on that second night of his great conferral with a president.

" 'You catch that dog food thief, Dr. Couch?'

"That's the first thing the president said to me when he saw me on North Delaware again, Frankie. I had to tell him my sad story. Then he peppered me with a series of sharp questions, but I couldn't quite figure out what he was getting at. Your dogs didn't bark? He asked me that, and I said no. Do they usually if a stranger approaches your house? Why yes, sir, they surely do. They're normally good guard dogs, as well as family pets, I told him. Tell me exactly where you placed this tin of dog food, Dr. Couch. Right under a window, sir. How high is the bottom of the window? I measured it with my hand to show him, Frankie, and it was probably a little taller than you are. Where did you sit to wait? Just inside the dining room, I told him, with the window right in front of me. What kind of chair did you sit in? An easy chair, my mistake! When you sat in that chair, what could you see outside? I could see right out that window, sir. Could you see to the sides? No, not much. Could you see above it? No, sir, I couldn't. What about underneath it, could you see the tin of dog food? No, sir, it was below my line of sight.

" 'You need to have it *in* your line of sight,' he told me. 'If you were going to shoot this thief, you'd want to be able to see him even if he came crawling up onto your porch on his belly, wouldn't you?'

" 'Are you advising me to shoot him, sir?'

" 'No, I am not! Not for dog food. I am advising you to line up your target in your sights.'

("This was a former Army corporal speaking, Frankie, so I paid heed.)

"'Yes, sir, I'll do that, but how do soldiers keep from falling asleep?'

"President Truman smiled a bit when I asked him that, and said with mock severity, 'Think of your mission, soldier, just keep your mind on your mission.' I had not served in the war, Frankie, and I hoped he did not think less of me for that. My deferment was granted because I was the sole support of my parents as well as of my own little family, but I was sorry I could not join the other men of my generation to serve our country in that way."

"I'm glad you didn't go, Grandpa," the child told him in her honest fashion.

"Why's that?" he replied, knowing that he was asking the obvious.

"Because you might not be here now," she said, which surprised him. He had thought she would say, "Because I might not be here now." But the child rarely thought of herself first if there were other creatures—including human ones—to consider.

Her grandfather shifted a bit in the big easy chair, and she automatically adjusted to his movements. When he reached for more Kisses, she held out her hands together, palms up, and waited for the treats to drop into them.

"Since the president was kind enough to enquire about my small problems, Frankie, I got up my nerve to ask about his. How's your mission going, sir, I said. And he rolled his eyes and said, 'I'm not advancing, Dr. Couch. In fact, I've been pushed back behind the lines.'

"I commiserated with him, not knowing what else to say, and soon we went our separate ways. It was snowing again and the wind picked up. I remember looking back at him once and noticing two things: one that he had a gloved hand on his hat to hold it on his head, and two, that the last Secret Service man was looking back at me. I nodded at him and hurried on, anxious to prove that I wasn't up to mischief behind their backs."

"Did you stay awake that night, Grandpa?"

"I did. The president had inspired me. I kept my mind on my mission."

"Did you catch the dog food thief?" she asked, excitedly.

"I'll tell you about that," he promised. "But let's skip on ahead to the very next night. I guess I don't have to set the scene for you again?"

"Snow. Wind. Cold. Night. Here comes the president."

The old man laughed. "Well done! Yes, there I was walking along again and here came the president again.

"'Good evening, Dr. Couch, and who have we here?' he said.

"'Good evening, Mr. President. This boy I have with me is Edward Johnson, Jr., who is eight years old. Eddie, say hello to the president of the United States.'"

"You had a boy with you, Grandpa?"

"I did, indeed, Frankie. I'd brought him with me especially to meet the president.

"'Hello,' the child mumbled, looking not particularly frightened at all.

"'How do you do, Eddie,' Mr. Truman said politely. 'And what else have we here?'

"'A puppy,' young Eddie told him."

("A puppy?" Frankie squealed.)

"'What kind of a puppy, Eddie?'

"'Mutt puppy.'

"'I'll bet that puppy eats a lot,' the president remarked, with a knowing glance at me.

"'He don't eat all that much,' Eddie explained. 'But him *and* his brothers and sisters and mother, they eat more than you could believe.'

"The president looked at me again, Frankie. As tactfully as I could, I explained the situation to him. 'Eddie's father was in the war, sir.' I gave the president of the United States a look to tell him that Mr. Johnson had not come home, and he was never coming home to support his family, much less a mother dog and eight small puppies, all of whom needed to be fed. 'Eddie's father is a hero.'

"'I'll say he is,' the president said in a husky voice. 'I'll say.'

"'Eddie is the oldest of three children, sir. He considers that he is now the man of the house, but unfortunately he is not old enough to quit school and get a job to support them all.'

"'Certainly not,' the president said with a kind but firm look aimed right at the boy. 'It is essential to the national interest that this young man remain in school to get his education. His father would want that. I want that. Jobs can come later. Do you understand that, Eddie?'

"'Yeah—'

"Yes, sir, Mr. President,' I prompted him.

"'Yes, sir, Mr. President, but—'

"'I understand,' the president said quickly, forestalling the need for the child to have to say the painful truth: families have to eat, buy clothes, families need money. 'And because I do understand, I am going to have one of these tall men write down your mother's name and phone number and your address and I am going to have somebody visit your mother tomorrow to work things out.'

"'What things—Mr. President, sir?'

"'Everything, Eddie. So you've needed dog food for your puppies, is that it?'

"'Yes, sir, Mr. President.'

"'And I'll bet that you come to just about here—' President Truman made a gesture with his hands to show the difference between two heights,'—in relation to the bottom of a certain window sill, so you would be impossible to see if a man didn't have you in his line of sight. And I'll also wager that you are friends with Dr. Couch's dogs, so they would not bark if there were to see you coming to—visit. Have I got it right so far?'

"'Yes, Sir, Mr. President,' the boy agreed. 'You got that right.'

"'But you're not going to have to do that anymore, are you, Eddie?'

"'Don't know, sir. Depends, I guess.'

"'It depends on what, lad?'

"'Depends on everything, I guess.'

"The president looked at me again. 'Smart lad. He'll go far, I predict. But Eddie, I want you to go far in the right direction, are we clear about that?'

"Finally intimidated just a bit, Eddie Johnson Jr. nodded: 'Yes, sir!'

"'Eddie,' I said then, 'why don't you walk over there and give that man your mother's name and telephone number and your address, if you can. Give me the puppy to hold, will you?'

"I had already talked to Eddie about this, without telling him the precise nature of the situation between Mr. and Mrs. Truman, so there was no problem there. I had even made sure to bring the cutest, cuddliest of the litter with us. When the child walked away, I said, feeling as hesitant as I ever had before or ever would afterwards, 'Sir, I think you ought to take this puppy.'

"Well, he backed off as if I'd kicked him, Frankie.

"'Not permanently,' I hastened to say. 'Just for a little while. I got to thinking, Mr. President, how all women love kitties and puppies. A cute little puppy will always melt a woman's heart, it seems to me. Maybe if you borrowed this little guy, it might get you back into someone's good graces.'

"'Dr. Couch, that's genius.' His eyes twinkled behind their glasses. "I think you may have missed your calling. If you ever get tired of being a vet, I hope you'll consider military strategy. You'll go far, too, I predict, no matter what you do in life.' But when I tried to hand him the dog, he put up his gloved hands to ward me off. 'No, no, not me. Give it to one of these fellas.'

"'Sir, I'm not sure that's going to work. I think you may have to get involved with this yourself.'

"'I know, but not until we get back to the house.'

"I grinned at the president of the United States. He wasn't an animal lover, but he sure wasn't anybody's fool, either. One of the Secret Service men took the dog from me, and they all turned to hurry back to the big white house before the dog could decide to have an accident in their arms. Even Secret Service men have a limit to their dignity, I expect."

Cuddled on his lap like a puppy, herself, Frankie sighed with pleasure.

"Did Mrs. Truman forgive him? Was she nice to him after that?"

"Well, that's what I sure wanted to know, Frankie, so I took a walk at the same time the next night to see if I could find out. Sure enough, at the exact same time as before, here came the president and the president's men. One of them was carrying a basket and when they got near enough to hand it over to me, I peeked under the blanket and saw the puppy in it.

"I looked at the president, as if to ask, So?

"'A disaster!' he exclaimed, and my heart sank."

"A disaster?" Frankie cried, sitting up straight. "But I thought you saved their marriage!"

Her grandfather shook his head, feigning a woebegone look.

"An unmitigated disaster, the president told me in no uncertain terms. 'Dr. Couch,' he said, 'I want you to know that not every woman loves kitties and puppies. I have learned the hard way that some women consider them to be as big a mess and bother as I do. This, it turns out, is one more thing I have in common with my lovely wife.)

"'Oh, Mr. President, I'm so sorry.'

"'Don't be sorry! My wife didn't want anything to do with the puppy, but our daughter was beside herself with joy, Doctor. Margaret adores puppies. The poor child has been enduring a Christmas with two grumpy parents and your puppy brought a night and a morning of sheer happiness to her.'

"'I'm glad of that, at least.'

"'But that's not all, Dr. Couch. There is nothing that pleases myself or The Boss more than making our daughter happy. When Bess saw Margaret smiling, heard her laughing, saw her playing on the floor with the puppy, she couldn't help but smile over at me.'

"The president shook his head, and sighed.

"'Doctor, I'm a realistic man. That's how I ended a war, by being realistic. I don't expect to see the sun on a day when the clouds are thick, but when I see a glimmer of sunshine, it gives me hope that the sun will shine again someday soon. You've given me a ray of sunshine, Doctor. I think there's hope.' The president of the United States peeled the glove off his right hand and stuck it out for me to shake. I returned the gesture and there we stood, a young vet and the most powerful man in the world, under a streetlight, in the snow on North Delaware Street. He thanked me, Frankie. I thanked him, too, and told him that a nice woman had already been to visit Eddie's mother to see what the government and private sources might be able to do to help. I'd taken over a supply of dog food and I was helping them find good homes for their pups, but I didn't see any reason to mention that to him."

"Then what happened, Grandpa?"

"Then he went on his way and I on mine and I never saw him again. Not in person, anyway. I saw him lots of time in the newspapers and such. And you know what I learned later, Frankie, from a book his daughter wrote?"

"No, Grandpa, what?"

"In her book, Margaret Truman said that after her father went back to Washington, D.C., that Christmas, he wrote Bess Truman the most important letter of their marriage. He told her how her support meant more to him than that of anybody else in all the world and that he just couldn't do his job as well without that support. She must have taken it to heart, Frankie, because I never heard a hint of problems after that."

"And the puppy started it?"

"I like to think the puppy was the tiny ray of sunshine that gave him the heart to go back and write that letter to his beloved wife. He knew she loved him. He just needed to see a hint of that in order to appeal to her best nature, too."

"Grandpa, you saved the day."

"Where ever did you hear that old saying, Frankie?"

"Mom lets me watch Superman reruns on Nick at Nite."

This child saved his days, Franklin Couch thought as he reached for the last Kisses in the bowl to give to her. The old vet had admired Harry Truman for being able to shower attention and affection on his wife and daughter even while running the free world. Franklin Couch deeply regretted that he had not, himself, mastered that knack when his own two daughters were growing up. It was not a mistake he was repeating with his granddaughter.

"Frankie," he said, "how much time have we got?"

"Forever, Grandpa."

"How I wish that were true. But until forever comes, have I ever told you the story of the snake that ate the Easter egg?"

Sax and the Single Cat

Carole Nelson Douglas

The day I get The Call, I am lounging on Miss Temple Barr's patio at the Circle Ritz condominiums in Las Vegas, trying to soak up what little January sunshine deigns to shed some pallid photosynthesis on my roommate's potted oleanders.

Next thing I know, some strange Tom in a marmalade-striped T-shirt is over the marble-faced wall and in my own face.

It is not hard to catch Midnight Louie napping these days, but I am on my feet and bristling the hair on my muscular nineteen-pound-plus frame before you can say "Muhammad Ali." My butterfly-dancing days may be on hold, but I still carry a full set of bee-stingers on every extremity.

Calm down, the intruder advises in a throaty tone I do not like. He is only a messenger, he tells me next; Ingram wants to see me.

This I take exception to. Ingram is one of my local sources, and usually the sock is on the other foot: I want to see Ingram. When I do, I trot up to the Thrill 'n' Quill bookstore on Charleston to accomplish this dubious pleasure in person.

I look over my yellow-coated visitor and ask, "Since when has Ingram used Western Union?"

Since, says the dude with a snarl, he has a message for me from Kitty Kong. The intruder then leaps back from whence he came—Gehenna, I hope, but the city pound will do—and is as gone as a catnip dream.

A shiver plays arpeggios on my spine, which does nothing to restore my ruffled body hair.

This Kitty Kong is nobody to mess with, having an ancestry that predates saber-toothed tigers, who are *really* nothing to mess with. They would make Siegfried and Roy's menagerie at the Mirage Hotel look like animated pow-der-room rugs.

Though the designated titleholder changes, there is always a Kitty Kong. Long ago and far away, in Europe in pre–New World days, this character was known as the King of Cats, but modern times have caught up even with such a venerable institution. Nowadays Kitty Kong can as easily be a She as a He, or even an It. Nobody knows who or what, but the word gets out.

Supposedly, a Kitty Kong rules on every continent, the Seven-plus Seas being the only deterrent to rapid communication. Even today, dudes and dolls of my ilk hate to get their feet wet. If the aforementioned saber-tooths had been as particular, they would have avoided a lot of tar pits, but these awesome types are legend and long gone. Only Midnight Louie remains to do the really tough jobs, and at least I resemble an escapee from a tar pit.

I follow my late visitor over the edge to the street two stories below and am soon padding the cold Las Vegas pavement. Nobody much notices me—except the occasional cooing female, whom I nimbly evade—which is the way I like it.

Ingram you cannot miss. He is usually to be found snoozing amongst the murder and mayhem displayed in the window of the Thrill 'n' Quill. Today is different. He is waiting on the stoop.

"You are late, Louie," he sniffs.

Such criticism coming from someone who never has to go anywhere but the vet's does not sit well. I give the rabies tags on his collar a warning tap, then ask for the straight poop.

"And vulgar," he comments, but out it comes. A problem of national significance to catkind has developed and Kitty Kong wants me in Washington to help.

No wonder Ingram is snottier than usual; he is jealous. But his long, languorous days give him plenty of time to keep up with current events.

I am not a political animal by nature, but even I have noticed that the new Democratic administration in Washington means the White House will be blessed with the first dude of my ilk in a long, long time, one Socks (somehow that name always makes my nose wrinkle like it had been stuffed in a dirty laundry basket). However, I am not so socially apathetic as to avoid a thrill of satisfaction that one of Our Own is back in power after a long period when the position of presidential pet had gone to the dogs.

This First Feline, as the press has so nauseatingly tagged the poor dude, is not the first of his kind to pussyfoot around the national premises. I recall a poly-toed type named Slippers was FDR's house cat and the White House's most recent First Adolescent, Amy Carter, had a Siamese named Misty Malarky Ying Yang. Come to think of it, Socks is not such a bad moniker at that.

Anyway, Ingram says the Inauguration is only two days away and a revolting development has occurred: The president's cat is missing; slipped out of the First Lady's Oldsmobile near the White House that very morning. We cannot have our national icon (Ingram uses phrases like that) going AWOL (he does not use expressions like that, but I do) at so elevated an occasion. The mission, should I choose to accept it (and there is nil choice when Kitty Kong calls): find this Socks character and get him back on the White House lawn doing his do-do where he is supposed to do it.

The reason Midnight Louie is regarded as a one-dude detection service is some modest fame I have in the missing persons department. A while back I hit the papers for finding a dead body at the American Booksellers convention, but I also solved the kidnapping of a couple of corporate kitties named Baker and Taylor. Things like that get back to Kitty Kong.

You would be surprised to know how fast cats like us can communicate. Fax machines may be zippy, but MCI (Multiple Cat Intelligence) can cross the country in a flash through a secret network of telecats who happen to look innocent and wear a lot of fur. These telecats are rare, but you can bet that they are well looked out for. I have never met one myself, but then I have never met a First Cat, either, and it looks like I will be doing that shortly.

After I leave Ingram, I ponder how to get to Washington, D.C. I could walk (and hitch a few rides along the way), but that is a dangerous and time-consuming trek. I prefer the direct route when possible.

Do I know anyone invited to the shindig? Not likely. Miss Temple Barr and her associates are nice folk but neither high nor low enough to come to this particular party. I doubt any of the Fifty Faces of America hail from Las Vegas (though several million such faces pass through here every year). I would have had better odds with the other guy and his "Thousand Points of Light."

But que será, será, and by the time I look up my feet have done their duty and taken me just where I need to be: Earl E. Byrd's Reprise storefront, a haven for secondhand instruments of a musical nature and Earl E. himself.

If anyone from my neck of the wilderness is going to Washington, it will be Earl E., owing to his sideline. I scratch at the door until he opens it. Earl E. stocks a great supply of meaty tidbits, for good reason, and I am a regular.

Of course, when I visit Earl E., I have to put up with Nose E.

I do not quite know how to describe this individual, and I am seldom at a loss for words. Nose E. resembles the product of an ill-advised mating between a goat-hair rug and a permanent wave machine of the old school. Imagine a white angora dust mop with a hyperactive hamster inside and a rakish red bow over one long, floppy ear. Say it tips the scale at four pounds, is purportedly male and canine. There you have Nose E., one of the primo dope-and-bomb-sniffing types in Las Vegas, even the U.S. You figure it.

Earl E. has a secret, and lucrative, sideline in playing with bands at celebrity do's all over the country. The lucrative is that Nose E. goes along in some undercover cop's grip, ready to squeal on any activities of an illegal nature among the guests, including those so rude as to disrupt the doings with an incendiary device.

Dudes and dolls of my particular persuasion are barred from this cushy job for moral reasons. Our well-known weakness for a bit of nip now and then supposedly makes us unreliable.

Oh. Did I mention Earl E.'s instrument of choice? Tenor sax. Will Earl E. be at the Inauguration? As sure as it rains cats and dogs (that look like dogs) in Arkansas.

* * *

Commercial airliners are not my favorite form of travel, but with Earl

E., I and Nose E. get separate but equal cardboard boxes and a seat in first class. (Actually, my box is bigger than Nose E.'s, since I outweigh this dust-mop dude almost five-to-one.)

Getting here is not hard—after I gnaw on the heavy cream parchment of Earl E.'s invitation for a few minutes he gets the idea and says, "What is happenin', Louie? You want to go to D.C. today with Nose E. and me and boogie?"

I look as adorable as a guy of my age and weight can stomach, and wait.

"All right. I am paying for an extra seat anyway for the sax and Nose E. A formerly homeless black cat like you should have a chance to see history made."

See it? I make it. But that is my little secret.

As per the usual, there is little room at the inn in D.C., but Earl E. has connections due to his vocations of music and marijuana sniffing. My carrier converts into a litter box for a few days in a motel room not too far from the Capitol with a king-size bed I much approve of and promptly fall asleep on for the night, despite the company. I also plan to use most of my facilities outdoors, reconnoitering.

Naturally, Earl E. has no intention of letting me out unchaperoned, though he takes that miserable Nose E. everywhere. Imagine a Hostess coconut cupcake sitting on some dude's elbow and squeaking every now and then. But there is not a hotel maid alive who can see past her ankles fast enough to contain Midnight Louie when he is doing a cha-cha between the door and a service cart.

I am a bit hazy on dates when denied access to the Daily Doormat, but I discover later that we arrived on the day before the Inauguration.

Washington in January is snowless, but my horizon is an expanse of gray pavement and looming white monuments, so the effect is wintery despite a delicate dome of blue backdropping it all.

I stroll past the White House unobserved except by a pair of German shepherds, whose handlers curb them swiftly when they bay and lunge at me.

"It is just a cat," one cop says in a tone of disgust, but the dogs know better. Luckily, nobody has much listened to dogs since Lassie was a TV star.

Socks is not officially resident at the Big White until after the swearing in, so I do not expect to find any clue in the vicinity. What I do expect is to be found. When I am, it is a most unexpectedly pleasant experience.

I am near the Justice Building when I hear my name whispered from the shade of a Dumpster. I whirl to see a figure stalking out of the shadow—a slim Havana Brown of impeccable ancestry.

"You the out-of-town muscle?" she asks, eying me backwards and forwards with a dismaying amount of doubt.

"My best muscle is not visible," I tell her smugly.

"Oh?" Her supple rear extremity arches into an insulting question mark.

I sit down and stroke my whiskers into place. "In my head."

That stops her. She circles me, pausing to sniff my whiskers, a greeting that need not be intimate but often is. Then she sits in front of me and curls her tail around her sleek little brown toes, paired as tight as a set of chocolate suede pumps in Miss Temple Barr's closet.

"You know my name," I tell her. "What is yours?"

"You could not pronounce my full, formal name," she informs me with a superior sniff. "My human companions call me Cheetah Habañera for short."

Cheetah, huh? She does look fast, but a bit effete for the undercover game.

"You sure you are not a Havana Red?" I growl.

She shrugs prettily. "Please. My people fled Cuba more than thirty years ago with my grandmother twelve-times removed. I am a citizen, and more than that, my family has been in government work ever since. What have you done to serve your country lately?"

Disdain definitely glimmers in those round orbs the color of old gold.

"They also serve who stand and wait," I quip. An apt quote often stands a fellow in good stead with the opposite sex. Not now.

She eyes my midsection. "More like sit and eat. But you managed to get here quickly, and that is something. Do you know the background of the subject?"

"What has grammar got to do with it?"

"The subject," she says with a bigger sigh, "Socks, is a domestic short-hair, about two years old; nine to ten pounds, slender and supple build."

She eyes me again with less than enchantment. "He has yellow eyes; wears black with a white shirtfront, a black face-mask, and, of course, white socks."

"Yeah, yeah. I know the type. A Uni-Que."

"Uni-Que? I never heard of that breed."

"It is not one," I inform her brusquely, "just a common type. That is what I call them. Street name is 'magpie.' I know a hundred guys who look like that. If this Socks wants to lose himself in a crowd, he picked the right color scheme for the job. You, on the other hand—"

"Stick to business," she spits, ruffling her neck fur into a flattering, chocolate-brown frill.

I refrain from telling her that she looks beautiful when she is angry. The female of my species is a hard sell who requires convincing even when in the grip of raging hormonal imbalance, and I do mean moan. This one is as cold as the Washington Monument.

"Fixed?" I ask.

"Do you mean has he had a politically correct procedure? Of course," she answers, "is not everybody 'fixed' these days?"

"Not everybody," I say. "What is the dude's routine?"

"He is not a performing cat—"

"I mean where does he hang out, what jerks his harness?"

"Oh. Squirrels."

"Squirrels?"

"He is from Arkansas. They must have simpler sports there."

"Nothing wrong with a good squirrel chase," I say in the absent dude's defense, "though I myself prefer lizards."

Her nose wrinkles derisively. "We D.C. cats have more serious races on our minds than with squirrels and lizards. Do you know how vital to our cause it is that an intelligent, independent, dignified cat with integrity inhabit the White House, rather than a drooling, run-in-all-directions dog, for the first time in years? The four major animal protection organizations have named 1993 the Year of the Cat, and the year is off to a disastrous start if Socks does not take residence ASAP."

"Huh? What is ASAP, some political interest group?"

Her lush-lashed eyes shudder shut. "Short for 'As Soon As Possible.' Do

Las Vegans know nothing?"

"Only odds, and it looks like Washington, D.C., is odder than anything on the Las Vegas Strip, and that is going some. Okay. We got a late-adolescent ex-tom who is a little squirrely. Any skeletons in the closet?"

"Like what?"

"Insanity in the family?"

For the first time she is silent, and idly paws the concrete, all the better to exhibit a slim foreleg. I can not tell if she is merely scratching her dainty pads, or thinking.

"Family unknown," she confesses. "Could be a plant by a foreign government. Odd how neatly he became First Cat of Arkansas. The Clintons had lost their dog Zeke to an auto accident—"

I nod soberly. "It happens, even to cats."

"The First Offspring, Chelsea, saw two orphaned kittens outside the house where she took piano lessons and begged for the one with white socks. The president and his wife are allergic to cats, but okayed Chelsea taking the male."

"Now that is the most encouraging sign of presidential timber I have seen yet," I could not help noting. "Ask not what you can sacrifice for your country when your own president and spouse will suffer stuffy noses so their little girl can take in a homeless dude. Kind of makes your eyes water."

"Mine are bone dry," Cheetah answers with enough ice in her tone to frost her brown whiskers white.

"What about the female?" I ask next.

"What female?"

"You said 'the male.' There were two orphans. Ergo, the other must be female."

She blinks, impressed by my faultless logic and investigative instincts, no doubt. Then she sighs.

"Taken in too, by a friend of the piano teacher who read about Socks and also had lost a pet dog. A Republican lady." She sniffs, whether at the political or former pet leanings of the other kit's adoptive family, I can not tell.

"Another Uni-Que?" I ask.

"No." Cheetah Habañera is proving oddly reluctant to reveal Socks's family connections. I soon discover why. "Jet black. All over. Now called "Midnight."

All right! Methinks a small detour to Arkansas on the way home might become necessary. I am not politically prejudiced. Republican cats are still superior to Democratic dogs. Midnight, huh. Nice name. At least Little Miss Midnight is not missing.

"She is also fixed?" I inquire.

"Who knows? Or cares? Listen, Mr. Midnight, better keep your nose to business. Without Socks found by tomorrow, your name will be Muddnight Louie. I do not know why Kitty Kong wanted out-of-town help anyway."

"To catch a thief, send a thief. To find a disoriented, disaffected out-of-towner—"

"Right. If you get a lead on Socks, you can find me here."

She sidles back into the Dumpster shadow like she was born there, and I start looking around Washington. My plan is serendipitous, which is to say, nonexistent.

I pace the terrain, sniff the chill winter air and generally observe how this place would strike a fellow from the country's heartland. Like a monumental chip off the big cold white berg on an iceman's truck.

Miles of hard pavement and towering buildings as white and bland as the grave markers in the National Cemetery would not seem welcoming to a junior good ole boy squirrel-chaser from Little Rock.

One other thing is clear. Not many cats hang out in these sterile public corridors. Even a down-home Uni-Que would stick out like a sore throat.

Naturally, I do not expect to stumble over the absent Socks on my first tour of the place, so I amble over to the Arkansas Ball Hotel for some forced-air heat and human company.

The place is a mess of activity, a snarl of hotel minions and party organizers in both senses of the word, a veritable snake pit of electrical cables and audio-visual equipment. Even the Secret Service wouldn't notice a stray cat in this mayhem and I make sure I am not noticeable when I want to be.

Earl E. is jamming on stage with the other boys in the band. (How come there are never girls? Even we cats make our night music coed.) He is rehearsing for the big Arkansas Ball tonight, where you can bet Clinton Inc. will be even if Socks is missing.

Nose E., wearing a Scotch-plaid vest to protect him from the winter chill, is lying like a discarded powder puff near Earl E.'s open burgundy-velvet-lined instrument case, eyes the usual coal-black glint behind the haystack hairdo, and black nose pillowed on furry toes. I presume the thing has toes.

I have been out pounding pavement all morning while this fluffpuff has been supine posing for a Johnny Walker Red ad.

Nose E. gives an obligatory growl of greeting, then admits that he has nothing to do. It seems that Earl E. and his buddies are too busy jiving and massaging their glittering brass saxes onstage to pay Nose E. any mind. Or is that saxi?

That is the trouble with a prima donna dog, whatever the gender: they get addicted to being the center of attention. So would I if I were carried everywhere, wore bows on my ears and was called "Sweetie Pie" by celebrities who never would dream that I am really a cross between a body guard and a snitch. Me, I like being Mr. Anonymous and underestimated.

Nose E.'s litany of ills goes on. Nothing is doing until six o'clock or so, he says. He has met his handler of the evening, and it is not the usual scintillating doll in rhinestones, but a former football player who holds him like a dumbbell, with one hammy hand around his rib cage.

Besides, Nose E. notes morosely, so many federal security types decorate the building, and indeed the entire town—they even seal the manholes along the Inauguration parade route—that not even a speck of fairy dust could escape notice. Nose E., in short, is redundant. For such a spoiled squirt, that is indeed hard to take.

So sunk is Nose E. in his imagined troubles that he does not think to ask about my mission; besides, to a dude after cocaine and TNT, normal, ordinary canine pursuits, such as finding and harassing cats, is low priority.

This is fine, for my observations during my meander, in which I have seen Socks's puss peeking out from every newspaper-dispensing machine, has given me an idea—not that anybody outside the Clinton inner circle knows that Socks is missing.

What is obvious, if not the whereabouts of Socks, is that this dude's overnight fame has made him a hard slice of salami to hide, no matter how commonplace his appearance. Now I know where to look.

I wander toward the river. I am not much for rivers, but I avoid the public portions bordered by leafless trees and bare expanses of brown-green lawn, heading for the fringes where I know I can find a population that inhabits every city—the homeless.

Even the homeless are hard to find in D.C. right now. Panhandlers know better than to haunt the populated areas when a major network event is unfolding; besides, half of them are dressing and duding up like the rest of the Inauguration influx, to play Cinderella and Prince Charming-for-a-day at the Homeless Ball.

At last I find a motley group wearing their designer hand-me-downs from Salvatore Arme. In their battered trench coats and tattered sweaters and mufflers, they resemble a huddle of war correspondents.

I do not expect any revelations as to the whereabouts of the missing Socks from these folks, but where the homeless gather, so do their animal companions of choice: dogs. And no one on the city streets knows the scuttlebutt like a dog that associates with a transient person.

Sure enough, I spot a Hispanic man in a cap with numerous news clips safety-pinned to it, surrounded by a bark of dogs, doing same. I look for the unseated Millie of White House fame among them, but these dogs' only visible pedigree is by puree. They are as awkward a conjunction of mutts as I have ever seen, and are barking and milling and twining their leashes until they resemble one of those seven-headed monsters of antiquity, but they are at least talkative and really rev up when I stroll into view.

I sit down, making clear that I will not depart without information. The people present view me with alarm, but I am used to being considered unlucky and even dog bait. Besides, should the pack lose their leashes, I have already spied the tree I would climb like a berserk staple gun.

"Cat," these morons yap at me and each other, growing evermore excited. (I do not speak street dog, a debased and monosyllabic language, but I understand enough to get by.)

"Yeah," I growl back, "I suppose you are not used to seeing such fine specimens of felinity."

They claw turf as their whines go up a register. The poor dude in the cap now has his arms twisted straitjacket-style as he tries to control his entourage, all the while yelling "Scat!"—only he pronounces it "Escat!"

The other homeless watch in hopes of some action entertainment shortly.

"Black cat," the dogs carol in chorus after rubbing their joint brain cell together.

"Bingo." I yawn. "See any black and white cats lately?"

They go berserk, baying out cats of all colors that they have seen and pursued. Not one is a magpie.

After a few more seconds of abuse, I am convinced that the street dogs have not sniffed hide nor hair of Socks, luckily for him. Further, I also learn that the humans present are not as ignorant of Socks's newfound celebrity as I had hoped.

A woman with a face as cracked as last year's mud edges toward me, a bare hand stretched out in the chill. "Here, Kitty. Stay away from those dogs. Come on. If you walked through whitewash you'd even look like that there Socks. Here, Kitty," she croons in that seductive tone of entrapment used upon my ancestors for millennia, "I got some food."

I remain amazed that people who have nothing, not even the basic fur coat my kind take for granted, are so eager to take kindred wanderers under their wings.

These homeless individuals may be sad, or deficient in some social or mental way, but they share a certain shrewd survival instinct and camaraderie also found among the legion of homeless of the feline and canine kind. Of course we all need and want a home, but most are not destined for such bounty and are not above appealing to the guilt of the more fortunate in making our lot more palatable. At least the homeless of the human kind are not corralled into the experimental laboratories or the animal processing pounds that ultimately offer little more than the lethal injection or the gas chamber in the name of mercy.

So I look upon this sweet old doll with fond regret, but I am a free spirit on a mission, and too well-fed (if not well-bred) to take advantage of a kind face despite the temptation of a free meal. I scamper away, leaving the battlefield to the dogs, and trudge back downtown, much dispirited.

If even the homeless have seen enough discarded newspapers to know about Socks, it will prove harder than I thought to turn up the little runaway. Will Socks vanish into the legions of homeless felines from which he came? Will the country and the Clintons survive such a tragic turn of events? Will Midnight Louie strike out?

I picture Cheetah Habañera's piquant but triumphant face as I trot back to Hoopla Central. The sun is shining; the brisk air hovers pleasantly above freezing. For some reason mobs of people are thronging down Pennsylvania Avenue. I manage to thread my way through a berserk bunch performing calisthenics with lawn chairs. People do the strangest things.

Still distracted, I return to the hotel that will host the Clintons' triumphant Arkansas Ball. Everybody in this town has something to celebrate, except for Socks and me.

The stage area is temporarily deserted; even Nose E. is gone, and I shudder to find that I miss the little snitch's foolish face. Earl E.'s instrument case is still cracked open like a fresh clam. I curl up on the burgundy velvet lining—an excellent background for one of my midnight-black leanings—and lose myself in a catnap. Maybe something will come to me in a dream.

*　*　*

The next thing I know I am being shaken out of my cushy bed like cockroach out of a shoe.

Earl E. Byrd is leaning over me, his longish locks pomaded into Michael Jackson tendrils and his best diamond earring glittering in one ear. I take in the white shirtfront and the jazzy black leather bolo tie with the real live dead scorpion embedded in acrylic in the slide. Earl E. looks snazzy, but a little shook up.

"The case is for the instrument, dude," he thunders, brushing a few handsome black hairs from the soft velvet. "Behave yourself or you will be ejected from the ball. How did you get here, anyway?"

Of course I am not talking, and I can see by the way the lights, camera, action and musicians are revving up that Earl E. has no time to escort me elsewhere. He has other things on his mind as he lays his precious sax back in my bed. Does a sax feel? Does a sax need shut-eye? Is a sax on a mission to save the First Feline? Is there no justice?

228 of White House Pet Detectives

Nose E. comes up to sniff at me in sneering rectitude, and I know that the last question was exceedingly foolish. Before Nose E. can really rub it in, a humongous man in an structurally challenged tuxedo swoops up the little dust bunny and moves into a room that has now filled with women in glitz and glitter and men in my classy colors—black with a touch of white about the face.

Let the ball begin.

Earl E. and the boys swing out. Although Earl E. is essaying the licorice stick at the moment, several musicians bear saxophones that shine brassy gold in the spotlights and wail, I'll admit, like the Forlorn Feline Choir in the darkest, bluesiest, funkiest alley on the planet. Folks foxtrot. The hip . . . hop. I settle grumpily next to the sax case from which I was so rudely evicted. All is lost. On the morrow the nation will wake to the news that it has a new president and a former First Feline. Bast knows what Kitty Kong will do.

While I am drowsing morosely, I start when the case beside me jolts. A burp of excitement bubbles just offstage. Someone knocks into Earl E.'s sax. So what. A pair of anonymous hands rights the big, shiny loudmouth thing. I see enough black wing-tips to shoe a centipede cluster onto the stage from the wings. When the phalanx of footwear suddenly parts, the First Couple stands there like a King and Queen in a Disney animated feature—Bill and Hillary dancing.

No doubt this is a festive and triumphal scene, and the First Lady's hair is rolled into a snazzy Ginger Rogers do, and they got rhythm and all's right with the world and I could go out in the garden and eat worms. . . .

As my bleary eyes balefully regard the hated sax that has usurped my spot, I spy an odd thing. Inside the deep, dark mouth of the instrument something shines—not bright and gold—but whitish-silver.

A snake of suspicion stirs in my entrails until it stings my brain fully awake. Why is Earl E. not playing the sax, when he brought it especially for that purpose?

Even as I speculate, Earl E. slips offstage and heads toward me. I expect another ejection, but he ignores me and reaches for the sax, his eyes on the stage where the First Couple have stopped dancing. The president is edging over to the band and microphone. He's going to talk, that's what presidents do, only when they do it, it's an address. He's going to address the crowd . . . my big green eyes flash to the approaching Earl E. The president is going to talk, then Earl E. is going to give him the sax and the president is going to play it!

The president is going to play a doctored sax in front of millions of TV-watching citizens.

Even as Earl E. grabs the sax I leap up, all sixteen claws full out and sink them into his arm.

He jumps back and mouths an expression that luckily is drowned out by all the bebopping going on, but it rhymes with "rich" if that word had a male offspring.

I can tell I drew blood, because Earl E. drops his precious sax and it hits the case sideways and something falls out of the mouth like a stale wad of gum.

Earl E.'s eyes get wide and worried. He whirls back to the stage, runs over to appropriate a sax from a startled fellow player and hands it to the president with a flourish.

Everybody plays. Saxophones wail in concert. Everybody laughs and applauds. Something rustles behind me. The Meat Locker has returned Nose E. to the vicinity. The creature stiffens on its tiny fuzzy legs as its nose gives several wild twitches. Nose E. rushes toward the fallen sax, sits up and cocks an adorable paw as he tilts his inquisitive little noggin one way, then the other.

Earl E. is over in a flash. This nauseating behavior is Nose E.'s signal that he has smelled a rat. Being an undercover canine, he can resort to nothing obvious like barking. (Besides, he squeaks like a castrated seal.)

Then Earl E. upends the sax to shake out a windfall of plastic baggies containing a substance that much resembles desiccated catnip. I come closer for a look-see, but am rudely shoved aside.

"Good dog," Earl E. croons several sickening times.

What about *my* early warning system? Except for rubbing a hand on his forearm, he seems to have forgotten my pivotal role in exposing the perfidy. Probably puts it down to mysterious feline behavior.

Two of the wing-tips come to crouch beside Earl E., taking custody of the bags, the sax and the case. There goes beddy-bye.

"Marijuana. Whoever did this," one comments softly, "wanted to make sure that this time the president would inhale."

"Saxophones don't work that way."

"Does not matter," the other wing-tip says. "The idea was to embarrass the president. The dog yours?"

"Yeah," Earl E. says modestly.

"Sharp pup." The wing-tip pats Nose E. on the cherry red bow.

Sure, the dogs always get the credit.

So I sit there, overlooked and ignored and Sockless, as the party goes on. The president surrenders the sax and the stage and leaves for another Inaugural Ball. I cannot even get excited at this one when Carole King comes on to sing "You've Got a Friend." Name one.

The band plays on. I recognize a couple tunes, like the ever tasteful "Your Mama Don't Dance and Your Daddy Don't Rock and Roll," and the ever inspirational "Amazing Grace."

I'll say inspirational. I rise amid the post-Inaugural hubbub and make my silent retreat. Nobody notices.

Outside it is dark, but I have already reconnoitered the city and I know where I am going. There is only one place in town where a dude as over-publicized as Socks Clinton could hang out and be overlooked.

"I once was blind but now I see." I see like a cat in the dark, and I see my unimpeded way to a certain street on which stands a certain civic building. Around back is the obligatory Dumpster.

I wait.

Soon a curious pair of electric green eyes catch a stray beam of sodium iodide street light. The dude's white shirtfront and feet look pretty silly tinted mercurochrome-pink as he steps out into the sliver of light. He looks okay, for a Uni-Que.

"Why did you do it?" I ask.

"How did you find me?" he retorts instead of answering. Then I realize that the poor dude has answered me.

"I figured out that there was only one place you could hang out and beg tidbits without being recognized: The Society for the Blind. Midnight Louie always gets his dude. You have to go back."

"Where? Home? I live in Little Rock."

"Not any more. You are a citizen of the nation now."

"I didn't ask to be First Cat."

I search through my memory bank of cliches but only find 'Life is no bed of Rose's.' (I do not know who this Rose individual was, but apparently she knew how to take a snooze, and that I can endorse.) I decide to appeal to his emotions.

"It seems to me that your human companion, Miss Chelsea Clinton, faces the same dislocation," I point out. "I would hate to see my delightful roommate, Miss Temple Barr, confront a barrage of public curiosity and a new and demanding role in life without my stalwart presence at her side."

"You would move here?" Socks asks incredulously. "Where are you from?"

"Las Vegas."

"Oh," he nods, as if that explains a lot. "I bet you do not even chase squirrels. Did you know the White House squirrels may be . . . rabid," he adds morosely.

"No!" I respond in horror. There is nothing worse than tainted grub. Poor little guy . . . no wonder he split.

"And," Socks adds in the same spiritless monotone, "you have not had the press shooting pictures down your tonsils for weeks, or getting you high on nip so you'll spill your guts to the press and embarrass your family. Then they dug up some rumor that my father was a notorious tomcat—"

"Shocking! But so was my old man."

"You are not First Feline," he spat glumly. "There's that instant book about me by that name, and all those T-shirts, then menu items named after me in places where I would not even be allowed to lap water. Can you believe that a local hotel concocted a Knock Your Socks Off drink?"

"Sounds like incitement to riot to me. What is in it?"

"Frangelico, Grand Marnier, half-and-half and creme de cacao."

"Does not sound half bad."

"I do not even know what most of those ingredients are. Now if they had made it from Dairy Queen ice cream—"

"Forget Dairy Queens. You are on a faster track now."

"I guess. They dug up some love letters I scratched in the sand to a certain lady named Fleur before I was fixed; I'm only an adolescent, for

Morris's sake—I should be allowed some privacy."

"Sacrifice of privacy is a small price to pay considering what you can do for the country and your kind. We need a good role model in a prominent position. You owe it to your little doll and cats everywhere to stick in there for four years."

"Eight," Socks says, a combative gleam dawning in his yellow eyes.

I swallow a smile (my kind are not supposed to smile or laugh, and I like to keep up appearances) and trot out my more grandiose sentiments. I begin to see that what this dude needs is a campaign speech.

"Remember, Socks, you represent millions of homeless cats, crowded masses yearning to breath free of the pounds and the lethal streets. We are a transient kind in a world that little notes nor long remembers our welfare. You may not have chosen prominence, but now you can use it to do good. Some are born great," I add, preening, "others have greatness thrust upon them by circumstance. You are one of these . . . circumstantial dudes. Do you want to drive your little doll into such loneliness at your defection that the First Kid goes turncoat and gets a dog to replace you? Do you want to be known as the first First Feline in history to abdicate?"

"No-o-o."

I have him. I brush near, give him a big brotherly tap of the tail on his shoulder. "What is really troubling you, kid? What made you snap and take off just as you got into town?"

Socks sighed. "I have been offered a book contract."

"Hey! That is good. I dabble in that pursuit myself."

"The book is to be called 'Socks: The Untold Story.'"

I am nudging him down the alleyway and into the full glare of the streetlight. The bustle of inaugural traffic rumbles in the distance along with faint sounds of revelry. D.C. could be the Big Easy tonight.

"What is so bad about that?" I ask.

Sock stops. "There is nothing untold left to tell! The press has squeezed every bit of juice out of my own life. I have nothing to say."

"Is that all? Big-time celebrity authors do not let that stop them from penning shoo-in bestsellers. You just think you are not interesting. What you need, my lad, is what they call a 'ghost writer'—someone discreet and more experienced who can help you bring out the most interesting facets of your life."

"Squirrels?"

"No. We must create a feline 'Roots.' We can call it 'Claws.' What do you know about your mom and dad? All cats in this country are descended from the Great Mayflower Mama, of course, but I have heard on good authority that your forebears were mousers around Mount Vernon. Did not Martha Washington herself have a cat-door installed there for somebody's ancestors? Why not yours? Obviously, there is a long tradition of presidential association in your family . . . . speaking of which, how about your sister, Midnight—nice name—where in Little Rock did you say she hung out?"

By now I have the dude heavily investing in his new career as raconteur and idol of his race. We reach the White House in no time, and I push him in. He admits that he could use the litter box in the engineering room. Aside from a few distraught aides—and aides are used to being distraught—no one need know of Socks' little escapade.

I trot back to my hotel, anticipating informing that snippy Cheetah Habañera of my success, and contemplating the fifty-fifty book deal I have just cut with Socks. Somebody has got to look our for a naive young dude in this cruel world.

Even though it is late, I have to wait outside the motel room door for at least an hour before Earl E. and Nose E. arrive, both a bit tipsy: Earl E. high on jamming and celebrity, Nose E. on all that marijuana he sniffed out.

I am in like Flynn and ensconced on the king-size before either of them gets a chance at it. Earl E. phones home before he retires, with news of his big adventure, which is how I learn who planted the weed in the presidential saxophone.

"PUFF," Earl E. explains to a benighted buddy on the phone while Nose E., half zonked, tries to curl up near me. I cuff the little spotlight-stealer away. "They called to claim responsibility. Can you believe it, man? PUFF is a radical wing of the pro-smoking types. I do not know what it stands for—People United For Fumes? Whatever, they were ticked off when Clinton made such a big deal about not inhaling once long ago and far away! They think it is unAmerican and namby-pamby to smoke anything without inhaling. Weird. We have had a weird time in this burg, man. What a gig. I cannot wait to get back to someplace normal like Las Vegas."

Amen.

Contributors

While still in high school, **Edward D. Hoch** was tempted to enter a short story contest announced by *Ellery Queen's Mystery Magazine*. He thought of writing a mystery to be solved by the President of the United States, but never got around to submitting it. The following year the winner of the contest was announced: "The President of the United States, Detective," by H. F. Heard. That was when he decided to become a writer. Since 1955 he has published some 850 short stories, appearing in every issue of *Ellery Queen's Mystery Magazine* since 1973. Being born on Washington's birthday he was naturally drawn to a story about the Washingtons' presidential pet for this anthology, even though Martha's parrot was never a favorite with the president. Hoch and his wife, Patricia, reside in Rochester, NY, and though they have no pets of their own they do tend to the neighbors' Old English sheepdog, Daphnee, letting her out at noon when the neighbors are at work. Previously honored with Edgar and Anthony Awards for best short story, as well as a life achievement award from the Private Eye Writers of America, Hoch was honored in 2001 with the Grand Master Award from Mystery Writers of America and the Lifetime Achievement Award from the Bouchercon World Mystery Conference.

Although the murder victim in "Martha's Parrot" is fictitious, he is based on one of Hamilton's aides who did indeed make a killing by using prior knowledge of Hamilton's proposal to Congress.

Lillian Stewart Carl has published multiple short stories and multiple novels in multiple genres. More stories and novels are in the pipeline, but she's pretty much run out of genres. *Publishers Weekly* says of her latest book, *Shadows in Scarlet*, "Carl delivers yet another immensely readable tale. She has created an engaging cast and a very entertaining plot, spicing the mix with some interesting twists on the ghostly romantic suspense novel." She has been intrigued for years by Thomas Jefferson and his intelligent, inquiring mind, not to mention his facility with a quill pen. In Colonial Williamsburg she's had the pleasure of hearing Jefferson, played by expert interpreter Bill Barker, speak of his life and times. While she's never had a chance to ask him about his mockingbirds, which he began keeping in the 1770s, Lillian enjoys the ones who live in her own backyard—even when they're teasing the cat.

Bill Crider is the author of several mystery series, including one featuring Sheriff Dan Rhodes and another about Dr. Sally Good, who teaches at a small Texas community college. The first Sheriff Rhodes book won the Anthony Award in 1987. Crider is a long-time alligator fan, and he once published an article about books whose storylines dealt with alligators in the New York sewers. Crider has a house full of 'gator memorabilia, so he was delighted to discover that John Quincy Adams kept an alligator in a bathtub in the presidential mansion (which wasn't called the White House in Adams's time). Where the alligator came from and how long it remained in the bathtub, Crider has no idea.

Brendan DuBois is the award-winning author of short stories and novels. His short fiction has appeared in *Playboy, Ellery Queen's Mystery Magazine, Alfred Hitchcock's Mystery Magazine, Mary Higgins Clark Mystery Magazine*, and numerous anthologies. He has twice received the Shamus Award from the Private Eye Writers of America for his short fiction and has been nominated three times for an Edgar Allan Poe Award by the Mystery Writers of America.

He's also the author of the Lewis Cole mystery series—*Dead Sand, Black Tide, Shattered Shell* and the upcoming *Killer Waves*. His most recent novel, *Resurrection Day*, is a suspense thriller that looks at what might have happened had the Cuban Missile Crisis of 1962 erupted into a nuclear war between the United States and the Soviet Union. This book also recently received the Sidewise Award for best alternative history novel of 1999. Most of his works of fiction show his deep interest in political and military history throughout the world. Please visit his website, www.BrendanDuBois.com.

He lives in New Hampshire with his wife, Mona. When asked about animals in his life, Brendan writes, "Growing up in a rural part of New Hampshire, our household was full of creatures underfoot. From a dark black 'mutt dog' called Princess, to a yellow Labrador retriever called Eric, and a brother-and-sister Siamese cat pile of fun called Charlie and Samantha, there was never a quiet time at home, much to our joy and my mom's dismay. Now, with my wife, we share quarters with a black and white cat named Oreo, who bites my ankle while I'm working in the office to demand dinner, or who sometimes jumps on my desk to share my water glass by dipping his paw into it. On weekends, at a vacation hideaway, my wife and I have been adopted by the neighbors: two Golden Retrievers and an overactive and playful Springer Spaniel called Mulligan, who moves in with us and has been known to spend a vacation from his family at our home."

Jan Grape has won both an Anthony and a Macavity award and has also been nominated for the Edgar, Shamus, and Agatha awards. Many of her short stories have been reprinted, including in Japan, and in December 2002 Five Star Mysteries will publish a collection of her stories titled *Found Dead in Texas*. Jan's first full-length novel, *Austin City Blue* (Five Star Mysteries), came out in October, 2001, to rave notices. In 1999, Jan and husband, Elmer, sold Mysteries & More bookstore in Austin, Texas, after nine years to travel with their cats, Nick and Nora, and spend time with their three children and five grandchildren.

Why Tad Lincoln and Tabby? Jan Grape says:

> I chose Tad Lincoln and his cat, Tabby, for three good reasons. First and most importantly, we have two cats, Nick and Nora, who insist I write about cats. Their yowling voices are nerve-wracking when they don't get their way. (As I write this note, Nora is in my lap making sure I mention her influence.) Second, I like the time period, having written an earlier story

with First Lady Julia Dent Grant, and felt familiar with the 1860s. Finally, I liked the idea of writing about the first "First Cat." (Note: the goats Nanny & Nanko did not actually come to live with the Lincolns until after Willie's death in 1862, and were only used for purposes of this story.)

How do I know Tabby was the first "First Cat?" In doing research, I discovered The Presidential Pet Museum in Washington, D.C., at the website www.presidentialpetmuseum.com. The website lists all the presidents and all the known family pets to live in or near the White House. I then phoned the curator of the museum, Claire McLean. She raises dogs, a breed known as Bouvier des Flanders, and held the position of White House groomer to the Reagans' dog Lucky. Claire verified Tabby's position as First Cat.

In late October when I was in D.C. for Bouchercon 2001, I went to see Claire and the museum. It's small but quite nice, with mostly recent presidential pet photographs, pictures, books, etc., but there are plans to expand. Donations, sales, and grants are the museum's only support.

Jeffrey Marks was born in Georgetown, Ohio, the boyhood home of Ulysses S. Grant. Although he moved with his family at an early age, the family frequently told stories about Grant and the people of the small farming community. The Grant legends frequently centered around horses, one of Grant's great loves in life.

Marks began freelancing after college, and wrote a number of interview articles with mystery writers. After numerous author profiles, he chose to chronicle the short but full life of mystery writer Craig Rice.

That Edgar- and Agatha-nominated biography (*Who Was That Lady?*) encouraged him to write mystery fiction. *The Ambush of My Name*, featuring Ulysses S. Grant, is his first published mystery novel, although he has edited several mystery short story anthologies.

His work has won a number of awards including the Barnes and Noble Prize given in conjunction with the Green River Writers for best mystery short story, and he was nominated for a Maxwell short story award by the

Dog Writers of America. He writes from his home in Cincinnati, which he shares with his dog, Ellery.

Carolyn Wheat has won the Agatha, Anthony, Shamus, and Macavity awards for her short stories. It's no wonder that her single-author collection, *Tales Out of School*, was nominated for the Anthony award in 2001. She is a defelined cat lady who once had four cats in a one-bedroom Brooklyn apartment (actually, she sent three cats out to play and four came back). She's taken a bit of historic liberty with this story, since Lucy Hayes didn't receive her Siamese cat (the first to come to America) until after she'd left the White House. Pickle and Colonel Prior are real, as is the expensive dress and the Hiawatha boat.

Jeanne M. Dams is a full-time mystery writer who lives in South Bend, Indiana. A lifelong Hoosier, she is also a rabid Anglophile; hence her first series of books is set in the British Isles. Featuring an American expatriate widow named Dorothy Martin, these books have garnered critical and popular acclaim. The first, *The Body in the Transept*, won the Agatha Award for Best First Novel of 1995. Seven more titles have followed. In 1998, her attention turned to her hometown and its history, and she began the first book in a new historical series featuring South Bend and the famous Studebaker family. Hilda Johansson, an intrepid immigrant Swede, is a fictitious (though fact-based) housemaid for the Studebakers in their mansion, Tippecanoe Place; she somehow finds time for quite a bit of sleuthing along the way.

Dams hated history as a child in school, finding it a boring succession of dates and battles. When she began to research the Hilda series, however, she came to the realization that history is nothing but people, and what could be more endlessly fascinating than people? The second book in the series, *Red, White, and Blue Murder*, is set around the 1901 assassination of President McKinley, which is how Dams came by her interest in him. She has been interested in cats since the age of five when her first pet, Whiskers, came into her life. Hence the story about Blanche and her people.

The McKinleys really did keep a white Angora cat at the White House, as well as a parrot that whistled "Yankee Doodle." Their names have been invented for "Remember the *Maine?*", but Dams has no doubt that their relationship was as stated.

Janet Pack submits non-fiction to a local magazine and a newspaper, but her greatest joy is concocting science-fiction and fantasy stories. She has more than two dozen in print—the latest are "Fire and Rain" in *The Mutant Files* and "Praxis" in *A Constellation of Cats*. "Should've Listened to the Cat" in *Vengeance Fantastic* will be out soon, as will "Snake Charmer" in Jean Rabe's anthology *Carnival*, which will be on CD from Lone Wolf Publishing. She's in the process of editing her own anthology entitled *Fairy Tails* from DAW (about cats, of course!). When not writing, Janet works as manager's assistant at Shadowlawn Stoneware Pottery in Delavan, WI, reads, hikes, cooks, designs jewelry, travels, and investigates history, especially ancient Egyptian.

Janet lives in Williams Bay, Wisconsin, with her long-haired French Blue, Baron Figaro di Shannivere, and black cats Tabirika Onyx and Syrannis Moonstone. The cats enjoy watching wildlife such as crows, cranes, raccoons, deer, fox, woodchucks, ducks, Canadian geese, and a great horned owl from the windows as Janet writes.

Esther M. Friesner has had thirty novels and over one hundred shorter works published. Best known for her humorous fantasy and science fiction work, most recently for creating and editing the popular Chicks in Chainmail anthology series, she nonetheless won the Science Fiction Writers of America's Nebula Award twice for her more serious works. Back in a humorous vein, she wrote the novelization of the screenplay for *Men in Black 2*, which will appear in Summer 2002. Bears are one of her favorite animals—besides cats and hamsters—and she owns an extensive collection of them in all their (inanimate) forms. When told that Calvin Coolidge had a pet bear, she simply had to do a story about the critter. Silent Cal voiced no objections to just coming along for the ride.

P. N. "Pat" Elrod has written twenty novels, including three with actor Nigel Bennett, a number of short stories, and has edited two anthologies. She is best known for the ongoing Vampire Files series featuring her Sam

Spade with fangs, P.I. Jack Fleming. Currently she is branching out into mystery and fantasy/comedy genres.

Elrod always thought that Herbert Hoover got a bum deal being blamed for the Depression, when he time and again warned against the follies that led to it. This anthology struck her as a great opportunity to show the human side of his family. Though highly dedicated in their endeavors at public service, they were a most private clan. Mrs. Hoover was never one to speak to reporters. But Allan Hoover did relent and let his picture be taken once in a while. He was indeed a very handsome young man, and obviously pleased and proud of his distinctive pets. One wonders how he managed with them while away at Harvard!

Virgin Islands resident **Kate Grilley** is the 2001 Anthony award–winning author of *Death Dances to a Reggae Beat*, the first novel in the Kelly Ryan/St. Chris Caribbean mystery series. Other books in the series include *Death Rides an Ill Wind* and *Death Lurks in the Bush* (to be published by Berkley Prime Crime in fall, 2002). She won a 1998 Derringer award for her short story "Guavaberry Christmas" and a 2000 Macavity award for "Maubi and the Jumbies."

"I particularly wanted to write about President Franklin Delano Roosevelt and his little dog Fala, the most famous White House pet, because I'd mentioned FDR in *Death Lurks in the Bush*," she said. "President Roosevelt's trip to the Virgin Islands is remembered fondly by St. Croix residents—FDR's birthday was once a local holiday—and documented in local history books, Eleanor Roosevelt's *This I Remember* and in the collection of FDR's personal letters edited by Elliott Roosevelt and Joseph P. Lash. But it was Maubi who told me the real story of what happened on that July day when President Roosevelt came to visit St. Croix with his little dog Fala."

Nancy Pickard is an award-winning and prolific mystery writer with ten books in the Jenny Cain series, three books in the Eugenia Potter series, and two books in her new Marie Lightfoot suspense series, *The Whole Truth* and *Ring of Truth*.

A founding member and former president of Sisters in Crime, she has won two Anthonys, two Macavitys, two Agathas, and her work has also had three Edgar nominations (two for Best Novel, one for Best Short Story) She lives in Prairie Village, Kansas, with two miniature dachshunds, two cats, and a teenager.

"I've always loved animals and I've always loved mysteries," Nancy says, "so when I get a chance to combine the two, I jump at it. When I was a child, the Dr. Doolittle stories were magic to me. I'm still convinced I could talk to the animals if I would just move my mouth right. I keep trying. My dogs look interested, but I think it's my cats who are really listening.

"I wanted to write about Harry Truman because he's my 'neighborhood President.' Independence, Missouri, his home town, is just a few miles over the state line from where I live. I've toured his house and walked down North Delaware Street, and I've read a lot about his life, so it comes naturally to me to write about him."

A former journalist and the author of more than forty novels, **Carole Nelson Douglas** has been nominated for or won fifty writing awards. Although she has written best-selling fantasy novels and women's fiction, she currently writes two mystery series. The Irene Adler historical suspense novels follow the adventures of the only woman to outwit Sherlock Holmes. The newest titles in the critically acclaimed series, including a *New York Times* Notable Book of the Year citation, are *Chapel Noir* and *Castle Rouge*. Douglas trades deerstalker for cat ears to write the Midnight Louie, PI mysteries, which feature the intermittent voice of a black-cat sleuth as well as four human crime solvers, both amateur and professional. *Cat in a Midnight Choir* and *Cat in a Neon Nightmare* are Louie's latest cases.

Douglas has been an animal lover as long as she can remember and collects vintage clothing, homeless cats, and the occasional stray dog. Her publisher, Forge Books, sponsors the Midnight Louie Adopt-a-Cat program of book tours, which finds good homes for cats and books and promotes animal shelters all over the country. She wrote "Sax and the Single Cat" when Socks Clinton became the First Cat in too long a time, and hopes that readers will note Socks's ultimate fate after eight years in office. When his owners moved, they took the dog but passed him along to a new owner across the country. When Socks vanished from there, he was lucky and got lots of publicity. Someone recognized and returned him after a few days. Louie hopes that Socks's sad story—from First Cat to lost cat—will convince people that domestic cats can and should lead happy lives as Indoor Cats Only, which Louie himself will be once he retires from his private eye career. Oh, and that Socks/Louie book deal fell apart. Seems there soon was more media interest in the shenanigans of Socks's owner than the mere confessions of an Arkansas alley cat.

Copyrights